Cupcakes and Cauldrons

Witch Haven Cozy Mystery - book 5

K.E. O'Connor

K.E. O'Connor Books

CUPCAKES AND CAULDRONS

ISBN: 978-1-915378-32-3

Written by: K.E. O'Connor

Preface

The Witch Haven series has been created so you spend time with four amazing witches:

Books 1-3 tell Indigo's story: Spells and Spooks, Hexes and Haunts, Curses and Corpses

Books 4-6 tell Luna's story: Muffins and Moonlight, Cupcakes and Cauldrons, Pancakes and Potions

Book 7-9 tell Odessa's story: Hauntings and High Jinx, Hauntings and Havoc, Hauntings and Hoaxes

Book 10-12 tell Storm's story: The Case of the Screaming Skull, The Case of the Poisoned Pumpkin, The Case of the Cursed Candy

And there are two bonus origin stories to enjoy: **Fire Fang** and **Silvaria**

Chapter 1

"Don't stick that rolling pin in your ear!" I dashed over and grabbed the floured rolling pin from Zek, a teenage gremlin with a chipped front tooth and bright green spiky hair.

He growled and hung onto the rolling pin before swinging it at my head.

I ducked and fell, bumping into two other gremlins on my way down as they carried cupcakes to the counter. Two dozen pale yellow cakes flew in the air and splatted to the floor of the reform school classroom.

Warm cupcake slid off my cheek as I stared at the ceiling. No one told me community service would be this challenging.

"Are you okay, miss?" Zek peered down at me. "You've got icing all over your face."

Vak, another of my teenage students, grabbed my arm and yanked me into a seated position.

I struggled up, careful not to stand on any cupcakes. I turned to the gremlins I'd bumped into. "Sorry about your cakes. They looked perfect."

They looked at the scattered cupcakes and shrugged.

"They'd have been gross," Vak said. "My mate replaced the sugar with salt to make you puke when you tried one."

The gremlins lunged at each other, growling and snarling as they rolled on the floor.

I left them to it as I scooped up squashed cakes. It took me most of my first day on community service trying to stop these fights before I learned that was how they settled their differences. No amount of reasoning or pleading did any good. And once the gremlins got it out of their system, they were fine.

A quick check of the time revealed class was almost done for the day. I clapped my hands together. "Everyone worked so hard today. I'll make sure that goes down on all your assessments."

The fighting gremlins pulled apart and grinned at each other before leaping up.

"We passed?" Vak said.

"You've all passed your domestic science course."

"Whoa! I never passed nothing."

"Congratulations."

He grinned at me, several of his teeth missing. "I liked it. Some of the others thought it was rubbish being forced to learn to bake, but I can use my skills to get girls. I'm now a master of lifting purses and making treats. I'll have them eating out of my hand."

"Um, maybe stick with the baking skills when you go wooing. Not all the ladies love light fingers."

He chuckled. "The ones I hang around with do."

"Everyone gather around with your cupcakes," I said. "We'll do a taste test to finish."

The group of six gremlins I'd been supervising over the last eight weeks bustled to the table. This was always their favorite part.

Four of them clutched trays of cupcakes. They placed them on the table, and after much shoving and growling to figure out where was the best place to put the cakes, they looked up at me expectantly.

"There's a lot of delicious cake here."

"I'm not touching anything Zek made," Vak said. "He picks his nose all the time and never washes his hands."

"I don't." Zek shoved his friend.

"No more shoving, or no one is eating cake! And no more picking noses when you're baking. Remember, clean hands at all times." I stared at the cakes. My students tried so hard, but their efforts looked as bad as mine when I'd had a terrible day using my baking magic.

I divided the cakes into six small piles then picked up one that was iced in brilliant green and sprinkled with something I hoped was chocolate and took a small bite. I chewed cautiously.

"That's mine," Cal said. "What do you think? It's rubbish, ain't it?"

It had an odd, sour taste, but it was edible. "Excellent work on the icing. The base is a little heavy. Cupcakes are usually lighter, but it's a solid six out of ten."

His face brightened. "I got a six. That's a pass?"

"It is. Well done."

He grabbed a cupcake, chewing it with a smile on his green face.

"I did way better than Cal." Zek shoved a cake at me. "You'll want to marry me after you've tried this."

I took a bite of the chocolate cupcake, and my eyes widened. "Zek! This is excellent."

"He cheated," Cal said. "I saw him."

Zek lobbed a cupcake at Cal's head. "Keep your lying mouth shut!"

"You did! You snuck in a packet mix this morning. He thought he got away with it, but I saw him tuck it under the kitchen counter. Miss, you should disqualify him."

The gremlins lunged at each other, snarling and snapping their sharp little teeth.

I ate more cake, waiting for the fighting fever to die down. "I'll have to fail you if you keep challenging each other. Fighting isn't allowed in class. You know the rules. They're on the wall if you need a reminder." Gremlins were almost as hierarchical as werewolves, always fighting for the top spot.

Vak snorted a laugh. "Zek can't even read."

"Can so." Zek broke away from the fight and glared at Vak. "It says no fighting. No swearing. No unauthorized magic."

"And no bringing in pre-made cake mixtures." Cal jabbed him in the ribs with a clawed finger.

"Did you bring in a packet mix?" I said to Zek.

He shrugged and looked defiant, although his cheeks colored pink. "There's no harm in it. I was using my initiative. You told us to be inventive."

"With the icing and the finished design." I looked at his too good to be true cupcakes. "Still, you get a mark for using your initiative."

"That's not fair!" Cal said.

I raised a hand. "But I'm deducting six marks for not using your own recipe. That gives you a two out of ten, Zek."

The gremlin scowled and swiped a cupcake off the counter before stomping away and glaring out the window.

I sampled more cupcakes, glad all of them tasted normal, although there was a hint of fried pickle in one. Maybe that was the cake from the nose picker.

"Who wins?" Vak said.

"I'm calling it a draw," I said. "You're all winners."

"That's not right. Zek cheated. He can't be a winner," Cal said.

Zek made a strange wheezing noise and staggered to the side, bumping into a table.

"Ignore him," Cal said. "He's angry because he came last."

Zek wheezed again and thumped his chest.

"Are you okay?" I hurried over to Zek. He was pale, and his green lips had lost their color.

He coughed and struck his chest again.

"He's choking!" I stood behind him, put my arms around his middle, and squeezed hard.

Cal gathered around with the other gremlins. "That's what you get for cheating."

"Don't be a horse's butt." Vak shoved him. "He's got cake lodged in his throat, dummy. It's probably one of yours."

"He stuffed a whole cupcake in his gob. That's why he's choking. It's not my fault he doesn't know what his teeth are for!"

It took me several hard squeezes before a large lump of slimy cake shot out of Zek's mouth and landed on the floor.

He gasped in a breath and slumped forward, resting his hands on his knees.

I patted him on the shoulder as he got his breath back, while his classmates examined the ejected piece of cake.

Zek lifted a hand and waved it in the air. "You saved me. No one's ever saved me before."

"Oh, Zek, I'm sure that's not true."

He kissed my cheek. "I owe you. I'll be in your debt until I save your life."

"There's no need. I'm happy to do my job."

Someone clearing their throat had me looking up. Devlin Goody, a meddling compliance auditor from the Magic Council, stood in the doorway, a sour expression on his face.

The gremlins froze for half a second and then scattered.

"Was that one of your cakes this young gremlin was choking on?" Devlin asked.

I stared at the gooey lump on the floor. "It's hard to tell. I don't think so."

"It had better not be. You've been in enough trouble with your dubious cake offerings."

I opened my mouth to protest. Devlin and I had history, and none of it good.

"Leave Miss Brimstone alone. She's a great teacher." Zek stood in front of me, his teeth bared at Devlin.

Devlin scowled at him. "Move back, unless you want your privileges taken away."

"I don't care about no privileges. Don't pick on Miss Brimstone." Cal joined him and was quickly followed by the rest. They surrounded me like a small, scaly army of righteousness.

I fought hard not to grin smugly at Devlin. "It looks like I'm getting a gold star for my teaching."

He walked over and slapped papers on the table, staying out of the reach of the snarling gremlins. "That's why I'm here. It's your final day of community service."

"You're signing me off?"

Devlin's thin lips pursed. "I was considering extending your sentence. Two months of teaching hardly seems a suitable punishment for your crimes."

"She's no criminal," Zek said. "Miss Brimstone is awesome. She's an inspiration. When I get out of here, I'm opening a catering van. I'll travel the world, selling gremlin snacks."

"Zek, that's a great idea," I said. "And I'm glad I inspired you."

"Hopefully, your time here will have inspired you to keep your nose out of things that don't concern you." Devlin scratched his signature at the bottom of the piece of paper.

"My brush with murder isn't something I plan to repeat."

"Did you kill someone, Miss?" Cal stared at me with excited eyes. "Who'd you whack?"

"No! I definitely didn't kill anyone. It was all a misunderstanding." I leaned down to my captive audience and lowered my voice. "Although Devlin thought I was guilty. And he worked hard to get me put in jail."

"Then he's a giant dirty horse's butt, thinking a nice witch like you could go around slaying people," Vak said.

"I heard that." Devlin pointed a finger at Vak. "You watch your manners, unless you want your file reviewed and your stay extended."

"I don't mind staying if Miss Brimstone is teaching. She's more fun than the others." Vak sneered at Devlin. "And you do look like a horse's butt with that tiny puckered mouth." He mimicked Devlin's expression.

Within seconds, six gremlins were leaping around with pinched faces as they brayed and trotted about the room.

Devlin gathered up the papers and checked my signature. "I can see your influence in these reprobates."

"Thanks. I take that as a huge compliment." I grinned as Vak whinnied so loudly it made Devlin jump.

"That's your copy." Devlin flipped me a piece of paper before stalking out.

"Horse Butt Face doesn't think much of you, does he?" Cal trotted past.

"He doesn't. But I've seen the last of him." I waved the paper in my hand. "I'm a free witch."

Cal trotted back to me. He dropped his chin to his chest. "Does that mean you won't be coming back? I mean, not that I care. You can do what you like, but your lessons aren't terrible. I don't hate you teaching us."

"They're a million times better than those boring woodwork lessons they insist we do." Zek cantered over.

I looked around the group as they assembled in front of me, and my heart felt warm. "Have you really enjoyed learning to bake?" It felt great to be wanted. And even though my baking skills were far from perfect, the gremlins didn't mind.

"You could teach us to make other stuff," Vak said. "We could come up with ideas for a three course meal. Starters, main course, and then pudding. We'd get to stuff our gobs."

"I want to do the pudding," Cal said. "I've got a sweet tooth."

I didn't hate the idea of carrying on the lessons, and I didn't want to let the gremlins down. It had been fun when I discounted the fighting, squabbles, and nose picking. "I'll speak to Sinbad and see what he has to say. Maybe they can move your schedule around and we can fit in a weekly cookery class."

"Then we can all go off and be world-class bakers," Zek said.

"You'll be a world class butthead." Cal ducked a punch from Zek.

I moved in between them. I had a genuine pang of affection for these little guys. "I love the way you always shoot for the moon, Zek. Never stop doing that."

He flashed his teeth at me. "One day, I'm gonna stick a pin in that sucker and claim it as mine."

The gremlins helped me clear up, and once the equipment and cakes were dealt with, I said goodbye to my class and headed out. I stopped by Sinbad's office and tapped on the door.

He looked up and smiled at me. "You survived your last day."

"It was touch and go a few times, but I've enjoyed myself." I stepped into his office. "And the gremlins asked if they can continue their cookery classes with me. Would that be possible?"

His grin widened. "You really want to do that? I know they can be a handful, and I've been in the class a couple of times and seen them be cheeky to you. A lot of teachers won't stand for that."

"I'm used to it. And if I can help them, I'd love to." I lifted a shoulder. "I know I'm not a proper teacher, so I'd understand if it doesn't work for you."

"You're a real teacher to them, no matter how you came to be here." He scratched his head as he glanced through a calendar on his desk. "We even have a small budget for lessons, so I can supply you with the ingredients. So long as you don't make Lobster Thermidor every week."

"I promise, it'll be simple home cooking. Recipes they can use every day once they're released. Knowing how to make a nutritious meal will be useful for them."

"Then consider it done. Life skills are crucial for our residents. Give me a few weeks to juggle things around, and I'll find the space. How does that suit?"

"That sounds great. I'm looking forward to it."

We said goodbye, and I headed out of the reform school and walked back to the center of Witch Haven. It felt good to get back to normal.

Well, things weren't quite normal.

I glanced around, relieved to see there was no sign of an angry werewolf stalking me. Ever since my misadventures with Cole Kellam, I'd been on the alert after he left a worrying message in my farmhouse.

I'd have to tackle him soon. That was, unless he tackled me first and chewed my arm off.

My forehead wrinkled as I spotted a large truck outside Fandango's, my Uncle Albert's bakery, where I worked when I wasn't doing my community service. The back was open, and people were carrying equipment out of it into the empty store next door.

Uncle Albert emerged from the doorway and hurried over the second he saw me. "They're early!"

"The film crew? I didn't think they were getting here until tomorrow."

"They've pushed everything forward." He clasped his hands together, his wispy hair blowing in the breeze. "We're not ready."

I caught hold of his shoulder and gave it a gentle squeeze. "We are ready. You've been making preparations for weeks."

"I wanted to run through everything one more time. What if I've forgotten something important? Will they want to interview me?"

"I don't know. But if you have, we'll fix it together. And you'll be a huge hit. Everyone will love Fandango's when they learn about the bakery."

My uncle's expression remained anxious. "I don't want anything going wrong. This is a once-in-a-lifetime opportunity to promote us."

I nudged him out of the way as two members of the film crew walked past with a large box between them. We'd been contacted three months ago and asked to take part in the prestigious baking contest, *The Bewitching Bakery Showdown*. It was a huge event in the magical baking community. Each year, the sponsor picked a venue to promote and live filmed the show in the area. It was a great platform to promote our desserts, and the orders would come flooding in.

Uncle Albert had almost fallen off his seat when he got a request for Fandango's to star in the show. It was hardly a surprise it was picked. My parents were world-renowned bakers, and Uncle Albert wasn't far behind, although he preferred to keep things small scale. I was a Brimstone, and he was a Black, but both bloodlines came with a hefty dose of natural baking magic. At least, that was the theory. I was the wonky reality.

"Albert, I've been looking for you." Mrs. Henriette DeVere, a tall witch with long white hair and brilliant amber eyes, strode over. She wore an expensively tailored black suit with a red blouse underneath.

"Mrs. DeVere. It's good to see you again." Uncle Albert stepped forward and shook her outstretched hand.

"Please, call me Henriette." She turned her attention to me and smiled. "I hope you've both been looking forward to this."

"Of course. We're glad to have you at Fandango's." Henriette had been to visit the bakery twice while making plans for the show.

"We're thrilled to be here. And I'm so looking forward to your father being a judge. We were delighted when he accepted our request to head up the judging panel. It's a treat."

"I'm looking forward to him visiting, too. Dad hasn't been to Witch Haven for a year."

Her eyebrows shot up, then she nodded. "His work must keep him busy. I saw the marvelous eight-tiered cake he made for Viscount Hornsbill. It was a work of art. It deserved its own private viewing gallery in an exhibition."

I grinned. My dad was a show-off with his cakes. "He's always enjoyed making unique designs."

"I'm hoping we can press him into making us something special for the show," Henriette said. "Nothing elaborate, because I know how many weeks it takes to make the decorations and come up with the concept, but something that will delight our viewers. It would be a ratings smash."

I glanced at Uncle Albert and bit my bottom lip. My dad hated surprises. He loved order and routine. He wouldn't be pulling any last minute surprises out of his chef's hat, but I didn't want to dash Henriette's hopes. "Maybe we have something in Fandango's you'd like to showcase? Uncle Albert is also an incredible baker. He comes from the Black family line."

"Of course. And they're excellent at what they do. I've already tried three of his cakes." Henriette smiled at Uncle Albert. "And I hope you don't mind us turning up early. We heard the venue next door was empty, so we decided to get ahead of ourselves. We're setting up live cooking stations with state-of-the-art equipment. Nothing but the best for our talented bakers."

I glanced at the store the crew hurried in and out of. It had once been a used book store and small café, but it had shut down months ago and stood empty ever since. "It's a perfect location."

"And we'd love to get shots of you and your uncle in action in your kitchen. You can wow the viewers with your special Brimstone baking talent."

I gulped down panic. "You should focus on Uncle Albert. He'll be a natural in front of the camera."

"You must be included, too," he said. "I'm sure your dad wants to see your baking star shine."

I hid a grimace. I didn't want my baking star appearing on screen. It was wonky and dull. My plan was to stay below the radar. Uncle Albert loved baking, so he was welcome to take center stage and show off Fandango's.

There was a yelp, and something crashed to the ground.

I looked up and gasped. Earl, my lazy black cat familiar, was flopped in the pathway of the crew. I raced over and scooped him off the ground, muttering apologies to everyone.

Earl grumbled and flipped himself up onto my shoulder.

"What are you doing?" I hissed at him.

"I don't like all these people hanging around." He booped his damp nose against my cheek and yawned fishy breath in my face. "They're making so much noise. I was having a nap in the empty store when they barged in. Who are they?"

"You can't have forgotten the baking show starts tomorrow. Uncle Albert has been talking about little else for the last few weeks. And this will be big business for the bakery. Imagine what'll happen to Fandango's when we get national exposure."

"It sounds like a lot of extra work." He wrapped himself around my neck and began snoring.

"I'm looking for Luna Brimstone and Henriette DeVere." A bike messenger stopped by the store.

"I'm Luna." I pointed over my shoulder. "And that's Henriette."

Henriette walked over to join me. "It's probably paperwork for the show. There's always last minute admin to deal with."

I took a letter and signed for it, and so did Henriette, before the bike messenger cycled off.

Henriette opened her letter first. She glanced at me. "It's good news for you, my dear."

I tore open my letter, and my heart sank to my boots as I read the contents. "Dad's not coming. He got an urgent commission he couldn't turn down."

"To bake for the royal family in the Elven kingdom." Henriette sighed. "He'll do such a wonderful job."

"Yep, I'm sure he will. It would have been great to see him, though." But that was my dad. Work was his life, and his family was an afterthought. I tried not to take it personally, but it stung that he always picked pudding over me.

"I'm disappointed he can't make it, but his replacement is almost as good."

"Oh! Who's his replacement?"

"Didn't he say in his note to you?" Henriette said.

I flipped it over. "Nope."

She smiled at me. "He nominated you to take his place as head judge. Congratulations."

Chapter 2

"There must be some mistake." I clutched the letter in my sweating hand. "Dad can't have meant me. Uncle Albert is the perfect choice. Uncle Albert! I need you." There was no way I could be a judge.

He walked over and joined us. "What's going on?"

"We've had wonderful news for Luna. She's now a judge on the show." Although Henriette sounded happy, her expression was strained. She must be bitterly disappointed to have me as a stand-in. I was a nobody compared to my dad, and when she tasted my food, she'd know I wasn't a natural baker.

"Are you going to be an extra judge?" Uncle Albert said.

"No, Dad can't make it. The Elven royal family needs him to provide desserts for some special event. He's already on his way there."

He frowned. "Your dad could have let us know before making these changes. You haven't seen him in such a long time."

I was disappointed not to see Dad, and my mom was supposed to be coming, too. I rarely saw them together. Work kept them apart for long periods.

"I see nothing but good in this situation," Henriette said. "A fresh, young-faced baker is just what we need. I'm sure you'll stun the viewers. And we can arrange a private audience with your father at a later date."

"That's good of you to take this so well," I said.

"We've had much worse to deal with on previous shows. And your father nominated you, so everything is fine." She leaned closer. "Some judges simply don't turn up. No note, no excuse, nothing. It's the height of bad manners."

Uncle Albert shook his head and tutted. "I can't imagine why anyone wouldn't want to be a part of this show. I've watched it ever since it started. Each season only gets better."

"You're too kind." Henriette fluttered her lashes. "I'm excited the DeVere Company could be this year's sponsor. I've also been a big fan for many years."

"Uncle Albert, you should step in as the new judge." I turned to Henriette, forcing myself to remain calm. "He has much more experience than me. And you've tasted his cakes, so you know how amazing they are. He's the true genius in the bakery."

She patted my arm. "No, you'll be perfect."

"You'll do great." Uncle Albert gave me a reassuring smile. "This is a great opportunity for us. And the audience won't want to see some bumbling old fool in the kitchen, missing his cue and forgetting his lines."

Henriette nodded. "It is a wonderful chance for the bakery to sparkle. And every second matters when you're on camera. Give me a few minutes, and I'll get you shown around the set and outline your duties as a judge."

"Duties? What will I need to do?"

"It won't be anything complicated. It's mainly about enjoying the excellent food our bakers will make." She looked over at the crew. "I must go. I'll be back soon."

I shoved my hair out of my face as a strong wind whipped along the street. "Uncle Albert, I shouldn't do this. I'm too busy."

He tilted his head. "The bakery isn't busy. I made sure people knew we weren't taking custom orders this week because of the show."

"It's not just the bakery. I've said I'll carry on teaching the gremlins. I don't have time to do that and be a judge." There had to be a way out of this nightmare. I couldn't be a judge. It felt wrong.

"It's just a few days, Luna. And you deserve time off from the reform school." He reached forward and plucked a piece of dried icing out of my hair. "Those gremlins have been tough on you. Take a break and enjoy yourself."

I doubted I'd enjoy myself at all, especially not when I was exposed as a baking fraud live on television.

"You can celebrate the good news with your friends." Uncle Albert pointed along the road to where Storm Winter, Indigo Ash, and Odessa Grimsbane were walking.

They headed over and stopped outside the bakery.

Odessa's eyes gleamed with excitement. "This all looks important."

"It's the baking show," Uncle Albert said. "If you'll excuse me, I need to check the buns in the oven." He hurried into the bakery.

"I thought they weren't getting here until tomorrow." Storm tossed her dark hair out of her eyes.

"They arrived early," I said. "And I've had terrible news."

"What's the problem?" Indigo smiled at me. She was my closest friend in the group, although I loved all my friends. We'd been through tough times together.

"No one is allowed to laugh." I took a deep breath. "I've been nominated as head judge for the baking competition."

"Oh! That's good," Odessa said. "Isn't it? Think of all the free cake."

"They want me to judge other top bakers' food. I can't do that. My scones sometimes turn out like rocks, and my Chelsea buns can taste of sour cream and chives. Who am I to judge anyone else's food?"

Storm chuckled. "Are you going to be baking anything in this contest?"

"Hopefully not, just judging others. But it feels wrong." I glanced around to make sure none of the crew were listening in. "You know my food magic has been a bit dodgy."

"Relax. You don't need your magic, just functioning taste buds," Indigo said. "What could go wrong?"

"The event sponsor was suggesting my dad make a special treat for the show. What if she asks me to do the same thing and I mess up?"

"Say you haven't got time," Storm said. "Don't let her pressure you into doing something you're not comfortable with. I know what you're like."

"I don't want to let her down."

"Just don't give her any of your food, and it won't be a problem," Storm said.

"If she asks, you know what you have to say," Indigo said.

I cringed. I was such a people pleaser. "I'll be happy to help you?"

Storm rolled her eyes. "Say no. Or you'll end up with exploding cake on your face."

"I could ask Uncle Albert to make something and then say it's mine."

Indigo groaned and shook her head. "Don't do that. You'll get in trouble."

"And have Devlin after you again," Odessa said. "Have you finished your community service yet?"

"Yes. The last class was today. I'm officially no longer a criminal."

"You are the way Devlin Goody looks at you," Storm said.

My mouth twisted to the side. "I don't think we'll ever be friends."

"Luna! I'm ready for you to look around the set." Henriette dashed over, and I made a quick introduction to everyone.

She pushed her white hair out of her eyes. "I don't know where this wind has come from. The weather was supposed to be glorious the whole time we were here."

"Witch Haven is unpredictable," Odessa said. "It's all the magic. If something is out of sync, the weather gets weird."

"Well, let's hope everything remains in sync," Henriette said. "I want backdrops of glorious sunrises and sunsets so I can show off the beauty of this village. Come on, Luna. I'll show you around the set."

I grimaced at my friends, but they shooed me away, so I had no choice but to follow Henriette.

I was so surprised when I walked through the store door that I stopped dead. The place had been transformed. There were separate units full of baking equipment being constructed, a lighting rig going up, and stunning artwork with a dessert theme covered the walls.

Henriette smiled at me and tugged my arm. "It spectacular, isn't it? The crew are experts. Most of them have worked on the show since it began, and many are baking aficionados."

"It's incredible. You've done all this in such a short amount of time."

"They've got the setup down like clockwork. This way. I've got something to show you." Henriette led me past the busy crew, to a unit at the back, where there was a counter, a range of top quality baking equipment, and a gold cauldron with fluted edges.

I sucked in a breath. "Is that a model three hundred series?" I hurried over, my hand hovering, too afraid to touch the cauldron in case it wasn't real.

"It is. Only the finest for our bakers. Most of them demand the newest equipment," Henriette said. "I don't blame them. The best equipment for the best bakers."

"It's so beautiful." The cauldron shone under the lights.

"And this one is yours to use on the show."

My head whipped around so fast I almost gave myself whiplash. "What do you mean?"

She grinned at me. "This is your surprise. Everyone is taking part in this edition of the show. The contestants and the judges will all be baking."

My mouth opened and closed several times, but the power of speech eluded me.

"Oh, don't worry. This is just for fun. And I'll be doing it, too. You, me, and Elwin La Croix. The three of us will do the official judging, but we'll also get to show off our own talents. Although my baking isn't spectacular. I'm what you call an enthusiastic amateur."

"Oh! You don't want me baking anything for the show."

"No modesty around here. Your family's reputation is exemplary."

"Sure, but I'm not an expert baker."

"You're a Brimstone. You have to be." She patted my shoulder. "Don't look so worried. This is just for the entertainment value."

I shook my head. I couldn't be on a TV show, screwing up my baking and ruining the family name. There had to be a way out.

"You won't be on the timer like the official contestants. And if you make a mistake, which I'm sure you won't, we'll give you a chance to have a second go. Remember, it's fun."

It felt like fate had stepped in and decided to reveal my baking fakery to the entire world. I was too stunned to say anything.

"Follow me. There's much more to see. And the contestants are already here, so I'll make the introductions." Henriette glanced over her shoulder at me. "Don't mind if they're distracted. They can get intensely focused on their baking and sometimes forget themselves."

I could do nothing but be dragged along by Henriette. We headed past the set and into a back room. There were four people in there. Henriette walked over to a tall guy with a shaved head and dark brown eyes. From his rotund figure, he must enjoy sampling his own baking.

"This is Cade Waters, one of our contestants." Henrietta gestured at me. "Cade, this is Luna Brimstone. She's our new judge."

He nodded at me. "I thought your dad was supposed to be judging us."

"We've had a change of plans," Henriette said. "Luna is extremely skilled. We're fortunate to have her join us."

He smiled. "Sure. Sounds good. Enjoy."

Henriette led me to a stunning, petite woman in her mid-twenties. She had an Elven look about her and long, silky dark hair.

"Meadow Eclair, meet Luna Brimstone, our new judge."

Meadow grabbed my hand, her eyes shining. "It's great to meet you. I'm so excited to be here. And I can't wait to try the food at Fandango's. Is it all your own work?"

"No, mainly my uncle's. He's the one who should really be here."

"Nonsense. Although your uncle is a fine baker." Henriette turned and gestured to a short, squat guy who looked to be around thirty. He had messy, sandy brown hair and was scowling as he stomped over.

"This is Troy Morelli." Henriette made the introductions.

Troy gave my hand a single shake. "You're young to be judging. You can't be much older than me."

"Luna is a Brimstone," Henriette said. "She could be a teenager and she'd be perfectly qualified to judge anything you make."

I didn't miss the sharpness in Henriette's tone as she spoke to Troy.

"Make sure you're fair with all of us." Troy's gaze cut to Meadow. "Some get preferential treatment around here."

"Come on, my dear." Henriette led me away. "Don't mind the talent. They can have big egos. Troy is definitely one to watch out for."

"He must be talented if he got through to the final."

"His talent isn't the issue. It's his attitude. He's mean to anyone he thinks can't give him an opportunity. I expect he'll be disgustingly charming to you. Don't let that fool you. Judge him on his food alone."

"Of course. I wouldn't do anything else."

"Oh! And here's Elwin," Henriette said. "Elwin! Our new judge is here. Come and meet Luna Brimstone."

I sucked in a breath as Elwin turned. He was as famous as my parents in the baking world. He was tall, well-built, and a silver fox, with neatly brushed back shoulder length hair and brilliant green eyes.

He strode over and shook my hand. "A Brimstone baker. What a delight." His voice was like warm molasses and had just a hint of an Irish accent.

"It's wonderful to meet you," I stammered. "You're a rock star in the baking community."

"You're too kind."

"Everyone loves the recipes you create. They're so inventive."

"It comes with years of experience, and of course, we all have our own little magic touch." He waved his fingers in front of me, and the smell of sugar and nutmeg filled the air.

"Elwin is giving away prizes during the show," Henriette said, "including signed hardback editions of his new book."

"You have a new recipe book coming out? How exciting," I said.

He lifted one shoulder, a trace of smugness on his face. "I can only ignore the demands of my most ardent fans for so long."

"It's been a while since you published. My uncle Albert has all of your books."

"It's not been that long," Elwin said.

"I always buy Uncle Albert your books as gifts for his birthday. I think it's been five years—"

Henriette made a show of clearing her throat. "Perfection takes time. And trust me, this recipe book is sensational. It'll take the bakery world by surprise."

The sour expression on Elwin's face faded, and he preened under Henriette's compliments. "The early feedback has been excellent."

"I'd love to buy a copy," I said.

"It's not on sale. The book won't be released until the end of the show."

"We're building up a huge buzz," Henriette said. "We're hoping it'll make the bestseller list."

"I'm sure it will," I said.

"Fawn! Where are you?" Elwin called out.

A short woman in her mid-twenties dashed over, a headset on, which squashed her blonde hair. Her green eyes looked tired, as if she hadn't had much sleep.

Elwin smiled at her. "There you are. I'd like to treat our new judge to an advanced copy of my recipe book. Go to my trailer and get a copy."

"Of course. I'll be right back." She dashed away.

"Wow! That's generous of you. You don't have to do that. I'm happy to buy a copy when it's available." Although baking didn't make me giddy with joy like Uncle Albert, I was excited to get a peek at the new collection.

"I insist. It's the least I can do for a Brimstone baker."

My cheeks grew warm, and I ducked my head. "I'm not half as talented as my dad. I'm sorry he couldn't be here to judge."

"He wouldn't have recommended you if he didn't think you weren't capable," Elwin said. "I know your father, and he's an ambitious and dedicated man, who expects the very best."

I nodded. It was a perfect description of my dad. He was always looking to improve himself and expected the same from others.

"I heard he's been baking for the Winstanley family. I once had a request to bake for them, but I was already booked."

"It's a hard life when you're so talented." There wasn't a hint of sarcasm in Henriette's voice as she gazed at Elwin.

Fawn raced back with a copy of a book in her hands.

Elwin took it with a nod of thanks. "I'll autograph it for you, Luna."

Fawn handed him a pen. He scrawled across the front page and handed the book to me. "Enjoy."

"I will. Thanks so much. We'd love to try some of the recipes in Fandango's."

"We can discuss that. It shouldn't be a problem. You'll just need to attribute the recipes to me."

"That won't be a problem." Uncle Albert would be over the moon if he could showcase these new dessert treats to customers.

"Fawn, please show Luna the run-through of the filming schedule. She'll need to know what's expected of her." Elwin's smile was a touch condescending. "Is this your first time on camera?"

"Yes. And I'm nervous."

"There's nothing to be nervous about," Henriette said. "The focus will be on the baking contestants.

Everyone wants to see who'll win the final. Of course, you'll have a few moments when you're testing the cakes, and everyone will look forward to trying your treats."

I bit my lip. They wouldn't want to try them again after they'd tasted them. I was sure I could figure out a way to get Uncle Albert to make my cakes and sneak them onto the set at the last minute.

"Henriette, I wanted to talk to you about a scheduling issue." Elwin caught hold of her elbow. "I'll see you tomorrow, Luna."

"Sure. Thanks again for the book."

He nodded and led Henriette away.

Fawn shifted from foot to foot. "Hey. So, you're a Brimstone baker?"

"Yep. What about you?"

"I'm nothing special. Just a Halliwell. We're not supposed to be any good in the kitchen." Something intense flickered in her eyes, but then it was gone. "Have you had a look around the set?"

"I have. It's impressive."

"There's more to see. I'll give you the tour."

"Thanks. Lead the way."

We headed around the rest of the set, which had almost been completed, and stood by a workstation. Fawn pulled out a pile of papers and set them in front of her.

"This is what you—"

"Fawn! Where's my triple shot cappuccino?" Meadow yelled from the other side of the set. "I've been waiting ten minutes."

She raised a hand. "I'll get right on that."

"It sounds like you're in demand."

Fawn let out a sigh. "There's supposed to be two assistants, but Margo quit a week ago. She couldn't take the pressure from the prima donnas who toot sugared icing and expect us to clear it up and congratulate them."

I stifled a smile. "I have heard mention of the egos on the show."

She glanced at me. "It's not just the contestants I need to look after. Henriette and Elwin also have me running around for them."

Cade strode over. "Fawn, we need to talk."

Her posture stiffened. "Can it wait? I'm showing the new judge the running order for tomorrow."

He frowned but then nodded. "We can speak later. Maybe grab something to eat together?"

"I'll let you know." Fawn didn't meet his gaze.

Cade sighed then turned and walked away.

"I don't mind doing this another time," I said.

"It won't take long. And I can talk fast."

"You must love baking to put up with all these demands."

A genuine smile crossed Fawn's face, and her shoulders relaxed. "I love it. More than anything. This is the best job in the world, being surrounded by so much talent. And I bake, too."

"Have you ever done anything for the show?"

"No, I don't have a family reputation to back me up." Her eyes widened. "I mean, sorry, that was thoughtless. Obviously, I know who you are, and I know all about your amazing family."

"They give me an impressive set of credentials to live up to."

"I'm sure you're amazing." Fawn jumped as something banged against the side of the building. "We're planning on doing outside filming for the judges' interviews, but the way this wind is kicking up, it won't be possible. The microphones are too sensitive."

"I'm sure it'll pass. Why don't you give me the details of the running order? I'll take it away and leave you to your work."

Fawn rifled through her papers and pulled out a sheet that she handed to me. "If you've got questions, just ask. I'll be here until the early hours, making sure everything is sorted."

"Be sure you take a break."

"The chance would be a fine thing." Fawn turned then looked back. "We're glad to have you here. I can't wait to see what a Brimstone baker creates for us."

I let out a soft sigh as she hurried away. So much for keeping a low profile.

Chapter 3

"It all sounds wonderful." Gloria Barkridge's knitting was nestled on her lap as she smiled at me. "You'll be on the television, showcasing the amazing food that comes out of Fandango's. How exciting."

"I'm not sure I can do it." I sat in the front parlor of my farmhouse with Gloria, Faye Calhoun, and Ridley Vandyke, my wonderful little magic harem. I'd been catching them up on the events of today, and my unexpected inclusion in the baking competition. They thought it was an amazing idea, but I was still in favor of finding an excuse to get out of it.

"Did you make these from the new recipe book Elwin gave you?" Ridley leaned forward and grabbed a cupcake off the tray I'd brought with me.

"Yes. Some of the ingredients were old-fashioned, but we had everything in the bakery store cupboards, so I thought I'd give them a try."

"They look tasty." Gloria picked up her own cupcake.

I handed one to Faye. "The recipe read like it came from a couple of hundred years ago. The wording was old-fashioned. Perhaps it's a new style Elwin is trying."

"He could be going back to the origins of each particular recipe, trying to find the inventor of the first genuine cupcake." Gloria sniffed her cake. "It smells nice."

"You don't have to try it." My unfortunate magic harem was often on the wrong side of my failed baking experiments, but they were always too polite to say how awful my food was.

The window rattled as the storm kicked outside. The wind had been getting steadily worse all day.

I went to the window, made sure it was secure, and drew the thick curtains to keep out the chill.

When I turned back, Ridley was chewing, a concentrated expression on his face, Gloria was looking around the room and humming under her breath, and Faye looked a little green.

"Is something wrong?"

"No, everything's great. The cupcake was amazing." Ridley smacked his lips together.

"Very nice, dear," Gloria said. "Ten out of ten for effort."

I glanced at her pile of knitting, which had developed a bulge. I grabbed the knitting and lifted it. Her cupcake was hiding underneath.

I groaned and dropped the knitting on her lap. "Was it really that terrible?"

Faye grabbed her mug of coffee and took a long drink. "Mine tasted earthy."

"My cupcakes taste of dirt?" I sank back into my chair and raised an eyebrow at Ridley. "Did you hide yours, too?" I glanced at the cushion beside him, which hadn't been there a moment ago.

"I had a bite." Ridley shrugged. "Faye is right. They don't taste good. Did you drop them on the way over here?"

The windows rattled again, and a howl of wind blasted down the open fireplace.

"It must have been the recipe. You said the ingredients were odd." Gloria nodded. "That'll be it."

"I'm sorry to inflict them on you." I rubbed my forehead. "I followed the instructions. I don't know what's wrong with me."

"Nothing is wrong with you." Gloria's smile was full of encouragement. "But you should take your fill of magic while you're here, just in case. You need to be at your best when you're on camera."

I loved my tight knit magic harem. This wasn't the kinky kind of harem from the Arabian nights stories, but my incredible magic users supplied me with just enough magic to hide my blunted baking ability. I was a magical blunt and would never grow into my powers.

But I'd found the perfect solution. Ridley, Gloria, and Faye needed a safe place, and I'd been happy to provide it for them in exchange for a small amount of their magic on a regular basis.

To begin with, it worked perfectly. The trouble was, I needed more and more magic to hide the fact my own powers malfunctioned more often than not.

"We'll make sure you're right on the day," Ridley said. "Do you want to do a naked magic transfer?" He raised his eyebrows and grinned.

"No!" Gloria and Faye said together.

"We aren't doing that again." Faye pressed a hand against her pink cheek. "It was inappropriate. I blame the sherry. I had two glasses that evening."

"Four glasses," Gloria said. "And you encouraged Ridley to get his clothes off. You even wolf whistled when he got down to his boxer shorts. I remember them so well. They had lipstick kisses on them."

Ridley chuckled. "They're my favorite. You get good air flow."

Faye covered her eyes for a second. "No more sherry for me. And no more looking at Ridley's undershorts."

"I agree with you, Faye. Naked magic transfer was a big mistake. Huge. It won't happen again," I said.

Ridley started cajoling Gloria and Faye into getting their clothes off, and they giggled and told him to behave. He was several decades younger than them, and he was lonely. I'd tried to get him some company of his own age, but that had spectacularly backfired.

I needed to fix Ridley up with a date. The guy was all on his own, and although Gloria and Faye were great company, they had different interests to Ridley.

I returned to the window and peered into the evening gloom.

"If you're looking for Cole, he's not been back," Ridley said. "I've been making checks around the farmhouse to see if he's been poking about."

Cole Kellam had been my spectacular backfire when attempting to expand my magic harem. In a moment of panic and insanity, I'd drained his magic and chained him up. I'd planned to speak to him and convince him to join the harem but got delayed after a misunderstanding involving a muffin and some poison. By the time I'd gotten back to the farmhouse, he'd escaped.

Since then, I'd been looking over my shoulder, expecting to be pounced upon by a vengeful werewolf.

"I'm sure he's calmed down by now," Gloria said. "It's been weeks."

"He was angry, though," Faye said. "He was growling most of the time he was here."

I turned away from the window. "I shouldn't have done it. I should have spoken to Cole, but he didn't leave me much choice. And his magic feels so good. Maybe I got a little greedy."

Gloria and Faye exchanged a glance.

Gloria settled her hands on her lap. "Are we not enough for you? Are you going to get rid of us?"

"No!" I returned to my seat. "I love having you here. And this will always be your home for as long as you want it."

Faye crossed her legs, making the chain around her ankle rattle. The chains were just a precaution. My harem could be a touch unstable at times. "We're not as strong as we used to be, but we don't want to let you down."

"I'm still strong, and I've got loads of magic," Ridley said. "You can take as much as you like from me."

"You're all perfect. And I'll just take a little from all of you tonight," I said. "I need to make sure my cupcakes taste less like dirt and more like... well, cupcakes."

"We'll help with that." Faye was already pushing up her sleeves.

"Although I was wondering about faking an illness. If I said I had an upset stomach, the other judges wouldn't let me near the food."

"You can't let your uncle down." Gloria shook her head. "You've told us how excited he is that the baking competition has come to Witch Haven."

I glanced at the window again. If it was just the competition to deal with, I could handle it, but there were too many other things going on that made my cozy existence feel less than secure.

"You're still worried about that puffed up werewolf, aren't you?" Ridley said. "I'll chase him off if he comes back."

"Cole doesn't live around here, though, does he?" Gloria said.

"No, he was visiting on pack business."

"Most likely, he left a long time ago. He won't be back."

I looked at the wall where I'd spent a long time scrubbing off his blood smeared threatening message. I didn't feel as positive as Gloria that Cole wouldn't come padding back into my life with a killer gleam in his werewolf eyes.

"How about a nice magic boost from all of us, a cup of tea, and then head home for a good night sleep?" Faye said. "Then tomorrow, you can focus on your baking."

I tensed at the thought of how tomorrow would turn out, but there was no getting out of it.

After grabbing a quick boost of magic from each of them, I said goodbye and left the farmhouse.

The night sky was cloudless as I stared at the stars. My magic didn't feel strong or stable. I missed the werewolf magic. And a part of me missed Cole. Even though he was growly and possessive, I hadn't forgotten his incredible kisses or the excited flutter he gave me.

I stepped off the porch, through the magic barrier concealing the farmhouse, and out the other side. I did a quick check of the barrier to make sure it was secure and then turned to leave.

My gaze dropped to the mud, and my breath caught in my throat. There were huge wolf pawprints in front of me. Cole had been here.

My knees wobbled. Cole was done waiting, and he was back to get his pound of witch flesh. I just hoped he didn't show up during the contest and eat the judges. Or me.

Chapter 4

I'd been up since dawn, stress pacing the kitchen. Uncle Albert found me just as I downed my third cup of coffee.

"You must be excited about today." He hugged me. "I can't wait to watch the filming if I get a quiet moment in the bakery."

Even though nerves rioted in my stomach, I felt a trickle of excitement. "I'll mention Fandango's as much as possible. We'll have a queue out the door next week. Everyone will want to try your food."

"And yours." Uncle Albert switched on the kettle. "Perhaps Elwin will encourage you to create your own recipe book. Imagine that. You could have a book alongside your father's."

"I wouldn't dare go up against Dad. You know what he's like."

Uncle Albert chuckled. "Baking before everything else. I'm sure he'd welcome anything you create, though."

A knock on the front door of the bakery had me turning. I hurried out and waved as I saw Fawn. I unlocked the door. "Hi, how's everything going?"

She gave me a thumbs-up. "All systems go. And you're wanted on set."

"Already? It's so early."

"We need to do sound and lighting checks. You won't have to do much, just stand at your workstation and smile. They'll want to do your make-up, too."

"Is that necessary? I won't be on camera much."

Fawn was already turning away. "I'm just following orders. Be there in five minutes. Oh, and Elwin wants to interview you on camera before the main filming starts."

"About what?"

She looked at me as though my sentence made little sense. "Your baking skills, I guess."

"Oh! Of course. I'll be there in a few minutes." I eased the door shut and closed my eyes. I was one big fraud, and it would take several serious miracles to get me out of this.

A thud at the door made me jump back, and my eyes flew open. Storm, Indigo, and Odessa stood outside staring at me. I pulled open the door.

"It's our famous friend!" Odessa flung her arms around me. "Everyone's talking about you being on the show, you lucky thing."

They filed into the bakery and headed to the counter.

I followed them, my feet heavy as I dragged them along. "I don't feel so good. Maybe I shouldn't be involved in the show."

"It's just nerves. I sometimes get a nervous stomach before an important event." Indigo turned to me. "Have fun. This is what you're good at."

"Sometimes." Storm leaned against the counter and arched an eyebrow.

"And that's the problem. Who knows what interesting cakes I'll reveal on the final cut?" I headed around the counter and switched on the coffee machine before lining up cherry and almond pastries, which my friends fell on.

"You're still just taste testing cakes, aren't you?" Odessa said around a mouthful of pastry. "Why should that worry you? We all know you can eat. I've seen you suck down a vat of pasta in less than ten minutes."

"I'm now baking, too. It's supposed to be fun, but it feels serious to me, and you can smell the rivalry on set. Everyone wants to make a winning cake." I picked apart my pastry, too anxious to eat. "I can't present anything I bake live on camera. What if it tastes like the dirt cakes I made yesterday?"

"Dirt cakes?" Storm shook her head and inspected her pastry. "Why would your food taste like dirt?"

I threw up my hands. "I've no idea, but it did. And I followed the recipe exactly."

"This will take your mind off the cakes," Indigo said. "A tornado alert just got released."

"Is it going to get that bad?" I said. "It's been windy all night, but we don't get tornados here."

"It's been brewing a couple of miles outside the village boundary," Storm said. "Whatever is causing this weather isn't natural."

"You think a magic user is shooting tornados our way?"

"Yep. And it's bad enough that the Magic Council has asked for help," Indigo said. "We're going to use our powers to divert it."

"It's heading straight for Witch Haven," Odessa said. "We're right in its path. We have to stop it, or my farmhouse and scarecrows will be destroyed."

"I can help! Stopping a tornado is more important than cake. I'll step back from being a judge."

"Luna!" Uncle Albert hurried from the kitchen. "Nothing is more important than cake. You can't miss this opportunity. Hello, girls." He nodded at my friends.

"Uncle Albert, this is important. Did you know about the tornados?"

"I heard an announcement on the radio, but it's under control. The Magic Council has told everyone to be on their guard and requested all elemental witches and those with advanced abilities to assist."

"A bunch of us are heading to the village border. We'll diffuse the magic," Storm said. "And then we'll find whoever's doing this and whip their butt."

"I should be there. I could be useful." My magic would be useless against something so powerful, but it was the perfect excuse to get out of the baking contest.

"You should be on set, showcasing your talent," Uncle Albert said. "We've worked hard for this, and this is Fandango's moment to shine. And yours."

"We've got this," Storm said. "You stick to the cakes."

"Although I'd love to help, I've got misbehaving scarecrows that need reminding it's bad to run through the play park rolling their heads and screaming. The children will have nightmares," Odessa said.

"I'll be there all morning, but then I have a case to work on," Storm said. "Someone's cheating spouse needs tailing and then tossing off a bridge with a heavy chain wrapped around his ankles."

"You're joking?" Indigo said.

Storm shrugged.

"She is. Storm wouldn't waste a good length of chain on a cheater." Odessa giggled.

The bakery door opened, and Olympus walked in.

Indigo greeted him with a kiss, and I handed him a pastry.

He nodded his thanks. "Are you all set for today, Luna?" He inclined his head at the door.

"No. I'm thinking about running away and changing my name."

"She's got stage fright," Indigo said.

"More like dirt cupcake fright." Storm shoved the last of the pastry into her mouth.

"Dirt cake?" Olympus said.

"Indigo can tell you," I said on a sigh. "And I need to get a move on, too. I'm wanted on set. Although... are you sure you don't need me to help deal with this weird weather magic?"

Storm glanced at Uncle Albert. "Nope. We're on it."

"Indigo, are you coming with us to the boundary? We need all magical hands on deck," Olympus said.

"Sure. I just wanted to wish Luna good luck."

"We'd better go. We've already got a crowd gathered at the edge of the village. Whoever has cast this magic is powerful," he said.

"Good luck," I said. "I hope you get it sorted."

"And to you," Indigo said.

"Break an egg," Odessa said.

Storm nodded at me. "Try not to make anything taste like dirt."

I waved goodbye as they headed out of the store.

Uncle Albert touched my arm. "Don't be nervous. You'll knock their socks off." He turned to the kitchen. "The crumpets are calling. I'll be back in a minute."

Fawn appeared by the door and beckoned to me. I was out of time. I had to face the cupcakes and hope I could pull this off.

I yelled a goodbye to Uncle Albert and headed next door.

The next couple of hours were spent smiling too much, standing under hot lights, and trying not to sweat. I kept forgetting not to stare at the cameras every time I talked, which made the camera crew sigh and shake their heads.

I was more than ready for a break when Elwin strolled over.

"Luna, it's time for your interview. It'll only take a few minutes. We do one with all the bakers and judges, so the viewers can get to know you."

"Sure. Fawn said you'd want to do an interview. Is here okay?"

"This is perfect." Elwin looked over at the camera and got the thumbs-up from the guy behind it. "Okay, just be natural. Talk to me like you're with an old friend and we're catching up. Do you think you can do that?"

"I'll give it a go."

"Excellent." He straightened his shoulders and smoothed a hand over his hair. "Viewers, we have a treat for you. Luna Brimstone has graciously stepped in as a judge at the last minute, and we couldn't be happier to have her here. The Brimstones need no introduction, but if you have been living under a stone for the last few hundred years, the family created the sparkling waterfall cake, the diamante prism layer cake, and the color changing pyramid cake. They have royal families in their thrall and bake for presidents and leaders across the world. Welcome to the show, Luna."

I resisted the urge to lick my lips. "Thanks. It's great to be here."

"I'd like to get your thoughts on being involved in this contest."

I glanced at the camera. "I'm hoping to judge some amazing cakes. It's a privilege to be a part of this."

"And we're delighted to have you. And we appreciate you stepping in to represent the Brimstone bakers. Your family must be so proud of you."

"I like to think they are."

"Everyone we spoke to in Witch Haven has nothing but good things to say about your uncle's bakery."

I nodded. This was the perfect opportunity to promote the business. "Fandango's bakery is incredible. My uncle created it with my auntie over thirty years ago. The cakes and pastries delight the most discerning palate."

"And you work there, too?"

"That's right. I've been helping my uncle for years."

Elwin arched an eyebrow and glanced at the camera. "When can we expect the Luna Brimstone patisserie? Surely you have plans to expand. It would be cruel to keep such talent in one place for too long."

I swallowed, careful to keep my voice level. "I'm happy helping with the family business. It keeps me busy."

"But you deprive so many people of your amazing food. That's a crime. You'd easily have a successful franchise."

I kept my smile serene. "Maybe one day, when I have more experience."

"That day can't come soon enough." Elwin glanced at the camera. "Now, for a surprise. As part of our baking challenge, I have a puzzle that needs solving."

"What kind of puzzle?"

"There is a recipe in my new book, *Classic Confectionery with a Tempting Twist*, which is unfinished. It's missing a key ingredient." He turned to the camera. "The challenge is to discover the missing ingredient in a cupcake recipe."

I smiled and nodded.

Elwin grinned at the camera. "Whichever baker finds the ingredient will receive a credit in the book for that recipe and ten percent of the profits from sales for the first six months."

"That's generous," I said. "Do you know what this missing ingredient is?"

The smile on his face jolted for a second before it returned full beam. "Aren't you excited? You could be a named recipe creator in an Elwin La Croix's cookbook."

"It's amazing. I'm sure one of the contestants will find it. They seem to have a huge amount of talent."

"They do. But you will be involved, too. The finalists and judges are all taking part."

I swallowed. "All of us? Baking on camera?"

"Absolutely. Even Henriette is taking part, and she doesn't have our natural talent. It seemed only right everyone on the show got a shot at this incredible prize. And it makes our finalists work even harder to achieve excellence." He gestured for me to say something, but my mind was a blank wall of panic.

"Uh... great. I mean, Henriette mentioned we'd bake, but not this. I, err..."

"You must be excited."

I couldn't think of a single thing to say as my brain flashed warnings to grab my passport and leave the country at the earliest opportunity.

"There we have it, viewers. Everyone's looking forward to seeing the amazing cupcakes created." Elwin shot me a curious look. "Thank you for your time, Luna. The viewers are excited to have a Brimstone baker on board."

I nodded a little too enthusiastically. "Yes, it's great to be here."

I waited until Elwin finished his piece to camera then stepped back. A trickle of sweat ran down my spine, and it wasn't because of the hot, overhead lights. How was I supposed to find a missing ingredient in some amazing cupcake recipe Elwin had created? Everything I touched in the kitchen recently turned into a disaster.

Elwin turned back to me. "You did well. Please, don't be so nervous. I know it's your first time on camera, but you're representing a legendary family. You have nothing to worry about."

"Of course not. Sorry, I'll be better next time."

"The editing will make everything look professional." He nodded at me before walking away.

I let out a long sigh. It was time to roll up my sleeves and hope for the best. So long as I didn't poison anyone, I'd call that a win.

***

My head ached, my eyes were sore, and I was less than happy with what I'd created during the day. I'd been baking for hours, trying different recipes to make the cupcakes taste acceptable and find the missing ingredient.

And I desperately needed a strong coffee. I'd asked Fawn for one over an hour ago, but she'd never come back. She was probably being harassed by a contestant, so I didn't blame her for forgetting about me. Every time someone wanted something, they yelled out her name, and she went scurrying.

I set my latest attempt at the cupcakes on a cooling rack and rolled my shoulders. I glanced at the camera crew who'd been filming me the entire time. Talk about pressure. "Is there any chance I can take a break?"

Dave's face appeared around the side of the camera and he nodded. "Sure. We've got loads of footage. You're like a baking robot. You never stop."

"I'm done here. I don't think I can make another thing."

He grinned. "Sure thing. I'll pause the filming."

I gave him a weary nod of thanks as I left. I had the workstation in the back corner, which meant I had to pass everyone else. I tried not to feel envious at how incredible their cupcakes looked.

Meadow had a glorious stack of pale yellow iced cupcakes. She was sprinkling something that looked like glitter over them. She caught my eye as I passed and smiled.

I slowed as I reached Cade's workstation. He'd created the largest cupcakes I'd ever seen. They were decorated with wavy white and green stripes. He also had a pile of cakes that looked like they'd been discarded. I stared at them for a second. Maybe I could borrow those and pretend they were mine.

"They're the rejects," he muttered as he continued icing his cupcakes.

"Rejects? But they look amazing."

"Of course they do. I made them."

I walked past Troy's counter next and stumbled over my own feet in amazement. His shimmering cakes looked incredible. "Are they waterfall velvet cupcakes?"

He looked up at me and grunted. "Of course not. That's not the recipe we have to figure out. And I'm not giving away my secrets. I'm determined to win this contest."

"I'm sure you will. They look great."

He grunted again and turned his back on me.

I waved at Elwin, who stood to one side, and gestured I was leaving the set.

He raised his hand in acknowledgement.

I headed outside and spotted Storm striding along the street. She saw me and walked over.

"Since we haven't been blown away, I'm assuming you held off the tornados," I said.

She nodded. "It was a close call. There were ten of us fighting it off all morning. The tornados were dead set on carving a path through the village. It would have destroyed buildings if we hadn't stopped it."

"Sorry I couldn't help." I glanced back at the set. "It won't be long until the judging takes place. The bakers have been busy all day."

Storm tilted her head. "Is that such a good idea?"

"You don't think my cupcakes are up to being judged?"

"You don't want to poison a famous baker on live TV."

I grimaced. "I'm not that bad."

"You're also not that good."

"Hey! I need a cheerleader to fight my cupcake corner."

"Then you're looking in the wrong place. The truth hurts, but you've got to admit, sometimes, your food sucks."

"It's hit and miss. But everything's under control, and my cupcakes look okay. Definitely edible. Probably." Tiredness seeped into my bones. I'd used a lot of magic during the day, and every time I'd cast a spell, it had fizzled out of me like a damp firework, grudging and unwilling to cooperate. No matter how much magic I borrowed from my farmhouse harem, it wasn't enough. I needed to find a more powerful source to help me.

I glanced at Storm. She was a super powerful witch. Her magic would have me firing on all cylinders. I shook my head. No, friends and family were off-limits.

"I was just doing this for fun." It hadn't felt like fun, and I'd been mopping my brow and crossing everything I could as I'd channeled my borrowed magic into the cakes.

"If you say so. Although your expression suggests you've been stuck in a torture chamber all day."

A groan slid from my lips. "If the worst happens, I could grab some cakes from Uncle Albert and sneak them on set. Nobody would know. And technically, they're almost mine. After all, I'd most likely sell them over-the-counter to customers."

"Help me!"

I turned as Henriette almost collided with me. Her normally smooth hair was windswept, and she was sweating. "What's wrong?"

"Is someone chasing you?" Storm glared over Henriette's shoulder.

"I found something terrible." She caught hold of my arm and hurried me away from the filming set.

Storm joined us. "What is it?"

"I... I can't believe it. I took a break from the set to meet up with her. I never expected this." The words tumbled out of Henriette as she hustled us along the sidewalk.

"Who are you talking about?" She was almost yanking my arm out of my socket as she charged around the corner and into the small play park beside the stores.

"Fawn! She said she needed to meet me here."

We entered the play park, and I stopped. The wooden play equipment was destroyed. Scattered all around were colorful plants that looked like they'd been ripped from the soil and torn apart.

But I wasn't focused on the destruction. My eyes were pinned to the body on the ground.

Chapter 5

A sob burst out of Henriette. "She's dead!"

Storm hurried over and checked the body. She looked up and nodded. "There's no pulse."

I pulled my gaze from Fawn and looked around. "What happened here?"

"It was like this when I arrived." Henriette clutched her arms around her middle as if comforting herself.

"Storm, are you certain the weird weather didn't get into the village?" I said. "A tornado has done this mess."

"That's not possible. The tornadoes faded as they reached the border of Witch Haven. Nothing got past us."

"So what the heck happened here?" I stepped closer to Fawn and looked down at her. She was on her back with her arms flung out, and there was a nasty open wound on her head.

Henriette let out another sob. "I can't believe this is happening."

"We need to inform the Magic Council," Storm muttered. "They need to see this."

I bit my bottom lip. I wasn't keen on getting the Magic Council involved, not given my track record with them, but they had to take charge of this situation. Olympus would know what to do.

"What should I do?" Henriette said. "Oh! I need to tell everyone on set. We'll have to halt the filming. There's so much to think about. Fawn was our only assistant. She loved her job."

"One thing at a time," I said. "Henriette, you deal with the business side of things. Stop the production and let everyone know there's been an accident. We also need the Magic Council here. They have a small office close to the bakery. Go there and tell them what you found. We'll wait here with Fawn and make sure nothing is disturbed."

"I... Yes, I can do that." Her gaze cut to Fawn. "She was only young. It's a tragedy." Henriette turned and dashed away.

"I agree, it's a tragedy," Storm said. "But was it an accident, right?"

I took a moment to look around the play park. "If a tornado didn't cause this, then Fawn had an epic fight with someone. It'll take weeks to put this place right."

I walked around slowly with Storm, looking at the torn up plants and ruined play equipment. None of it could be saved. It had been smashed by a tremendous power.

Storm stopped by Fawn's body. "If there was a fight, she didn't defend herself. Look at her hands."

I steeled myself and crept over to the body, being careful not to step on anything that looked important. "There are no marks on Fawn's hands or forearms. If someone came at her, she'd protect herself, even if she didn't fight back."

Storm nodded. "We'd see red marks or bruising. And even if they'd mainly used magic to fight, you'd see burns on her skin from the spells. And look at the wound on her head. Something hit her."

I looked around and spotted a metal pole with blood on it. "That would work."

She looked at the pole and grimaced.

I turned on my heel, taking in the whole scene again. The body, the head wound, the bloody pole left for anyone to find, and all the damage. "This looks almost too perfect."

"How do you figure that? It looks like chaos to me."

"When we arrived, my first thought was that this mess came from tornado damage. Fawn got killed by flying debris."

"I thought the same thing until we looked at her body. What are you suggesting?"

"Everyone was talking about the tornadoes hitting Witch Haven, and it was all over the news. What if someone took advantage of that? They figured they'd get rid of Fawn and set her murder up to make it look like an accident. If those tornadoes had hit, it would have done this kind of damage. When Fawn's body was discovered, she'd have been seen as a victim of Mother Nature."

Storm nodded slowly as she also looked around the scene. "So the killer assumed we wouldn't be able to stop the bad weather. They took a chance, and it didn't pay off."

"Why else would they leave that bloody pole? There could be fingerprints or magic residue on it. It will be easy to find out who hit Fawn."

"So long as their details are on file." Storm knelt beside the body.

"Maybe they created the tornado. It was their cover. But it went wrong because they didn't know how many powerful magic users live here."

"Maybe. Look. There's something sticking out of her jeans pocket."

I leaned closer and gently tweaked a small piece of paper out of Fawn's pocket.

"Be careful," Storm said. "If your fingerprints get on crime scene evidence, Devlin will be after you again."

I opened the piece of paper. The number eighty-seven was written on it, along with the words *Galangal Star*. I turned it over, but there was nothing else on the paper. I showed it to Storm.

"Does that mean anything to you?"

"I know about galangal. It's a rare herb and tastes a bit like ginger. It's hard to get hold of. I don't know what the number has to do with this or the word star. Maybe Fawn needed a supply of this herb for the show." I tucked the paper back in her pocket, and we both stepped away.

The air around us heated, and a second later, three members of the Magic Council appeared.

I just about suppressed a groan as I spotted Devlin Goody. Why couldn't it have been Olympus sent to investigate this case? Devlin seemed to be muscling in on his territory.

"What are you both doing here?" He stomped over, his wide-brimmed hat pulled down so low I could barely see his eyes.

"Henriette found us after she discovered Fawn's body," I said. "She was panicked and upset and needed help."

"Why did she come to you two for help?"

"Because we're nice witches." Storm crossed her arms over her chest and glowered at Devlin.

I touched her arm. "We were outside the recording set. We were the first people Henriette found."

"I hope you haven't touched anything," he said.

"We know not to mess with a crime scene," Storm said.

His eyebrows flashed up. "How do you know it's a crime scene?"

She smirked. "We'll let you figure that out."

"Keep out of our way. Especially you." Devlin pointed at me. "Unless you want to find yourself in the middle of another murder investigation."

I held up my hands and backed away. "I was just helping Henriette. We figured we'd stay here until someone arrived so things didn't get disturbed."

Devlin gestured to his two colleagues. "Have a look around, see if you can find anything out of place."

"This whole scene is out of place," Storm said.

"You can both leave." Devlin turned away from us.

"Don't you want to take our statements?" I said. "We were some of the first people on the scene."

"Did you know the victim?"

"No, not really. We only met yesterday."

"I've never met her," Storm said.

"Did you see anyone at the scene when you arrived?"

"Nope," I said.

"Do you have a connection to the victim?"

"No! But I liked Fawn. She was nice to me. I—"

"Then leave me to do my job," Devlin snapped.

"Let's get out of here," Storm said. "Devlin doesn't deserve our help. He can blunder about and figure this out on his own."

"We should stay," I whispered. "I want to make sure he doesn't mess things up. I didn't know Fawn well, but she was sweet."

Storm huffed out a breath. "If Devlin keeps being a jerk, I'm calling Fire Fang and setting him loose."

"I support that idea." I smiled at Devlin. "We're staying. Make use of us. At least get our statements, then we won't bother you anymore."

His cheeks flushed red. "Move out of the play park and stay out of the way while we do our jobs. I'll speak to you once I've taken in the initial findings."

Devlin walked around for ten minutes, muttering under his breath, and then consulted with his colleagues.

"He has to see what's going on here," Storm muttered. "He can't be that dense. This isn't your average tornado related death scene."

"When Devlin gets an idea in his head, he has trouble changing his mind. It took him days to figure out I wasn't Jinti Calrook's killer, even though I had no motive."

We waited a few more minutes, then he walked over to us.

"I'll take your statements now. You said Henriette came to you for help when she discovered the body?" He took out a notepad and opened it.

I nodded. "Henriette was panicked. Everyone else was still on set, and I'd just taken a break. We're filming an episode of a baking show."

"And you didn't know this woman well?"

"Not really," I said.

"I didn't know her at all. I was just in the wrong place at the wrong time when Henriette rocked up," Storm said.

"Her name's Fawn Halliwell. She was an assistant on The Bewitching Bakery Showdown. I wondered where she'd gone. I hadn't seen her for at least an hour."

"I heard the show was in the village," Devlin said. "You say she's been missing for an hour?"

"I asked her to get me a coffee. That was the last time I saw her. I paused the filming so I could get myself a drink, and that's when Henriette found me and Storm."

"Do you know why Fawn was in this park?"

"Henriette said she was meeting her here, but when she got to the play park, Fawn was dead."

Devlin glanced around briefly. "Did Henriette's behavior seemed unusual?"

"Of course. She'd just found Fawn's body," I said. "She was crying and shaking."

"That's to be expected." He scratched his chin as he looked back at the play park. "Although I don't think she was involved. This looks like an accident. You must have heard the tornado warning."

"That's what we thought at first, but then we took a proper look around."

His head whipped back to me, his eyes narrowed. "What do you think we've been doing? Having a picnic on top of the body?"

"Oh! I didn't mean you weren't doing your job properly, but Fawn's death wasn't an accident."

"Did you see what happened? Did you have something to do with it?"

"No! And I have an alibi. I was being filmed in front of a crew of people. You can check the tapes."

"I will." He jerked his chin at Storm. "And you?"

"I was at the magic barrier all morning, saving your butt from a killer tornado."

Devlin made an odd noise in the back of his throat. "Everything points to storm damage."

"It wasn't me," Storm said.

"Not you!" Devlin waved his hands around. "Wind damage. Everyone was worried about the sudden change in weather. Fawn obviously ignored the warning not to go outside unless it was essential."

"This scene has been staged," I said. "A tornado didn't do this."

"I disagree. Fawn must have been struck on the head with that pole. It could have come from the play equipment that was ripped out of the ground. The damage is consistent with a spot tornado landing."

"You're wrong," Storm said. "We prevented the tornadoes from getting here."

Devlin gestured around. "Maybe your magic isn't as good as you think it is."

"Take another look." Storm practically growled at Devlin. "Like Luna said, it's too perfect. You can ask any of the other nine witches and warlocks who helped stop the bad weather from arriving. It didn't make it over the border. No tornadoes set down here."

"That you saw."

"I know they didn't. We killed the weather. It nearly drained us all, but we did it."

"I'll consult the other magic users who assisted in that task," Devlin said after a few seconds of tense standoff, "but there's nothing here to suggest foul play."

"There are no defensive wounds on Fawn's arms," I said.

"How would you know that?"

"I... I can see from here. Her skin's unblemished. If Fawn was caught in a tornado, she'd have broken bones and bruises all over her body. She wouldn't have a single head wound."

"Perhaps she has injuries that can't yet be seen," Devlin said. "We'll know more when we've moved her."

"But you will investigate the possibility this wasn't an act of nature?" I said.

"Everything so far suggests it was an accident."

I glanced at Storm and bit my lip. "Don't dismiss the possibility of murder."

"Unless you witnessed a crime, you're of no value. It's time you both left." Devlin snapped his notebook shut. "There's no need to complicate things at this early stage."

"We should stay longer," Storm said. "Just to make sure you're doing your job. We don't want you picking an easy option if there's a killer out there."

"I assure you, I know how to do my job." He glared at me. "And unless you want more community service, you'll stop interfering in this investigation."

"You can't do that." Storm leaped to my defense before I uttered a word of protest. "Luna's a free witch. You can't slap extra time on her sentence because she's helping you."

"This is the opposite of help." He gestured to the broken gate. "Gather everyone who's involved in the filming so I can inform them what's happened. And make sure no one leaves until I've spoken to them."

"So now Luna's your unpaid assistant?" Storm said. "I thought you didn't want her involved?"

"No! I just..." Devlin drew in a deep breath. "Luna, I'd appreciate it if you'd get everyone together. It would save me time, and I can draw this tragedy to a close faster."

"I didn't hear a please in any of that," Storm said.

I nudged her. She was pushing her luck with Devlin, but it was fun to see him squirm.

He looked at the sky, as if seeking divine intervention. "Please, Luna."

"Of course. I'm always happy to help." I beamed at him.

He nodded then strode back to his colleagues.

"Let's get out of here," Storm said.

We walked away, but I turned back when we got to the end of the road. "I won't accept the accident verdict."

Storm tilted her head, and a smile slid across her face. "So, what are you going to do about it?"

"Find out who killed Fawn and why."

Chapter 6

An hour later, I was gathered on the set with the rest of the bakers, the judges, and the film crew. Devlin and one of his colleagues stood in front of us. I was eager to see what he had to say about Fawn's murder.

He cleared his throat and looked around the group. "I'm sorry I'm not meeting you under better circumstances, but as all of you will have learned, there's been a death. The body of Fawn Halliwell was discovered two hours ago in the play park."

Even though everyone had been told the news by Henriette, several people sucked in air or shook their heads.

"What happened to her?" Elwin said.

"The scene suggests it was an accident. Freak weather made its way into Witch Haven. Although I have yet to make my final report, it's possible a spot tornado landed on the play park. If the tornado hit Fawn, she wouldn't have been able to protect herself."

"It was an accident?" Henriette's voice wobbled.

"That's my belief," Devlin said.

I stood from my seat. "You're wrong. This was no accident."

All eyes turned to me.

"What are you talking about?" Henriette said. "We both saw what happened to Fawn and the mess in the park. What else could it have been?"

I made sure not to look at Devlin, who no doubt wanted to kill me. "It did look like an accident, but it couldn't have been a tornado. Several of my friends were in the group that stopped the bad weather. No tornadoes got into Witch Haven."

"That's enough, Luna. I understand you're distressed about discovering a body, but there's no need to worry everyone. Some unnatural weather could have snuck into the village."

The icy snap in Devlin's voice made me flinch, but I wasn't backing down. "Tornados don't sneak. You need to check with the magic users who settled the weather. They'll all confirm what Storm told you."

"Is this true?" Elwin said. "I noticed the winds easing while we were filming. I kept an eye on the weather to make sure there was no damage to the vehicles and the noise wouldn't interrupt the recording."

"Rest assured, I'll check the weather situation, but this is the most logical explanation. Fawn was in the wrong place at the wrong time." Devlin looked at Henriette. "Why were you meeting in the park?"

She glanced around. "I don't know the purpose of the meeting, but I got a note from Fawn this morning. It said she had important information to share about the integrity of the show. It didn't say more than that. I wondered if she was unhappy with the working conditions or was thinking of resigning and wanted to speak to me in private."

"She was miserable most of the time," Troy muttered. "Fawn hated it here."

I looked at Troy in interest. She'd seemed harassed and overworked, but Fawn hadn't seemed miserable to me.

"Do you know when Fawn died?" Elwin asked.

"Around two hours ago," Devlin said. "She hadn't been dead for long when Henriette discovered her."

"If I'd found her earlier, maybe I could have helped," Henriette said. "I saw the cut on her head. Was that what killed her?"

"It's unlikely you could have helped her, and you'd have been injured yourself. Fawn received a punishing blow to the side of her head from flying debris. She died instantly," Devlin said.

Cade winced while Meadow clutched her stomach and grimaced.

"Devlin, you're not listening to me," I said. "Fawn was murdered. There wasn't a tornado in the play park."

"Were you there?" Meadow said. "Did you see something?"

I shook my head. "But other than the head wound, there were no injury marks on Fawn's body. If she'd gotten slammed into by a tornado—"

Devlin glared at me. "Luna! You're upsetting people with these wild accusations."

"They're not accusations. They're facts. I'm no expert—"

"Exactly. Leave this investigation to the Magic Council. We've secured the scene and moved Fawn.

We'll see what other injuries she has. At this time, we aren't looking at this death as suspicious."

"I bet you a month's supply of chocolate cupcakes you won't find any other injuries on her body. If Fawn had been in that storm, she'd be covered in wounds."

Several of the group muttered to each other, all of them looking at me with worry in their eyes.

"Luna has a point," Elwin said. "We shouldn't be too quick to dismiss the idea something unpleasant happened. And if the tornados didn't reach Witch Haven, then how did Fawn get injured?"

Devlin looked around the group, the exasperation clear on his face. "What motive would anyone have for killing Fawn?"

"She was smug," Troy said.

"She could be a show off," Meadow said. "And she was the teacher's pet."

"Meadow, that's hardly fair. Fawn was an ambitious young woman. Sometimes those ambitions made her less than popular, but that's no reason to kill her," Elwin said.

"I'm not sorry she's gone," Troy said. "And she made terrible coffee."

Devlin glared at me as if it was my fault everyone was coming up with motives, but I refused to back down under his mean stare.

"It would be wise to look at this from all angles," Elwin said. "We shouldn't rule anything out, in case the worst happened. And Fawn was a valued member of the crew. It's the right thing to do, don't you agree?"

Devlin huffed out a breath. "Of course, Mr. La Croix. That was always my plan. We're still gathering evidence at this stage."

My eyes widened, and I pressed my lips together to stop from yelling at Devlin. Every time I suggested it was murder, he'd practically accused me of being a moron. Now an older authority figure was telling him what to do, and Devlin was agreeing with him.

"That's all the information I have for you. For now, if everyone can remain here, I might have questions," Devlin said.

"We're not going anywhere," Henriette said.

"We need to push back the filming schedule," Elwin said. "Everyone is in shock about Fawn. Perhaps we should cancel."

"Oh! No, we can't afford to do that. I mean, we're all sad about what happened, but we have to keep going," Henriette said.

"I'm not sad," Troy said. "It doesn't matter to me that Fawn is dead."

Meadow shrugged then nodded.

Cade's head was down. He hadn't spoken a word since Devlin arrived. He wiped a hand across his face.

"Let's put everything on pause for now," Elwin said. "We need to give the Magic Council time to investigate, and we must show Fawn the proper respect. Everyone needs time to come to terms with what happened to her."

None of the baking contestants looked happy with this decision, although I was secretly relieved. It meant the unveiling of my terrible baked goods could be put off. And a large part of me hoped they would cancel the whole thing.

Devlin left with his colleague but not before glaring at me. I didn't give a flying pig if he hated me for giving him extra work. Whoever did this wasn't getting away with it.

I walked over to Henriette, who looked pale, and her hand shook as she lifted a mug to her lips. "How are you doing?"

"I'm still processing." She blinked red-rimmed eyes at me. "Do you really think it was murder?"

"We shouldn't talk about this." Elwin joined us. "Let the Magic Council figure things out. Now that young warlock is on the case, it'll be sorted soon enough."

"I don't want to cause any trouble," I said, "but when I saw the scene, something felt wrong. It looked staged."

Elwin patted my arm. "You did a good thing. Even if it turns out to be a freak weather accident, we'll leave no stone unturned until we find out what happened to Fawn."

I glanced at the other bakers. "No one seemed to like her that much."

He tilted his head from side to side as if working out a kink in his neck. "Fawn could be prickly, but she was competent. And she loved this show. It was her life. I can't imagine she was meeting with Henriette to resign."

Henriette shrugged. "I can't think what else it could be. But you're right. She was passionate about baking. Fawn would sometimes bring in things she'd made at home, and they were always incredible. It put a few contestants' noses out of joint because her food was better than theirs. I don't believe Fawn had formal training, but she had talent."

"She did, despite her family name. Fawn asked me once if she could be on the show when a contestant was ill." Elwin chuckled and shook his head. "Of course, I had to turn her down. But that was her ambition. She didn't want to be a show runner. Fawn wanted to be in front of the camera, showcasing her baking creations."

"I had no idea she had such a talent," I said. "I don't know any Halliwells in the baking community."

"There aren't any. Fawn was an anomaly. But she had big plans for herself. None of that will happen now."

"Are you really thinking about canceling the show?" I tried not to sound hopeful.

Henriette's gaze flickered around the set. "We've got a lot of money invested in this show."

Elwin was quiet for a moment. "We should continue. Fawn wouldn't see it as disrespectful. She'd have wanted the show to carry on. But let's take the rest of the day to remember Fawn and think of a fitting tribute for her."

Henriette brightened. "I agree. We could showcase her recipes in a future show. It would be a nice way to remember her."

"I love that idea. But no one else knew of her talent. Fawn was always behind the scenes. And as Luna said, the Halliwells are no-names in our community. I'm not sure viewers would care about recipes from an unknown." Elwin's smile was rueful.

"You're right. And this show is all about fun and lightheartedness. Having a show dedicated to someone who was murdered would give out the wrong impression."

"You should do something for her, though," I said. "Even if Fawn rubbed people the wrong way now and again, you don't want to forget her."

"I have an idea." Elwin rapped his knuckles on the counter. "My new book is about to hit the bestseller lists, and the publisher is certain it'll be a smash. I'll use a percentage of the book profits to set up a fund in Fawn's name. It could help aspiring bakers who don't have the right credentials or family name to support them."

"Oh! That's wonderful." Henriette's eyes filled with tears. "Fawn would love that. She'd adore knowing she helped future generations of bakers. She was so frustrated with her position and wanted more. In this industry, it's all about your history and connections, along with your talent." She glanced at me. "Of course, I mean no offense to the Brimstone bakers. You're all excellent at what you do."

"I understand. There are always high expectations because of my name. They're hard to live up to."

"I'm sure you have no problems in that department," Henriette said. "Your baking is exemplary. But I love the idea of a fund. We could announce it at the beginning of a show and then move on to something light-hearted, maybe a recipe of Fawn's to entertain the audience. That seems appropriate."

"We'll figure things out over the next few weeks, once the Magic Council has completed their investigation," Elwin said.

"However Fawn died, we should still do it. Let's get started now," Henriette said. "Since we can't do any filming, there's not much else to do."

I excused myself as they plotted out Fawn's fund and the memorial show. It was time for me to get plotting, too. I didn't trust Devlin to get to the bottom of this murder, but I was determined to find out the truth.

Chapter 7

My gaze was forlorn as I stared at my sad little cupcakes on the workstation. I'd spent the last hour tidying up, then walking between the filming set and the bakery to occupy my time. But I couldn't settle on anything. My thoughts were full of what happened to Fawn.

I was convinced Devlin wouldn't budge from his belief her death was an accident. If that happened, I'd have to call him out. And the more I thought about the scene Storm and I discovered in the play park, the more I was certain that someone killed her.

My attention shifted back to my cupcakes. They seemed to sneer at me in all their lumpen glory, highlighting my lack of talent. But I had a legitimate reason for not being on top form. The murder had distracted me, and I'd had no opportunity to replace these monstrosities with cake from the bakery. I should throw them in the trash before anyone inspected them.

Henriette walked over. Her hair was neat and tidy, and she'd freshened her make-up, but her eyes were still red from crying. She gave me a small smile, then her gaze cut to my cupcakes. "Are these yours?"

"Um, yeah. I made them earlier."

Her forehead furrowed as she leaned over the plate. "They look interesting. What concept have they been designed around? Is it a rustic theme?"

"You could call them experimental abstract." I turned my back on the offensive cakes. "Is there any update from the Magic Council? I've been watching out for Devlin to come back."

"No, we're still waiting to hear from them. But I thought you'd appreciate an update on the show schedule, so you can juggle things around at the bakery."

"I don't mind if you want me to back out. Given everything that's going on, I assumed the show wouldn't go ahead as planned."

A flash of alarm crossed Henriette's face. "It's absolutely going ahead, and we need you as a judge. Don't think me mercenary, but I have too much money invested to cancel. And Elwin is expecting a huge boost in sales by promoting his book."

"Oh! Right. Are you sure you should?"

"We can't let our audience down. There'll be complaints if we don't air the show when they expect it."

"Viewers will understand the need to postpone." And it was a perfect chance for me to get out of this uncomfortable situation. "If you do delay, perhaps my dad can step in and take on the judging role. I'm sure you'd prefer him. He might be finished with his commission if you wait."

"No, that won't be necessary. And I'm sure your uncle can spare you for another day or two. We only pushed back filming until tomorrow. The contestants have been informed and will all make a fresh batch of cakes." Her gaze cut to my cupcakes again. "I imagine you got distracted when you made those."

My cheeks flushed as I glared at the embarrassing cakes. They were my best effort. "After seeing Fawn, I couldn't concentrate on baking. You know what it's like when your attention is elsewhere."

"I had no idea your talents were so sensitive. Still, every baker is unique. They use different techniques to keep themselves centered. Of course, finding a dead body would knock you off-kilter. It's understandable your cakes turned out looking like that." Henriette's expression suggested she wanted to incinerate my offensive offerings.

"I'm not proud of them. I can do much better." I was a terrible fraud. Any second now, I expected the truth to come out.

"Everyone will understand. And you're here to judge, not be judged. Your entry is simply for fun, along with mine and Elwin's. Perhaps you could have another go in the morning."

I forced a smile. "I don't want anyone to think I'm being given favorable treatment. It would be easier for me to grab something from the bakery."

"You can start again, just like everyone else. We want to see some of that Brimstone magic in action."

"Can someone get this cat off the camera?" Dave, the cameraman, was peering up at Earl.

I hurried over, stepped onto the ledge around the huge camera on wheels, and gathered up Earl. As usual, he was asleep. "Sorry, he'll sleep anywhere warm."

Dave tickled Earl between the ears. "He's cute."

"Thanks. He's also incredibly lazy." I carried Earl back to Henriette.

He yawned and flipped out of my arms, landing on the plate of cupcakes with a soggy thump.

"Earl! You clumsy boy." I was secretly grateful he'd ruined my cupcakes.

With a flip of one paw, he dislodged a cupcake, and it splatted on the floor. "Where am I?" His whiskers were bent on one side of his face and his eyes unfocused.

"On the filming set. Don't you remember coming in here?"

He licked cupcake frosting off his paw then wrinkled his nose. "The last few hours have been hazy."

"Too much catnip?"

Earl dropped to the floor. "You can never have too much of a good thing." He trotted away with a cupcake paper case stuck to his back.

Henriette stared at the icing paw prints he left behind. "You'll definitely have to bake something new now. Fawn, can you... Oh! I forgot. I'm so used to her helping when we have a problem." Her eyes flooded with tears.

I slid the cupcakes in the trash then handed her a hankie. "You said Fawn wanted to meet with you the day she died. Do you really have no idea what it was about?"

Henriette sniffed as she dabbed her nose. "Not really. I had a few theories, but whatever it was, it sounded important. And Fawn never exaggerated. She was a levelheaded young woman."

"Do you still have the note she sent you? That could give you a clue."

"I threw it away. It might still be in the trash. Do you think it's important?"

"I'm just curious what her concerns were."

Henriette rubbed her hands together as if they were cold. "I was worried it might be about the show. We have to make sure everything goes smoothly. Elwin's been working on his new recipe book for such a long time, and it would be a tragedy if his fans ignored the book and focused on the murder. If it even is a murder." Her worried gaze traveled over me. "You seemed to think it was."

"It's a possibility. And Fawn's death needs to be properly investigated. It's only right we find out what happened to her."

She closed her eyes for a second. "Of course. Sorry, that was thoughtless of me. I've been in this business for such a long time that my focus is always on the bottom line. Fawn's death won't become an afterthought. I still feel bad I never got to meet her to find out what she needed to tell me."

"When you went to the play park, did you see anyone else around? From what Devlin told us, she hadn't been dead long before you found her."

"I didn't notice anyone. My attention was taken by the mess in the play park. It even took me a few seconds to see Fawn. After that, I was in shock. Maybe I missed something, though."

"Was there anyone she worked with who might have had a problem with her? When Devlin asked if there were any motives for killing Fawn, the contestants were swift enough to come up with suggestions."

Henriette pressed her lips together. "I'll admit, there have been tensions on set. There are lots of strong egos, and they clash. Everyone wants to be the best. And you don't get to be a finalist on a show like this without being certain you're excellent at what you do."

"The finalists trod on toes to get their places?"

"Nothing illegal and certainly nothing that broke the rules of the contest. But this is their passion, and they'll do everything they can to make sure they don't lose their spot." She shook her head. "I feel the most sorry for Elwin in all of this."

"Why?"

"Fawn's father passed away a year ago. Ever since then, Elwin took her under his wing. We all saw she was lost and struggling with no parental guidance, so he did something about it. He never said, but I got the impression he thought of Fawn almost like a daughter. Elwin doesn't have any children."

"That was a nice thing to do." I empathized with Fawn's situation. Having ambitious parents who put cake before their only child was hard to accept.

"Elwin was always looking out for Fawn. He even showed her early versions of the recipes he worked on. And he took pleasure in making sure she had a satisfying job. It couldn't have been much fun running around after all of us, but Elwin kept an eye on things."

"Was that why he suggested the memorial fund? It was a kind gesture."

"Most likely. He's a good man. That's not to say he doesn't have an ego like the rest of the bakers, but he had a soft spot for Fawn."

"Is that why Meadow said Fawn was a teacher's pet? Was she jealous of their relationship?"

Henriette smiled and looked away. "It's possible. Meadow is as ambitious as the rest of them. But she deserves to be here. She's got a great talent, and I see good things in her future, even if she doesn't win this show."

"Troy was blunt about not liking Fawn."

"Oh, take no notice of him. Troy doesn't like anyone," Henriette said. "His bad attitude won't get him to the top. He needs to learn some manners. You can get away with being abrupt in this industry, but he's just rude. And he's the oldest in the group of contestants, so he assumes the role of alpha."

"You don't think much of him?"

"It wouldn't be wise to pass judgment on the contestants, in case I appear favorable to some of them. I judge purely on their baking creations, despite the bad attitudes."

"What about Cade? He seems the quiet one in the group. Did he ever have any problems with Fawn?"

"He's a sweet young man. And he is quiet. I'm not certain, but I believe he dated Fawn for a short time. The relationship didn't go on for long. But perhaps that's why he's not talking. He cared for her."

"What about other members of the crew? Fawn must have worked with them. Any problems there?"

"Not really. And we were her focus. She was the only show runner to the contestants and the judges and had little to do with the camera crew or anyone else on set." Henriette stood. "I need to get on with some work. Even though it's getting late, we have a lot to plan to keep this show on the road."

"Of course. And this will all get sorted soon. The Magic Council will figure out what happened to Fawn." And if they didn't, I would.

"Let's hope so." Henriette turned to me just before she walked away. "We'll do more filming tomorrow and finalize the new judging schedule. And you must make your cupcakes again with no distractions or cats falling on them. Won't that be nice?"

"Yes, I can't wait." A groan slid from my lips once Henriette was out of earshot.

I pondered what she'd told me about the baking finalists. There were several motives floating about for wanting Fawn dead. There was the grumpy alpha baker who had his nose put out of joint, Meadow not accepting Fawn's relationship with Elwin, and Cade and Fawn's romantic relationship that had broken down. Were any of those strong enough motives for murder?

Or maybe Henriette was hiding something. She really knew what Fawn wanted to talk to her about and was scared. Could Fawn have had dirt on Henriette or the show? Henriette made it clear she had to make this a success, so was Fawn a barrier she had to remove?

I stepped away from the workstation. Nothing would get figured out by sitting around here.

There was a stack of clean cake tins on the side, so I picked them up. I opened the cupboard and stared into a large brownie tray. Earl had wedged himself inside, his ears flat against his head and his tail tucked in tight. "I thought you left."

"I snuck in here and found this perfect cat bed no one was occupying. The door was open, and you were busy talking, so you didn't see me."

"Someone might want to use that brownie tray tomorrow."

Earl blinked slowly. "Give it a rinse out and it'll be fine. I barely shed any fur." He rolled out of the tray and stretched. "And she didn't do it."

I pulled out the brownie tray and gave it a thorough wash with dish soap and hot water. "Who are you talking about?"

"I was listening to your conversation with Henriette. She didn't kill Fawn." He still had a blob of cupcake icing on his side.

"How do you know that? Were you in the play park when it happened?"

"No, I was picking up a new blend of catnip from Ulric's store. It's mixed with caffeine. It should give me a boost." He bounced on his paws. "You're always moaning about me sleeping."

"Not always. But you sleep a lot. Even for a cat."

"There's nothing else to do."

I dried the brownie tin and placed it back in the cupboard, along with the rest of the trays. "Tell me your theory about Henriette."

"She found Fawn."

"I know that."

"If you're right, and the killer set up the murder to make it look like Fawn was a tornado victim, then Henriette couldn't have done it."

I leaned against the counter. "If Henriette set up the scene, she wouldn't have rushed back and found me and Storm. She'd have waited until the contest was over in the hope the tornado would blow through and destroy the evidence."

"Yep. See? She's not the killer."

I cocked my head at him. "How do you know about the murder, anyway? I've barely seen you since it happened."

"I'm always around. You just never notice me. And when I'm awake, I'm listening. And I found a warm place on the top of a cupboard in the bakery. I hear almost everything from there, and I get to stay nice and toasty."

"Good work, Earl. Thanks to your sleuthing skills, I'll move Henriette to the bottom of the list and focus on other suspects."

Earl scratched behind his ear with a back paw. "We could team up and solve this case together."

"We could. Are you sure you want to? You'll be missing valuable sleeping time."

"Sleep is for wimps. Once I've snuffed up enough caffeine infused catnip, I'll be unstoppable. Who's the next suspect?"

I grinned. It would be fun to have a partner to help figure out this mystery. "We've got several people to talk to."

"The other contestants?"

"They're all on my list. From what I can gather, none of them liked Fawn."

"Who shall we interrogate first?" Earl finally noticed the icing on his side and picked it off with his teeth.

"Let's see who's around and start asking questions. We'll begin at the top and go from there."

Chapter 8

Earl was settled over my shoulder, looking around with an uncharacteristic interest as I searched for Elwin. I wanted to learn more about his relationship with Fawn. If they'd been as close as Henriette said, he'd be devastated about Fawn's murder.

I ducked behind a crew van as Devlin came into view. I didn't want him to know I was poking around. He'd only tell me off.

"What are we doing?" Earl said.

"Hiding from trouble." I caught hold of him as he squirmed off my shoulder. "We need to stay out of sight of Devlin Goody."

A second later, Devlin's face appeared around the side of the van and he scowled at me. "I thought I heard your voice. What are you doing here?"

"I work at the bakery. You know that." My hiding had spectacularly failed. "I'm also a judge on the baking show. Yay, cupcakes!"

"Then shouldn't you be baking or judging, instead of lurking about on the street looking suspicious?"

"I'm done for the day." I leaned against the van, trying to look relaxed. "How are things going with the investigation? Do you still think it was an accident? Any evidence on the bloody pole that could be useful?"

The scowl remained on his face. "After consulting with other colleagues, and following the initial autopsy findings, it looks like murder."

I didn't grin. I really wanted to, and I wanted it to be a huge, smug grin. And I longed to tell Devlin I told him so. Instead, I calmly nodded. "What about the bad weather? Have you confirmed it didn't reach Witch Haven?"

He crossed his arms over his chest. "The other magic users confirmed the tornadoes petered out before reaching the village boundary. Nothing slipped through."

"So it had to be a murder. It's the only explanation. And the scene was staged to look like an accident." I pursed my lips. "It's clever in an evil way. If those tornadoes had whipped through the village, no one would have thought twice about what happened to Fawn."

"Yes. Very clever."

Since Devlin was talking, I'd keep asking questions. "What about the murder weapon?"

"It was most likely the pole."

"And..."

He tilted his head. "What?"

"Any fingerprints? Magic residue? Hints to who used it?"

"I can't disclose that."

"Would you if you could?"

He huffed out a breath. "The pole isn't useful in this investigation."

I was surprised. I'd expected Devlin to tell me to mind my business. "Huh! It really is genius. We have a smart killer on our hands if they removed all clues leading back to them."

"Indeed, I do. And I'm talking to everyone involved in the baking show, so I might as well start with you. Then you won't need to hang around and get in my way."

"Perfect. I've got new information you'll find useful."

"About what happened to Fawn?"

"Not so much, but I was talking to Henriette. She's not the killer."

"I've yet to eliminate you. Why don't we start there?"

"Me! Devlin, you know it wasn't me. I was being live filmed in front of a camera crew. Then I took a break and met Storm outside the set. That's when Henriette found us. I was never alone. It would have been impossible to sneak to the play park, kill Fawn, a woman I'd only just met, and return to the set without being spotted."

He grumbled under his breath as he made notes on a pad in his hand. "You're always in the middle of these problems. Why is that?"

"One time! I got involved in a murder once. And I wouldn't have been so involved if you hadn't been convinced my muffins were poisonous."

"I had every right to think you were the killer on that occasion. You looked guilty. And you certainly acted guilty." His eyes narrowed. "You always behave like you have something to hide."

"Not me. I'm an open book. Anyway, we've moved past that. I wasn't the murderer then, and I'm not the murderer now. But I could be helpful since I'm in the middle of this situation."

"You don't have to be. I'll get the information I need from you, but then you take a step back. A big one, so I don't see you."

"I'm a judge on the show. I have to be involved."

A faint growl rumbled in Devlin's chest, making Earl's head shoot up. "Be involved in the cake making but keep out of my murder investigation."

"Of course. Just listen to one thing I have to tell you, and then I'll be on my way. Henriette didn't do it. You're wasting your time by talking to her. She found the body. If she was the—"

"That's enough. I've got the information I need from you, and I don't need any wild speculations. Remember what happened the last time you got tangled in a murder and broke the law?"

"You insisted I do community service?" I grinned at him. "And I should thank you for that. I'll be teaching the gremlins every week soon. I'd have never thought about doing that if it wasn't for you."

"I wanted you put in jail, but the judge was lenient when he passed sentence. Don't think I'm unaware Olympus put in a good word for you. You manipulated your friendship with him to avoid serving time."

"Serving time for a tiny mix up of baking spells and a small cell escape is extreme. No one would have passed such a harsh sentence. Jails are for serious criminals. I'm only ever serious about my cakes."

"And that's only when she's having a good day," Earl muttered.

I petted him to encourage him to stop talking before we got in trouble.

"It was more than a tiny mix up. Your cake samples had multiple kinds of magic in them. And you still haven't explained that to my satisfaction."

I patted Devlin's arm and made him flinch. "That's ancient history. You should concentrate your energies on finding who killed Fawn. That's a serious crime. Solve this, and you might get a promotion."

"I'm warning you, Luna, stay out of this. If you obstruct this investigation, I'll arrest you."

I gave him my biggest smile. "You won't do that. I know you secretly like me."

"Just stay out of my way." He turned and strode away, his shoulders tight and his hands in fists. Devlin really had a problem with me.

"I don't think you got through to him," Earl said.

"Agreed. He didn't listen to a word I had to say about Henriette." I shrugged. "It's not my problem if he wants to waste time interviewing innocent people."

"So long as he stays away from us, I don't mind how Devlin spins his wheels."

I headed to the bakery but slowed when I got to the door, and my heart skipped a beat. "Earl, we might have a problem."

He jerked his head up and looked around. "Did someone steal my catnip?"

"No! The other suspects. They have the same alibi as me. We were all being live filmed when the murder took place. At least, the baking contestants were. If it wasn't one of them, that only leaves Henriette."

"Who I helped you discount."

"That's right. Or Elwin. But Fawn and Elwin had a great relationship, and I saw him on the set." I glanced at several of the film crew who were packing equipment in the truck. Was I looking in the wrong place? Was someone hiding in the shadows who I'd yet to identify?

Uncle Albert raised his hand as I walked through the bakery door, and I locked it behind me. The bakery had just closed for the evening.

"We have guests," Uncle Albert said.

I was already smiling as I made my way to the table where Indigo, Storm, and Odessa sat. "I didn't forget a meetup, did I?"

"No, but we wanted to find out what's going on with the murder investigation," Indigo said. "Olympus isn't impressed Devlin took over. Apparently, he pulled strings to make sure he could get this case."

Earl hopped down. "I'm going to try that new catnip."

I settled in a seat and hung my jacket over the back. "I was just trying to be helpful to Devlin, but he's not interested. He told me to keep my nose out, or he'll arrest me. I had useful information for him on a suspect, but he wouldn't listen."

"So long as he doesn't consider you a suspect again, that's the main thing." Odessa leaned back in her seat.

"He'd love to, but there's no way he can find me guilty. And I've convinced him I had nothing to do with it."

"You should still keep an eye on him," Storm said. "He loves causing trouble for you."

"That's because he's got a crush on you." Odessa giggled and batted her lashes. "It's like a playground relationship. He yanks on your pigtails to get a reaction."

I grimaced. "Don't say that. I've had enough of complicated men."

"Dinner will be ready in five minutes, ladies," Uncle Albert said from behind the counter.

"Thanks. You don't have to feed us all," I said.

"He absolutely does. He's promised us chicken pot pie with mashed potato and battered onion rings." Odessa smacked her lips together. "I can't wait."

My stomach grumbled. Uncle Albert's food was the best, and he loved having people to cook for.

"You mentioned complicated men. Who are you dating this month?" Storm said.

"No one! None of the guys I was sort of seeing worked out."

"What about the cute guy who didn't have his shirt on when we met him?" Odessa said. "I liked him."

"Ridley's a great guy, but we're only friends."

"And then there's—"

I cut off Odessa before she could go further. "I've come up with a problem for most of the murder suspects."

"Go on," Indigo said. "What's the problem?"

"Nearly all of them have the same alibi as me."

"You think a baking contestant killed Fawn?" Storm said.

"She wasn't popular with them. They described her as a teacher's pet or annoying." I tapped my fingers on the table. "The problem I've discovered is that all of us were being live filmed. I was on set baking, alongside the finalists, and Elwin was also there. He was being filmed but not continuously."

"Elwin is..." Indigo raised her eyebrows.

"Elwin La Croix! He's an incredible baker and an artist who makes stunning desserts. He's been a judge on this show for a decade. He owns a string of cake creative studios all over the world."

"I've heard of him. Didn't he make an edible replica of the Leaning Tower of Pisa?" Odessa's eyes sparkled. "I'd have loved that to fall into my mouth."

"He did. It took him three weeks. He's also got a new recipe book coming out and gave me an advanced copy. Elwin's at the top of his game."

"He could make magic cakes out of unicorn poop, but he still needs to be a suspect." Storm wasn't the tiniest bit impressed by Elwin's kitchen magic.

"He's on my list, but from everything I've heard, he had a great relationship with Fawn. When her dad died, he took her under his wing and made sure she was doing okay."

"Who else is on the suspect list?" Odessa said.

"Henriette. She found the body."

"Any killer vibes oozing out of her?"

Storm was shaking her head along with me. "It can't be her. If Henriette killed Fawn, she'd have kept quiet. When she raced over to us, she was in a state. She was crying and sweating and could barely get her words out."

"I agree, I don't think Henriette did it," I said.

"So you've only got one suspect," Indigo said. "It must be Mr. Fancy Pants baker, Elwin La Crotch."

"La Croix! I plan to speak to him next and find out what his relationship with Fawn was really like."

"So you're snooping?" Storm grinned at me.

"It's my duty to snoop. Fawn deserves justice, and I'm worried Devlin might not be able to deliver."

Uncle Albert arrived with our delicious plates of food, and we spent a few minutes enjoying the chicken pot pie and crispy onion rings.

"Maybe Elwin's relationship with Fawn crossed the line," Indigo said. "He wanted more from her, and when she refused, things turned nasty."

"He doesn't give out the vibe of being a sexual predator. You know how you meet a guy, and his eyes roam all over you, looking anywhere but your face," I said. "Elwin didn't do that when we met. He came over kind of fatherly. And no one's mentioned they were having an intimate relationship or that he likes to proposition women he works with."

"It's still worth considering," Storm said. "He's a famous guy, and some women get weird around that kind of thing. Elwin could have turned on the charm and dirty talked Fawn with complicated dessert recipes."

"Oooh, baby, let me show you my recipe for strawberry pavlova. I can guarantee a stiff peak." Indigo chuckled.

Odessa dropped her onion ring and giggled. "My sponge cake always rises to the occasion."

Storm snorted a laugh. "Maybe they got busy over the chocolate fountain."

"Many people consider him a silver fox." Odessa sprinkled powdered pumpkin all over her food. "And he's a handsome older man."

"You should date him." Indigo's smile was wicked as she looked at me. "You have a thing for old guys."

I whacked her arm. "My old guy dating days are over. I called time on my friendship with Englebert ages ago. I haven't seen him in weeks."

"He's walking around with Ayla Bellflower on his arm." Storm gave us all an evil grin.

My fork hit the table. "She's twenty-five! That's just wrong."

"Ayla is only five years younger than you," Indigo said. "And you didn't mind hanging out with Englebert."

"That was different. I had... needs to fulfill."

Storm snort laughed. "I don't want to hear about how your needs were met by Englebert's wrinkled old hands."

"That's just nasty." Odessa threw half an onion ring at Storm. "You didn't see any wrinkly bits, did you?"

"No! No wrinkled bits were exposed as part of our deal."

Indigo leaned back in her seat. "It's for the best you called time on Englebert. Find someone your own age."

"Or where there's a maximum of two decades difference between you," Storm said.

I arched an eyebrow at Indigo. "Should I find someone like Olympus?"

She raised a hand. "Hey! My first impressions of Olympus weren't great, but he grew on me. I definitely don't hate him hanging around anymore."

"You're such a sweet couple," Odessa said. "Seeing you together almost makes me believe in love again." She sighed as she picked an onion ring off her plate and chewed it.

"You'll find someone when the time is right," Indigo said. "And there's no rush. You're young, gorgeous, and you have a thriving business. You're a catch."

"Two thriving businesses. I'm booked solid for the next three months creating new scarecrows. And after that, it'll be pumpkin harvest time. I might even hire an assistant. A woman can only haul and carve so many pumpkins on her own."

"That's what you need. Some rugged farm hand to sweep you off your feet," Storm said. "And show you a great time in the bedroom."

Odessa looked away and stared at the chalkboard covered in descriptions of delicious desserts. "Will your uncle treat us to pudding?"

"I'm sure he will. He loves feeding us." Odessa had lost the love of her life years ago and hadn't seriously looked at another guy since then. We all hoped she'd move on, but her heart was stuck in the past, pining for a love she could never have.

Uncle Albert walked over and cleared our empty plates. "Who's for dessert?"

Odessa's hand shot up. "Me, please! I'd love a chocolate eclair."

"Coming right up. How about everyone else?"

We all agreed eclairs were the best choice, and he hurried away with our plates.

"I wouldn't mind someone like your uncle," Odessa said. "He's a caregiver. We all need a little extra looking after at times."

"Don't chase after Uncle Albert," I said. "It would be weird if you became my stepmom."

Odessa cackled a laugh. "I'd get to boss you around and be the evil stepmom."

I glanced at Uncle Albert as he pulled our desserts from the chiller cabinet. He must get lonely. He'd lost my auntie years ago and hadn't dated since. I should let him know I was fine with him being in a relationship. I hated the thought of him being alone.

He walked back with a tray containing our eclairs and a small brown wrapped package. He passed around the plates and then handed me the package. "This was left for you today."

"I haven't ordered anything." I pulled off the packaging to find a small black box inside.

"That looks like a jewelry box," Odessa said. "Has one of your admirers bought you a gift?"

"I don't have any admirers." I flipped open the box lid, and my breath caught in my throat.

"What is it?" Indigo leaned over. "Is that a silver wolf?"

I extracted the beautiful silver pendant shaped like a wolf. His head was tipped back, frozen in a howl.

"Does it say who it's from?" Storm said.

"Nope. I don't see any card." I checked the packaging, but I didn't need a note to tell me the sender's details. This was from Cole. But why was he sending me something so beautiful? He hated me.

"Put it on. It's pretty." Odessa helped me fasten the pendant around my neck.

I clasped it in my hand. I wasn't sure what message Cole was sending me with this gift, but it made my spine tingle. He was closing in, and I had a feeling he was about to make his move.

Chapter 9

The next morning, I was up early and headed to the farmhouse with a basket of supplies for my magic harem.

I hadn't slept well the previous evening after receiving Cole's gift. I hadn't been sure what to do with the pendant and in the end decided to wear it. I couldn't escape what was coming for me.

Once the magic barrier was lowered, I headed to the farmhouse and knocked on the door before entering. "It's only me. I've brought food and entertainment."

"We're in the front parlor," Gloria called out.

I entered the room to find Gloria and Faye settled in their usual comfortable armchairs.

"Have you had breakfast yet?" I settled the basket on the floor.

"No, we were just discussing what to eat." Faye patted her neat gray hair. "What have you brought us?"

Ridley appeared a few seconds later with a mug of coffee in his hand. He scratched his fingers through his bed messy hair. "Hey, Luna. What's in the basket?"

"I've got fresh croissants, and there are two loaves of bread and milk, plus plenty of dried goods to keep you going for the next few days. I also brought new magazines and books because I knew you were getting low, Faye."

"Thank you. I was running out of new romances to read." Faye pawed through the basket.

"I don't have much time." I settled in a seat. "You won't have heard, but someone was killed yesterday."

"Goodness! Is it anyone we know?" Gloria set down her knitting.

"No, it was an assistant on the baking show. I've got a lot to catch you up on." I spent the next ten minutes telling them about my involvement in the show, and what happened to Fawn in the play park.

They listened with rapt attention. I was their main source of village gossip, so I left nothing out.

"That poor young girl," Faye said. "What a deceitful person to hide her murder."

"They're a clever person," I said. "They almost got away with it."

"Do you think it was someone she worked with?" Gloria said.

"I doubt it was anyone from the village. Fawn's not from around here. And there are some good motives floating about the recording set. The Magic Council is investigating, but I'm worried they won't do a good job."

"Be careful you don't get in trouble," Gloria said. "We'd be lost without you. We'd have to leave the farmhouse if anything happened to you."

"We wouldn't have anyone protecting us." Faye clutched the book she'd extracted from my basket.

I leaned forward and patted her knee. "Don't worry about me. And we'll look out for each other. And if it's not too much trouble, I wouldn't mind a quick hit of magic. I was baking most of yesterday, and I'm exhausted."

"You can take mine." Ridley settled on the couch and set down his mug.

I wrinkled my nose. His magic always made my food taste sharp. Although I could use that to my advantage in lemon drizzle cupcakes. "You're on. I must make sure I don't make a mess of my baking like yesterday."

"Your cakes didn't come out well?" Gloria said.

I shook my head. "The magic didn't want to take. It slid off five times before I got some to stick."

"That's my fault. I was tired when you borrowed magic from me. You didn't get a good hit. I'm a silly old woman who isn't strong enough to help you anymore." Gloria's bottom lip jutted out.

"It's not you. I think it's me." I grabbed Ridley's hand and channeled his magic into me. "I seem to need more and more magic just to stay stable."

"We're not enough for you." Faye lowered her head. "I knew this day would come. Everything good gets taken away in the end. We'll have to move out, and the Magic Council will find us and lock us away. We'll never be seen again."

"Faye, no! I value all of you, and you'll always have a place here. I'd never turn you out. You're so good to me, sharing your magic, and I'd be lost without all of you. You're my extended family."

Faye dabbed at her eyes. "You're such a good girl. We were lucky to find you."

Gloria gave a firm nod. "And we don't mind if you need to add more people to the group. There's plenty of room, and it would be nice to have new company."

"We could make up the bedroom that overlooks the yard." Faye brightened as she warmed to the idea. "The windows have lovely views. Anyone would be proud to live here."

"I'm thinking about it. It's difficult to find people willing to join a household full time and donate their magic." My hand tightened around Ridley's.

"You've heard nothing from that werewolf who escaped?" Gloria said. "He had plenty of power."

My fingers brushed across the wolf pendant, and I was surprised to feel it was warm. "Not directly. He's not a good candidate, though. Werewolves like their freedom and being kept here would drive him crazy."

"He'd have plenty of woodland to run around in. I don't see the problem," Faye said. "And he was handsome."

"Once the baking show has left the village, and this murder has been figured out, I'll find someone suitable to join you. Someone we can all get along with."

Ridley groaned and slumped back in his seat.

I yanked my hand away. I'd been so busy talking, I hadn't noticed how much magic I'd drained from him. His face was pale and sweating, and his closed eyes flickered behind his eyelids.

I hurried to his side, making sure not to touch him so I didn't take more magic. "Ridley, are you okay?"

He tossed his head from side to side.

"Gloria, can you help me? I don't want to touch Ridley again." I bit my bottom lip. Curse my inability to cast real spells.

Gloria bustled over. She had a glass of water in one hand and smelling salts in the other. "He'll be fine. It's not the first time this has happened. We know what to do to get him back."

I inched away, my guilt making me queasy. This was happening too often. It hadn't always been like this. We'd had a great balance when I'd set up the farmhouse harem. A hit from any of them would have seen me through a week. Now, I needed a concentrated hit of their magic before I felt any effect. And even having just practically drained Ridley, I could have taken more.

My gaze shifted to Faye, who watched Ridley with interest as Gloria applied the smelling salts under his nose. I shook my head and squeezed my eyes shut. No! No more magic. I needed better control. That was the problem. I was pulling in magic and feeding it out too quickly. This was about balance. That was the only thing wrong here. Once I got a better balance in my life, everything would be fine.

After waiting anxiously for several minutes for Ridley to regain consciousness, I was rewarded when he opened his eyes, a dazed look on his face.

"I'm so sorry." I went to grab his hand but stopped myself. "You should have told me I was being greedy."

He tried to lift his head from the back of the couch but slumped back after several failed attempts. "You're good. It's what I'm here for."

"We'll set a timer the next time so I don't take too much."

"We'll make sure he's back to his normal self in no time," Gloria said. "You've nothing to worry about."

I was worried. My magic harem was a lifeline I couldn't do without.

Faye leaned over and squeezed my arm. "Won't the bakery be open soon? You don't want to be late. And aren't you doing more filming today?"

I checked the time and nodded. "I do need to get back. So long as you're okay, Ridley."

His nod was feeble as he sipped from a glass of water Gloria held for him.

Feeling like the biggest monster in the world, I said goodbye and left the farmhouse, my head down.

I hurried back to the bakery, slowing when Elwin came out of the filming set next door.

He raised a hand in greeting. "Morning, Luna. Are you up for a new challenge today?"

"I will be later, so long as you still need me."

"Absolutely. Your skills are invaluable. We're not planning on filming until later, so you have the day free if you need to be in the bakery."

"Thanks. I don't like leaving Uncle Albert for too long. We're already getting extra customers because they're so interested in what you're doing on set."

He smiled. "Wherever we go, we always draw a crowd. I sometimes get hand cramp from signing so many autographs."

I fell into step with him as he headed back onto the set. "Have you had an update from the Magic Council about Fawn?"

His smile slipped. "No, nothing since yesterday. Although Devlin confirmed it was murder late last night. I still can't believe she was killed."

"It must have been a big shock for you. Henriette mentioned you looked out for her."

"I did. Fawn could be a spiky little thing, and if you didn't take the time to get to know her, it was easy to assume she was cold. But I saw something in her as soon as she joined the crew."

"She was a good assistant?"

Elwin tilted his head from side to side. "She was an average assistant. But Fawn had a startlingly wide knowledge of baking techniques." He led me to one of the workstations. "When she thought no one was watching, she'd come over and ask me questions. It didn't take me long to realize her passion was in baking."

"It's good you kept an eye on her. She lost her dad recently, didn't she?"

He nodded. "I took more of an interest in her after that. She was only young, and her mom wasn't in her life, so she didn't have a support network. I don't like to think too highly of myself, but I hoped she saw me as a father figure. She'd talk about baking for hours, and we even tried a few recipes together."

"I heard from some of the others that Fawn wasn't popular with everyone, though."

Elwin leafed through a pile of paper on the workstation. "She wasn't. Anyone will tell you that. That's another reason I watched out for her. I won't have bullying on this show. Healthy competition is fine, but it's unacceptable to pick on anyone."

"Who bullied her?"

He glanced up from the papers. "There were harsh words spoken now and again, but they came from jealousy more than anything else."

"Who was jealous of Fawn?"

He discarded the papers and glanced around the set. "I expect they all were. There's competition in cupcakes, and those were her specialty. They always tasted like an angel had touched them. They were sweet and delicious, and I could never stop at one. I always knew when Fawn made the cupcakes and left them on the food table. She was almost as good as me."

"Were any of the contestants threatened by Fawn's talent? You said she'd never take part in a show like this because of her background."

"And she wouldn't. Fawn would never have been a finalist on this show, or any show, but there are other ways to get your recipes out there. She was always scribbling ideas and showing them to me. I had an inkling she was considering putting together a book of recipes."

"Maybe the contestants didn't like that idea. They thought it was wrong for someone with no qualifications or the right family name to promote themselves."

His eyebrows rose. "It's possible. But they had nothing to concern themselves with. They should have been focused on their baking challenges."

"No one raised any objections to you about Fawn baking?"

"The only contestant who made it clear she hated Fawn's food was Meadow. And she made life difficult for her. She'd order Fawn to get refreshments and then complain that she'd brought the wrong thing. I had a quiet word with Meadow because I could see what she was doing. Fawn was busy looking after all of us and didn't have time to play Meadow's games."

"Did you see Meadow talking to Fawn before she left the set on the day she was killed?"

"No, I didn't notice that. If Meadow wasn't yelling at her, she ignored her."

"Do you have suspicions about anyone who might have wanted to kill Fawn?"

His expression turned regretful. "I'm afraid I don't. And I was doing pieces to camera most of the day. They're used as inserts for commercials and fill-in sections when the baking is going on. I was focused on that. Maybe if I'd seen something, I could have stopped it from happening."

"No one knew what was going to happen."

"I suppose not." His gaze turned sharp. "You're very interested in this mystery, even though you didn't know Fawn."

"Her murder happened in my village, and I used to play in that park when I was a child. I want to make sure everything is properly investigated." I smiled. "And I might be a bit nosy."

"Curiosity is an asset in our line of work." He tapped the papers in front of him. "These are notes about my experiments into the missing cupcake ingredient. I've tried hundreds of variations. Bakers need to be tenacious and take risks."

"You really don't know what the missing ingredient is?"

"Let's just say, there are several paths to perfection. I'll be intrigued to see what you and the finalists come up with. You never know, you might get to be in my recipe book."

"I'm sure it won't be me who finds the secret ingredient, but I'll give it my best shot. Maybe Fawn would have figured it out if she'd been alive."

Elwin's head lowered. "Nothing would have surprised me about Fawn. She was a rare talent. It was a shame she had no support to enable her to bloom."

"She had you. That must have helped her."

A smile flickered across his face. "I like to think so."

I glanced around the set. "Has anyone from the Magic Council spoken to the contestants about Fawn?"

"Yes, I believe everyone has been spoken to. It's a mystery to me how any of them could have done this, though."

That had me puzzled as well since everyone had an alibi. "Was there anyone else in Fawn's life she was having trouble with?"

"If there was, she said nothing to me. Fawn only talked about the things she wanted to. Everything else was off-limits. Her conversations mainly revolved around baking."

"There were no ex-boyfriends on the scene she was scared of?"

"No, although she dated Cade for a while, but it wasn't serious. I asked about the relationship once, and Fawn shrugged it off. She said it wasn't important, and she was focused on her career. And she was young, so she had plenty of time to get serious with someone. But you never know. Young men can sometimes get the wrong impression."

I needed to speak to Cade and get his side of the story. Maybe their relationship had been more intense than anyone realized.

"How are you getting on with the recipe book I gave you?" Elwin said. "Have you tried anything?"

"I tested a cupcake recipe. And Uncle Albert has been looking through it. We're excited to get an advanced copy."

"Show it to your father, too. It might encourage him to come on a future show."

"I will. I'll let him know about it the next time I speak to him." Which wouldn't be for weeks. Sometimes, my parents were difficult to get hold of.

"I must get on," Elwin said. "Drop by the set after you've finished in the bakery. If the weather stays stable, we'll be able to squeeze in a few hours of filming tonight."

"Sure, I'll come back then. I'll see you later." I left the set and walked into the bakery.

Uncle Albert smiled as I approached the counter. He held aloft a tray of beautiful red velvet cupcakes. "Are we all set for a day of baking?"

"Always. Let's get to work."

Chapter 10

My apron was hung up, and I was just washing my hands when there was a knock on the kitchen door. A few seconds later, Henriette appeared.

"Your uncle told me you were back here," she said. "We're ready on set. I hope you're free for the rest of the evening."

"I was just on my way." I dried my hands, grabbed my jacket, and walked out of the bakery with Henriette after giving Uncle Albert a wave goodbye.

"It's taken us a while to figure out the new schedule, but we've jiggled everything around and can get back on track, so long as we film tonight." Henriette looked at me. "Will that be too much for you? After all, you've spent all day in the bakery."

"No, that's not a problem. I saw Elwin earlier today, and he told me what was going on."

"I expect a Brimstone witch never tires of baking. I hear it's invigorating to those with a natural ability. The more you bake, the more powerful you become."

I scrubbed the back of my neck with my hand. "Something like that. Although it can get tiring if you use too much magic in a short space of time."

She shot me a quizzical look. "I've never heard that before. Usually, at the end of a long day of baking, the contestants are bouncing off the wall with excitement. I guess it's different for every family, though."

I nodded, pretending it absolutely was, and I wasn't the biggest fibber in the universe.

We entered the set. The finalists were all there, along with Elwin, who was talking to the camera crew.

Henriette touched my arm. "Go see the contestants. I just need to speak to Elwin. I won't be long." She hurried away.

I walked over to Troy, who stood apart from the others. I gave him my friendliest smile, which he didn't return. "Are you all set for more baking?"

He scowled at me. "We wasted a whole day yesterday. The stuff I made is no good now. I had to toss all my cupcakes."

"You don't like baking?"

He looked at me as if I was a moron. "I wouldn't be here if I didn't like it. The Morelli family has been doing this for hundreds of years. What else am I supposed to do?"

"Um, something that makes you happy?"

He shrugged. "I'll be happy when I have a string of successful businesses and a team to do the donkey work."

"You have big ambitions."

"There's no point stopping at one tiny bakery." He glanced at me and smirked. "Some of us don't shy away from a challenge."

Troy was a charmless individual. "I've heard that said about Fawn. She was forging a path in the baking community despite not having the right credentials."

"Yeah, you would hear that. She was always bleating about how unfair it was she wasn't born into the right family." Troy straightened, his hands clenched. "Like I was expected to do something about it. She'd always butt in on things that had nothing to do with her, and she'd interfere with recipes and make suggestions for improvements. Fawn even had the nerve to bring her own creations on set."

"Were her cakes any good? I heard cupcakes were her specialty."

He made a gagging sound. "As if I'd touch anything she made. Gutter trash doesn't get to show off some freak talent they shouldn't even have. It was unnatural."

"But you admit Fawn had talent?"

"Maybe. She probably cheated."

"Why do that? And Fawn must have thought her baking was amazing if she brought it here, where there are so many talented bakers."

"She did that because she was an idiot. Fawn thought she was better than any of us. I could never understand why. No name, no prospects, and no hope of getting a decent job."

I crossed my arms over my chest, sorely tempted to find something to whack Troy with. "Why shouldn't she have had audacious goals, like you?"

He smirked. "She'd get nowhere with no name and no qualifications. Fawn had zero chance of ever being on a show like this. And I know she was wheedling Elwin to get on air. Like that would ever happen. She was a nobody."

"Fawn must have been a somebody to someone, since she was killed."

"That means nothing. She probably said the wrong thing to the wrong person. Fawn was always putting her foot in it or getting involved when she wasn't needed. Her job was our assistant. She was here to look after us and nothing else."

"You never got along with Fawn?"

"No, and I told the Magic Council that when they questioned me. They've been asking around to see what happened to her, but I've no clue what they expect to find on the set."

"Who do you think killed her?"

Troy stretched his arms over his head. "She probably ran into the wrong warlock when she was poking around the village. He snapped his fingers and got rid of her. Good thing, too. Now they'll have to hire someone who can make a decent coffee."

My hands clenched into fists. "Did you see Fawn leave the set the day she was killed?"

"Why would I pay any attention to her? I was being filmed, just like everyone else."

That's what I thought he'd say. "Even though you didn't get along, did you ever notice her having trouble with anyone on set or after work?"

He looked at the rest of the contestants and yawned. "Fawn argued with most of us, but that was what she did. She loved making herself the center of attention."

"Was there anyone in particular who got annoyed with her?"

Troy glanced at me and leaned in close. "Why are you so interested in Little Miss Nobody? You want her job?"

I stepped into his personal space. "Fawn was worth caring about. I want to know what happened to her. Even if you don't think she was a nice person, her death shouldn't be swept under the rug."

"It won't be. That's what the Magic Council is here for. And it's not just me. None of us liked her. I asked Elwin to get a different assistant, but he said Fawn was an asset." Troy leaned against the counter and started doing push-ups. "Maybe she looked after him in a particular way, if you know what I mean?"

My nose wrinkled. "You're suggesting Elwin and Fawn were in a relationship?"

He huffed out air as he continued his press-ups. "I didn't say that. But why else would he keep her around? It wasn't for her sparkling personality. And she used to bug the heck out of Meadow."

"Did they fight recently?"

"I saw them arguing a few days ago." His laugh was hard. "Meadow looked so red in the face, I thought she'd blow a gasket."

"What was the argument about?"

"I don't know, and I don't care. I just heard raised voices, went to look, and there they were. I kept out of it." Troy stopped his press-ups and started squatting. "Meadow thought Fawn was a teacher's pet. She was always hanging around Elwin and talking to him. I'm surprised she didn't get fired for that. Elwin is a judge you don't mess with." He finally stopped his counter workout.

"Was Meadow filming when Fawn was killed?"

"Most likely. The same as all of us." He lifted his mug and looked at it. "I need another coffee." He stomped away.

Troy was one thoroughly unpleasant individual, but he wasn't hiding his hatred for Fawn. And, unfortunately, he had an alibi. He couldn't be in two places at once.

I looked around and spotted Meadow. I was about to walk over and talk to her, when Elwin clapped his hands.

"Everyone gather around. This won't take long. I want to give you an update on the filming and judging schedule." He gestured for us to draw closer.

Everyone hurried over and joined Elwin and Henriette, and I moved to stand alongside them.

"As you're all aware, things have gotten off-track because of our tragic loss." Elwin lowered his head.

Troy snorted into his mug. Meadow glared at him, while Cade stared at his shoes.

"We're all saddened by what happened to Fawn. The Magic Council is investigating, and they're likely to be back asking more questions so we can find out what happened."

"We can't help them," Meadow said. "I've already told them everything I know. They'll get in the way of filming if they keep poking around."

"We'll have to accept that," Elwin said. "We must ensure they can do their job. It's only right they have full access to the set and all of you. I'm sure none of you will mind cooperating. This is all for Fawn."

The contestants grumbled under their breaths, but no one else protested.

"Excellent. I knew you'd all understand." Elwin glanced at Henriette. "I've been talking with our wonderful sponsor and the crew, and we've found a way to make up the time lost. And the good news is, you all get a second chance to create perfection. And this time, we must take it seriously."

I tensed as his gaze flicked to me. Did he think I hadn't been taking my baking seriously? Maybe he'd seen my terrible cupcakes. I'd buried them deep in the trash, but he could have passed my workstation when I hadn't noticed.

"You'll all have a chance to revise your recipes if you wish before we resume filming. And remember, we're looking for that crucial missing ingredient for the recipe in my book. Don't forget, anyone who finds the perfect combination will have a credit on that recipe and a percentage of the profits. This is a once-in-a-lifetime opportunity to get your name out there and have everyone know who you are." Elwin rubbed his hands together. "The winner will have their life changed."

The contestants glanced at each other. Troy looked smug, Cade looked sad, and Meadow appeared worried.

"And of course, just for fun, I'll also be taking part, alongside the other two judges. Our efforts won't be formally judged, but we'll sample each other's baked goods, and you'll get to see the extraordinary talent we have among our judges."

Henriette chuckled. "You'll have to excuse my entry. I don't have the natural baking abilities of any of you. Of course, I'll give it my best go, but be lenient. I don't want to make a fool of myself by offering inedible cupcakes."

"You'll do a wonderful job," Elwin said. "We all will."

I was convinced Henriette's cupcakes would be better than mine. Still, I'd been working on my lemon drizzle cupcakes in the bakery for most of the day and had the recipe almost perfect.

So long as I focused on the spells as I put them into the cakes, they'd be edible. That was my target. Make them edible, don't make anyone choke, and don't humiliate the Brimstone family name. The contestants could focus on finding the missing ingredient and getting the glory. The bar was low, but I aimed to meet it.

"You all have an hour to review your recipes and see if you want to make any changes, then we'll get started on the filming." Elwin glanced out the window. "Although I don't like the look of that cloud bank forming. We're not in for more bad weather, are we?"

I looked out the window and frowned. "No. It's supposed to be quiet. No more tornados heading our way." A flash of lightning flickered among the dark, heavy clouds.

"We'll keep an eye on the situation. Providing the weather stays true, and we've got adequate lighting, we hope to get four hours filming done tonight. We're also starting early tomorrow and running late into the evening to stay on track. Everything can go to editing as planned, and the show will go out in its scheduled spot."

The contestants were already edging away to their workstations.

Elwin smiled indulgently. "I see you're all eager to begin, so I won't hold you any longer."

Meadow, Troy, and Cade raced away, grabbing aprons and ingredients off the shelves.

Elwin looked over at me. "Is there anything you need to do before we get started? Have you got everything covered at the bakery?"

"I just need to let Uncle Albert know what's going on," I said. "I already know what cupcakes I'm baking, so I won't make any last-minute changes, just in case it all goes wrong."

He laughed. "You're funny. As if a Brimstone baker could mess up a cupcake. I'll see you back here within the hour."

"I'm looking forward to it." I turned and raced off the set.

I'd just reached the door to the bakery when a large shape stepped out of the shadows at the side of the building. My eyes widened, and I froze to the spot, my heart doing a somersault.

It was Bram Vexx, the debt collector, and he looked as angry as the looming storm clouds.

I swallowed my fear and pushed back my shoulders. "What are you doing here? You got everything you wanted when you broke into the bakery."

"I only got a fraction of what you owe after robbing this place, so I'm back to get the rest. And remember, you promised me double for covering for you." There was a nasty glint in Bram's eyes.

"That deal is off. You could have harmed Uncle Albert when you broke in. What if he'd found you when you were taking money from the register?" I glanced around, but no one was listening to the conversation.

"I'd never hurt a defenseless old guy. And I wouldn't have hurt you, but you tried to stop me. I was only taking what I was entitled to. It's your fault for getting in my way."

"You need to leave. I've got nothing to give you."

"Yes, you have. I gave all the money to Sylvester, but he's not happy. He's demanding it all. It's time to pay up."

I glanced in the bakery's window. Uncle Albert was pottering around in the back, writing out the menu on the chalkboard. I didn't want him knowing about this, so I had to get rid of Bram. "Not here. I don't have any money stashed on the premises."

"Why don't I take it from the till again?" His hand went to the door.

I grabbed hold of the door and shoved him back. "No! This is my debt. Uncle Albert's not to know about this."

Bram shook his head. "It's bad to keep secrets from your family. People get hurt when you lie to them."

"You'd know. You don't know what the word honest means."

"Hey, that's not nice. I always put in an honest hard day's work when I have to chase down those who forget about their debts." His smile was sly. "It's a common theme with people who get in trouble, though. They hide the truth. They think they can solve everything on their own, and when it all goes wrong, they look around for someone else to blame. Just like you're doing."

"I'm not forgetting my debt. And I plan to fix it. I've been saving up."

His laugh suggested he didn't believe me. "You've saved all the money you owe in a few short weeks?"

"Why not? I've been working overtime. And I have some savings." Savings he was never getting hold of.

"Then let's go get this money. You hand it over, and you'll never see me again."

My fingers flexed as I glared at him. I had to stand up to this bully and fix this problem.

Bram stepped closer. "I'm waiting for the cash, little witch, and I'm not prepared to wait any longer. When Sylvester gets angry, everyone suffers."

I gulped down panic. I could do this. "The money's not here. It's at the farmhouse."

He grinned. "I remember that place. Another one of your secrets."

"It's not a secret. Follow me if you want the cash."

Bram Vexx was going down, and I was getting rid of this problem for good.

Chapter 11

I had less than an hour to deal with Bram, and the solution I had planned needed to be permanent, or he'd keep coming back and making more demands. And every time he visited, he risked revealing my magic problem to my loved ones. That wasn't happening.

I glanced at Bram as he strode along beside me, his expression smug. He was big, with broad shoulders and muscles that looked like they could do damage. His nose had been broken at least once, and he had a faded scar on his neck. This guy wouldn't go down easily.

But I had to embrace this opportunity. If I tamed this troublesome debt collector, I could keep him at the farmhouse and make him mine. I had strong chains and a small team of magic users who would defend me to the death if I asked them.

Bram glanced at me as if sensing my appraisal. "I hope that werewolf jerk of yours isn't still hanging around."

"Nope. He's not." I clutched the pendant around my neck and noticed it was warm.

"You're into furry guys, huh?"

"That's none of your business."

"I've made you my business. I always like the interesting cases, and yours has been fascinating." Bram's grin looked feral. "And I've been asking around about you."

I clenched my fists. "Who have you been talking to? And what have you been telling them about me?"

He chuckled. "I've been asking questions, not answering them. And I've always kept things friendly. I can be a nice guy when I need to be."

"Not to me."

"Hey, now. You've had chances. I didn't immediately take the money you owed. You had time and fair warning, but you ignored me." He shrugged and lifted his hands. "I had to do my job."

"You need a new job."

"And you should stop hiding your secrets. Look where it's gotten you." He laughed when I didn't reply. "You've had an interesting life. When you're not hiding your weird baking magic, you're chasing guys old enough to be your grandad. What's the deal with that? Is that some weird kink? Like the fur?"

"It's not weird. And everyone knows guys mature much slower than women. I like to have sensible conversations about interesting things and not pretend to be impressed by fart noises and beer pong."

Bram snorted a laugh. "Yeah, but Englebert Whistletop is older than dirt, and from what I've heard, you've spent loads of time with him."

"You heard wrong. We're just friends."

"He's also loaded. I bet that's a bonus." He nudged me. "Hey, he could lend you the money you owe Sylvester."

I huffed out a breath, not intending to share anymore of my relationship history with this jerk.

My silence only made Bram laugh more.

We reached the edge of the track leading to the farmhouse.

Bram grabbed my arm and pulled me close. "You know, if you're short of money, we could come to an arrangement. I have much more stamina than that old dude." His gaze tracked down my body.

I shuddered and shook off his arm. "Get that disgusting idea out of your head."

"It's not disgusting. I won't even make you play beer pong, although alcohol might make this easier on you. And it would be a simple way to repay the favor you owe me, along with the money."

He was lying. Bram had previously admitted my debt couldn't be wiped out. He was taking advantage of a witch in a difficult situation.

"You'll get your money. I'm not sleeping with you."

"And my favor. That was a part of the deal. I keep my mouth zipped to your friends, and you owe me."

"I... Nothing illegal."

Bram's easy expression hardened, and danger flashed in his eyes. "I'll be clear about this. You got yourself in this mess. You need to get yourself out. Don't think the boss is a pushover just because we left you alone for a couple of weeks. He shoves me, and I look for someone to shove. And right now, my attention is just on you. You're only making it harder by not giving back what belongs to us."

I stepped away and glared at him. I was still in shock over how quickly I'd gotten into magical debt. I only meant to borrow on credit a couple of times, then it got out of hand, and I lost track of what I was doing. It had been simple to ask for something and give nothing back. Now, the debt was back to bite me hard on the butt. And those teeth were sharp.

"Let's go in and get this over with." My palms were sweating as I lowered the magic barrier that revealed the farmhouse. I glanced back at Bram as he stood behind me. "Are you coming in?"

There was a howl in the slowly encroaching gloom, and Bram jumped and hurried forward. "The money had better be here. I hate having my time wasted."

"It won't be wasted. You'll get what you need." I had no money here, but I had a hastily put together plan in my head to fix two problems with one sneaky move.

He grunted an acknowledgement and followed me to the door.

I opened it and stepped inside. "It's only me. I've brought someone with me."

"Come in. We love company," Gloria called out. "Is it a new recruit?"

"Have you still got those old girls in here?" Bram said. "I figured you'd have drained them so hard, they wouldn't still be breathing."

"Of course they're still alive. Be nice to them."

"If you get me my money, I won't even need to see them."

"Go in the front parlor and sit down. I've got the money stored in several places, so it'll take me a few minutes to get it together." I discreetly dabbed the fear sweat on my upper lip as I led him into the parlor.

Gloria and Faye were in their usual seats, and Ridley was lounging on the couch, looking much better than the last time I'd seen him.

"How you doing, Ridley?" I said.

He lifted a thumb. "Almost back to normal. I even went for a run earlier. The magic is at full strength if you need any. Who's the new guy?"

"This is Bram. The last time he was in Witch Haven, he robbed the bakery and took Uncle Albert's money. He also injured me with magic."

"Huh? Why are you telling them that?" Bram scowled at me.

Ridley was already sitting up, glaring at Bram. "Why steal from Uncle Albert? The guy's a legend. And you hurt Luna? She's a great witch. What's wrong with you?"

"He's here for more money. And Bram just indecently propositioned me. He suggested I work off my debt by giving him favors." I made big air quotes around the word.

Ridley growled and stood slowly, uncoiling his solid, muscular form to its full height. "You shouldn't disrespect Luna. She's a good witch. She looks out for us. And we do the same for her."

Bram snorted. "I don't have time for this. Give me the money."

"You watch your manners, young man." Gloria's hands were clasped around her long metal knitting needles. "It sounds like your mother raised you wrong."

Faye was also frowning. "We don't like troublemakers, especially not when they're unkind to Luna."

Bram slid me a glare. "Get the money."

I stepped closer to him. "You're rude, disrespectful, and mean. You hurt me, scared me, and stole from my family. That can't go unpunished."

"Are you out of your mind? You owe us money!"

"Gloria, use your needles," Faye said.

Gloria flicked her hands, and her huge knitting needles flew through the air and speared through Bram's thighs.

He howled and dropped to the floor as blood bloomed on his jeans. "You crazy old bird! What's the matter with you?"

"Ridley, get him," I yelled.

Ridley threw himself on top of Bram, and jagged sparks of red magic flew out and slammed into Bram's chest as they tussled.

Faye calmly lifted her oversized purse from beside her chair. She pulled out a bottle, uncorked it, and blew a dark green mist over Bram. "Hold your breath, Ridley. This is going to hurt."

Ridley slammed one more blast of magic into Bram's chest and rolled away just before the mist enveloped him.

Bram lay on the floor, his limbs spasming as Faye's incredible magic took hold of him.

My eyes were wide with shock. Faye rarely ever used magic. "What spell is that?"

She smiled as Bram flailed and jerked around. "Just a little something I've been working on for fun.

It freezes muscles while making you believe you're covered in fire ants. Those little guys know how to nip."

"Whoa! You're scary."

Her smile widened. "Thank you."

Bram howled and scratched at his skin, arching his back and flapping like a beached halibut.

"Steady on, Faye. We don't want him dead. Maybe ease back your spell," I said.

She pouted. "Are you sure about that? He was being so rude to you."

I hesitated. Killing Bram would remove him permanently, but he had something I needed. All I had to do was keep him docile and I could use his magic to remain stable.

Ridley stood over Bram as the green mist drifted away. "We should put him out of his misery. He's a bad guy, talking to you like that. And I can't believe he stole from your uncle."

Bram grabbed Ridley's leg and knocked him to the floor. There was a flurry of fists and a blast of magic from Ridley as they rolled over together, locked in a violent embrace that left blood on the floor.

I caught hold of Ridley's leg and yanked him away, patting out the flames that had ignited in his hair.

"That's enough, young man." Faye yelped an ear splitting battle cry. She flew out of her easy chair and dropped an elbow into Bram's groin.

Ridley and I winced as she slammed her elbow down several more times.

Bram stopped moaning, a keening sound coming out of his mouth.

Faye shuffled away and dusted off her elbow. "That'll show him not to disrespect women. He won't be using his battered sausage and two pickled onions for a while."

"That was an amazing elbow slam, Faye. Where did you learn to do that?" I said.

"Summer camp."

"She means, the summer camp she was court ordered to attend five years in a row for being a rebellious teen," Gloria whispered.

Faye grinned. "It's the same thing. I was there over the summer."

Bram curled into a ball and tucked his thumb into his mouth.

I knelt beside him and brushed a hand across his face. "He's powerful. I'm thinking about keeping him."

"Are you sure that's wise?" Gloria said. "What if his magic makes you bad like him? And you don't want to get the urge to proposition men to blow away the cobwebs in your undercarriage like he did to you."

"Gloria! It's not that dusty down there." I stroked a finger across his cheekbone. Bram wouldn't make me bad, just magically strong and stable. "Needs must. I'm having trouble holding onto the magic I take from all of you. I need something with a bit more of an edge."

"My magic is edgy," Ridley said.

"Your magic is amazing, but I can't keep taking from you all the time." I placed my hands on either side of Bram's head. "Let's see what you have to offer."

Tendrils of warm magic flowed through my arms and across my chest.

"How does it feel?" Gloria said. "It's not giving you dark thoughts, is it?"

"No, it feels good. He's strong. I can use this magic."

Gloria flicked up her hands, and the knitting needles impaled in Bram's thighs shot out and returned to her. She inspected them and shook her head. "These will need a boil in hot water before I'm using them again."

Bram jerked around for a few seconds as I continued to drain him then settled on the floor.

"Ridley, get some chains from the basement," I said. "Bram won't be happy when he wakes and realizes what's happened to him."

"I'm on it." Ridley dashed out of the room.

"I'm not talking to him," Faye said. "I want nothing to do with him if he's staying here."

"Try not to be too mean to him. He's helping me out, even if he doesn't realize it." Bram looked almost cute with his thumb still wedged in his mouth.

"I'll never help you," he muttered around his thumb.

I tightened my grip on his head. "You just relax. I've given you a new purpose, one that means you'll never hurt anyone again. No more chasing innocent women for money."

"Or stealing from their families," Gloria said. "Luna is good like that. She puts people on the right path and makes sure they're looked after." Her gaze ran over Bram. "We'll convince him this is the right thing to do. He'll be on your side before you know it."

"And if he doesn't come around to our way of thinking, Gloria can stab him with her knitting needles again," Faye said.

Gloria nodded. "I'm always happy to do a little stabbing when it's called for."

Ridley returned with the chains and attached them to a sturdy chain link set in the floor.

I checked the time. I needed to hustle if I was getting back to the baking contest in time. I sucked in a last blast of Bram's magic and, with Ridley's help, moved him to the wall and propped him against it.

Ridley stood back as I looped the chains around Bram's ankle.

His eyes flicked open, and he shoved me away with surprising force. "Hey! What are you doing? Get away from me."

Gloria gasped. "Quick! Take more of his magic."

Bram scrambled to his feet, his gaze shooting around the room. "What happened? What are you doing with those chains?" He kicked them free from his ankle.

I gulped down my panic. Bram was more powerful than I realized, and I hadn't expected him to wake for at least twelve hours after taking so much magic. "This is the farmhouse. Remember, you came here with me. You want to be a part of this."

He slid along the wall, his hands raised, unsteady looking magic sparking across his palms. "Where's the money? I came for that."

"You're not taking anything from Luna," Faye said.

"She... she owes me." Bram touched his thighs and hissed. "You stabbed me."

"You're staying here." Ridley advanced on Bram. "We're keeping an eye on you so you can't cause more trouble for Luna."

"You were planning on holding me here?" Bram's gaze flicked to the chains. "That could get you in a lot of trouble. My boss would send people to find me."

"You get used to the chains," Gloria said. "I like mine. They give me a sense of security."

"You're out of your mind. Can't you see what Luna's doing to you? You're prisoners. She's got you chained up in this place, and you can't escape."

"We knew what we were signing up to." Gloria inspected her knitting needles and made jabbing motions in the air.

Bram licked his lips. "What about that barrier around the house? She's keeping you under her control. Why can't you see that?"

I was proud when they shook their heads, although doubt flickered through me. An outsider looking in on this situation would see the worst. They'd see the magic barrier, the chains, and the way I kept my harem drained. But this setup helped everyone. It wasn't a one-sided deal.

"Gloria, use your knitting needles again," Faye said. "He's not behaving himself."

Gloria launched the needles at Bram, but he dodged out of the way, and they embedded in the wall behind him.

Ridley chased after Bram. He smashed into him so hard that they flew through the window.

Gloria and Faye shrieked and covered their eyes with their hands.

I raced to the broken window and peered outside. Ridley and Bram were rolling around, magic flying between them.

"Is Ridley injured?" Gloria lowered her hands. "Don't let him get hurt."

I briefly considered jumping through the window, but there were shards of glass jutting out, and I'd cut myself to pieces. I raced out the front parlor and through the main door.

"Stop him! He's getting away," Ridley yelled from behind the farmhouse.

I rounded the corner and slammed into Bram. He took me off my feet, and I smashed to the ground, seeing stars as my head bounced off the hard dirt.

He growled in my face. "You'll pay for this. I'll make sure you're sorry." Then he was gone.

I groaned as I rolled onto my side, horror hitting me in the gut as Bram ran straight through the barrier. I must not have put it up properly when we'd come through, and now he was escaping.

Ridley appeared beside me and grabbed my arm. One side of his face was coated in blood, and he was holding his ribs. "Sorry for messing up. I didn't mean to damage the window, but that jerk made me angry." He helped me to my feet.

"None of this is your fault. I underestimated Bram and didn't realize he was so strong. I thought I'd taken enough magic to subdue him." I touched Ridley's bloody face. "And you're hurt."

"This is all my fault. You were being careful not to drain Bram too much because of what happened to me." Ridley looked crestfallen. "I'm not strong enough for you and made you take a dangerous risk."

I turned my gaze to the trees as Bram sprinted away. There was no point in chasing him. Someone would see us, and awkward questions would get asked. "You did great. I shouldn't have brought my problem to the farmhouse. I thought I was fixing things, but I've only made it worse."

"I'll get the window fixed," Ridley said. "I don't want Gloria and Faye to catch a chill. If you order the new glass and frame, I'll make the repairs. I'm handy like that."

"Thanks. There's plywood in the shed if you want to make a temporary repair."

"I'll get on that." He squeezed my arm. "I'll make our home right. You'll never know what happened tonight."

I kissed Ridley's cheek. "I appreciate that. And so you know, you didn't screw up. This is all on me."

Gloria and Faye appeared in the doorway, and they peered around.

"Where's he gone?" Gloria said.

"He got away. I didn't put up the barrier properly." I was heading back to the house when a movement among the trees caught my eyes. My breath caught as a huge silver gray wolf slid among the trees, following Bram.

Was that Cole? Had he seen the fight? I bit my bottom lip. I'd never seen Cole in werewolf form, so I had no idea if it was him or a random werewolf interested in what was going on. Anyone running as fast as Bram would catch the attention of a predator.

Maybe I'd get a hit of luck, and the werewolf would catch Bram and make him his tasty evening meal. I grimaced. That was a bad thought to have, but it would solve the big problem I'd just given myself.

I settled Gloria and Faye in their seats with strong cups of tea and a plate of cookies. After making sure they were happy, I said a quick goodbye to them all, leaving Ridley fixing a temporary cover on the window.

I couldn't worry about Bram, the broken window, or the mysterious werewolf. I had a cake contest not to ruin.

Chapter 12

"Meadow, how did you get your cupcakes to rise so well? They're huge." I'd been hanging around her workstation for five minutes since returning from my failed attempt to capture Bram, pretending to admire her handiwork. It wasn't hard. Her cupcakes smelled of tangy lemon and cherries and looked so tempting I wanted to sneak one off the cooling rack.

She shot me an irritated glare. "Shouldn't you be watching your own cupcakes?"

"The mix is done. I'm letting it rest for a few minutes."

Her head shot up, and she glanced at my workstation. "That makes a difference?"

"Oh, yes. My family has been doing that with their cupcakes for generations." It wasn't true, but it gave me an excuse to loiter and ask questions instead of bake.

Meadow stared at her cakes. "I should make another batch and try that. Thanks for the tip."

"You're welcome." It was only a tiny fib, so I didn't feel bad.

Dave poked his head out from behind the camera. "We'll be doing more filming in a few minutes, so the set needs to be cleared."

"I won't get in the way when you're ready to roll," I said.

"This must be easy for you." Meadow pulled out a fresh mixing bowl and tightened the string on her white apron. "You've got that family name backing you up. I bet you make cupcakes in your sleep, and they taste incredible."

"You know how it goes. Having a name associated with amazing cakes always helps. You're an Eclair, aren't you?"

She nodded. "We're not one of the bigger names in the industry, but we hold our own."

"You wouldn't be here if you weren't great at making cakes."

"I'm amazing." Meadow pulled out flour, eggs, and milk. "I've already got a joint credit on one of Elwin's recipes. It'll be in the next collection he releases. Not the one being pushed during the show, but he promised me it would happen. He's already showcased it to a group of celebrities, and they loved it."

"That's a huge accolade. It's an honor to be associated with Elwin La Croix."

"Getting that credit helped me secure a place in this final." She shrugged as she measured out the cupcake ingredients. "You know what our community is like, everyone gossips. The recipe was supposed to be a secret, but the rumor is out there. I can't say it's done me any harm that people know I'm creating for Elwin."

I arched an eyebrow. Perhaps Meadow put that rumor out to give her reputation a boost. "I heard Fawn worked with Elwin on his recipes."

Meadow missed the mixing bowl, sending flour cascading across her workstation and clouding around us. "Who told you that?"

"He did. I think Elwin was worried about her after she lost her dad, so he helped her out."

"He shouldn't have bothered. Fawn had nothing good to say about her family. She'd go on about wishing she'd been born to a baking dynasty because then she'd have had a shot at the big time. She was always complaining about something."

"Elwin must have seen the good in Fawn. Otherwise, he wouldn't have kept her around."

"If you say so." Meadow's whisking became manic, and batter splashed over the side of the bowl.

I took a step back to avoid being splattered with cake mixture. "I heard a rumor Elwin and Fawn might have had a more intimate relationship."

Meadow smirked. "Let me guess where you heard that. It was Troy. He's only ever got one thing on his mind. Well, two things if you include baking."

"Has Elwin ever been inappropriate with you?"

She blurted a laugh. "No! Elwin's not like that. He'd never do that."

"And Troy?"

Meadow lifted one shoulder. "The guy's a pest. He's always making suggestions and reckons everyone's getting it on with each other. He's like a teenage boy after reading his first dirty magazine.

It's pathetic. If he tried anything with me, I'd make sure it was the only time."

"And you never saw anything going on with Fawn and Elwin? Anything that made you think they were dating?"

"They never dated. Elwin can have his pick of A-list celebrities. He'd never pick a boring grump like Fawn. She'd never satisfy him. And he could hardly take her to a premier or show her off in front of the cameras. She'd be an embarrassment. No, they were never involved."

"But they spent time together?"

"Now and again. But she was his assistant. Elwin had no option but to be around her."

"More than the rest of you were? Did he enjoy spending time with Fawn?"

Meadow cracked an egg so hard it made me wince. "I paid her no attention, so I can't answer that. Why the interest in their relationship? Are you into Elwin and glad the competition is out of the way?"

"Err, nope, nothing like that." I went to pick up a silicone cupcake case off the counter, but Meadow slapped the back of my hand.

"Leave it. That's clean."

"Sorry. I was just interested in the cases you use."

"Be interested somewhere else. I have to get these new cupcakes mixed. Then I'm trying your resting method. Are you sure it'll make them better? I need an edge, especially over Troy."

"Oh, sure. It works every time." I remained by her workstation.

She thumped down her spoon. "What? Why do you keep watching me? Is this a trick to put me off? Do you want one of the other finalists to win?"

"I'm a judge, not a contestant. Why would I want to put you off? I'm simply interested in your methods."

Meadow heaved out a sigh. "Sorry, but you're younger than the other judges, and this is stressful. Troy has been hounding me, Cade has been hiding in his room and refusing to say a word, and all this chaos Fawn caused... well, I didn't sleep much last night. I didn't mean to be spiteful. Of course, you can inspect what you like."

"Thanks. And I understand why you're stressed. There's a lot riding on this." I glanced around. "Troy mentioned you argued with Fawn recently. What was that about?"

Her forehead furrowed, and her beating arm sped up. "Why do you care?"

"I'm curious about Fawn. I'd like to know more about her."

"You're wasting your time. She was boring."

"Not boring enough for you to ignore, though. Not if you argued."

Meadow added yellow color to the cupcake mix and stirred it through carefully. "Fawn had issues. She should never have worked on the show."

"What kind of issues?"

"She was opinionated, rude, and never got my drink order right. One day, I called her on it, and she didn't like it. And she was jealous of me."

"Jealous about what?"

"The recipe I'd be getting credit for. Fawn was convinced she'd helped Elwin with it. She said it wasn't fair." Meadow shrugged. "This is magical baking. It's not about fairness. It's about who you know and how much money you have to spend on training to finesse your baking magic."

"Did she help Elwin with that recipe?"

"No! Nothing Fawn could tell him would be useful in creating a new recipe. But she had the cheek to say I didn't deserve to be in that book. Like she'd know a decent recipe if it penciled itself across her forehead."

"That couldn't have been fun, fighting over a recipe."

"It wasn't for her. I told Fawn exactly what I thought of her. I threatened to have her fired from the set. She backed off after that."

"Did you two often argue?"

"Now and again when she got in my way, but she argued with everyone. Fawn enjoyed it. She was nothing but trouble. Just like everyone else, I'm glad she's gone. We don't have to put up with the sour looks and her stamping around when she didn't get her own way."

"We need to start filming now," Dave said. "Sorry, Luna. I need to get live action shots with just Meadow."

I wanted a few more minutes to question Meadow but was out of time. I stepped out of shot but remained close by.

"Filming in five, four, three." Dave lifted two fingers and then one and pointed at Meadow.

She transformed, her scowl vanishing as a radiant smile appeared. Meadow even stood differently the second the camera rolled.

I watched for a couple of minutes, then Meadow dropped her fork. "Cut! We have to do that again."

"It's fine. Keep rolling," Dave said. "We can take that out in edits."

"No! We're doing it from the top. Erase that. I don't want to end up on a bloopers show." Meadow grabbed the fork.

"We'll need to reset if I erase the recording. Just carry on."

She slung the fork at him. "Then reset. That's what you're here for. And you weren't filming my best side. I keep telling you, keep the camera angle on my left side. And what's wrong with these lights? I'm being blinded."

"Yes, princess." Dave sat back on the fixed seat behind his camera. "Everyone take a minute while we do a reset."

I raced back to my workstation, made sure the oven was up to temperature, then put my cupcakes in it. I returned to Meadow's workstation to ask her more questions, but she'd already left.

I walked over to Dave. "Does that often happen?"

He scraped a hand through his hair. "It sure does. Especially when you're dealing with prima donnas like Meadow. She's the worst one here, and that's saying something."

"Sorry we're so hard to deal with."

He waved a hand in the air. "No, not you. You've been great. You haven't asked for anything. You just get on with it. I wish everyone was as easy to work with as you."

"I'm not used to the cameras. They're intimidating. I keep looking at the lens when I'm not supposed to. I feel like a fraud."

"Once you've been around them a while, you forget they're there. That is, unless you're Meadow La De Da Eclair. She knows every angle. She wants the lighting just so to make her hair shine and insists on certain angles because apparently her nose looks crooked with a shadow." Dave shook his head, a tight smile on his face. "She even keeps throat spray under the counter so she always sounds clear or some rubbish. I don't pay her attention most of the time. It's the only way you can get through this."

"Where's Meadow gone?"

"To touchup her make-up again. She does it all the time. With these high definition TVs everyone's getting, she's worried about every wrinkle and pore. You know what that's called?" He leaned closer. "Real life. We've all got them. Why hide reality under an inch of make-up and pretend to be something you're not?"

I grinned at him. "You must like your job if you stick with it, despite the baking prima donnas."

"I do. And you get to see all sorts of interesting things. I have the most fun when I'm filming people and they forget we're here. They're always doing it. Sometimes, I keep rolling and catch hilarious things. And they're always forgetting to turn their mics off, so I hear them bitching about each other."

"Have you heard anything interesting while filming on this set?"

"The usual. Mainly nasty comments about a rival's cakes."

"Anything about Fawn?"

His smile faded. "Ah, no. Well, nothing nice. No one seemed to like her."

"What did you think of her?"

"Nothing. I didn't know her. Fawn stayed away from the rest of the crew and spent most of her time with Elwin or on her own. She didn't have any friends. I felt sorry for her. I tried to talk to her a few times, but she made it clear she wanted nothing to do with me." He shrugged. "I didn't take it personally. Fawn was into her cakes, and nothing else interested her."

"That seems to be her one true passion. It's so sad what happened to her."

Dave nodded, then grinned at me. "Do you want to have a go on the camera while you wait for Princess Meadow to come back? The crew needs to make changes before we can start up again, so I'm just twiddling my thumbs."

"I wouldn't mind. Thanks."

He shifted out of the raised seat behind the camera. "Hop on. I'll show you how it works."

I spent the next ten minutes getting a beginner's guide to how to operate a camera. It was complicated, and I was overwhelmed with the skills needed to use it.

"And that's what it takes to become an amazing camera dude. Or dudette." Dave tucked his thumbs through his belt loops and rocked back on his heels.

"I'm impressed with everything you have to remember. Does it ever get boring when you have long shoots like this? It can't be exciting watching us standing in the kitchen and baking."

"I don't mind. And I get to sit. It's not like the old days, when I was lugging a heavy camera on one shoulder." Dave rubbed at his right shoulder.

"But we can be here for hours just baking. That must get dull."

"Sure, it's not the most thrilling part of the job. But as you saw, Meadow's always going off and fixing her face or complaining about angles and wanting retakes, so we get breaks."

A thought hit me full in the face. "Did she do that on the first day of filming?"

"Of course. We had breaks so she could put on more lip gloss and fluff her hair, even though it should be tied up. She's baking. This isn't a fashion show."

My chest felt tight. How could I have missed this? "How long did those breaks last? It can't take long to put on lip gloss."

"You'd think it wouldn't, but each time, she'd be gone about twenty or thirty minutes."

"And Meadow left the set to do this?" My heart was pounding like a captured toad's pulse that was about to end up in a bubbling cauldron.

Dave nodded. "I think so. And you can do that if you like when we're filming you. I don't think you've ever asked for a break."

"I didn't know we could. I thought live filming was continuous, so you captured everything."

This new knowledge meant the contestants' alibis were worthless. I'd been so focused on getting my baking right that first day that I hadn't noticed filming being paused.

If Meadow, Troy, and Cade were able to leave the set, any of them had an opportunity to kill Fawn. But I had a feeling Meadow had the real problem with her.

"Is everything okay? You've got a strange look on your face," Dave said. "Has my camera talk bored you?"

"No! I'm great, actually. I've just found the solution to a puzzle I've been struggling to figure out."

"And I helped you do that?"

"You did. And thanks for letting me look over the camera. It's been helpful. I learned a lot." Including what an idiot I was.

"Any time." He looked over and grimaced. "I'd better get on it. The princess is back, and she's not looking happy."

I smiled as I walked away. This was the breakthrough I needed. Now, I just had to find out which baker slipped off the set after Fawn, and I'd find the killer.

There was a cry of alarm and running feet headed my way. "Luna! Your cupcakes are on fire."

Chapter 13

I stood by my workstation, staring forlornly at my ruined, smoking cupcakes. I'd gotten distracted talking to Dave, and I'd forgotten about them. There was nothing I could do to save them. Even cutting off the burnt bits wouldn't be enough to salvage these disasters.

Elwin patted my shoulder. "Don't worry. Your involvement in the contest was only for fun. We figured it might up the finalists' game when they saw you hard at work. It's such a shame to see these delicious cakes ruined."

Henriette walked over and joined us. Her nose wrinkled as she stared at my cakes. "Did the oven malfunction?"

"It was my fault. I wasn't paying attention. I put the cupcakes in the oven and then got talking to the crew."

"I'll have a word with them," Henriette said. "They shouldn't be bothering judges. They're here to work, not distract you. Who was it?"

"No, I went to talk to them. This isn't their fault."

"Didn't you get the feeling?" Elwin said.

I glanced at him and shook my head. I knew what he meant, but I never got the feeling. Not once. Uncle Albert often talked about it, how he would put something in the oven, be serving at the counter, and have to dash away when his cakes magically informed him they were ready to come out. The only feeling I got when I looked at my baked goods was intense disappointment and lingering failure.

"Everyone can get distracted." Elwin's smile was reassuring. "I remember in my first year of advanced bakery skills, I once turned a cake bright green. I had to pretend it was vegetable inspired."

I forced myself to chuckle along with them, but I was mortified. And when I looked closely at the cupcakes, they looked lumpy as well as charred. Maybe Bram's magic wasn't good when it came to creating baked goods.

"I'm embarrassed by mine, too. Wait here. I'll show you what I've created." Henriette dashed off and returned with an amazing plate of pale yellow cupcakes topped with tiny iced flowers. "Aren't they just awful?"

"They look good to me," I said.

"You're too kind. I might have another go, see if I can do better." Henriette took a look at my cakes again and shook her head. "Maybe you should, too."

The last thing I wanted to do was make even more terrible cupcakes. "I'll deal with these first."

"Don't look so sad," Elwin said. "Even the best of the best needs a learning experience. This is yours. And I can guarantee you won't get distracted again."

I gave him my best smile. I could guarantee I would. Baking didn't make my heart sing. It simply made it want to take a long vacation somewhere hot, where I didn't have to lift a finger when it came to making the desserts.

Elwin checked the time and clapped his hands together. "Everyone, it's time to stop baking. We've done enough filming for the day."

There were several relieved groans from the camera crew around us.

"Store your cakes away, and tomorrow you'll decorate them. After that, we'll judge your edible works of art." He turned to me. "That's always my favorite part. I usually gain about a stone during these competitions. I have such a sweet tooth."

"I'll enjoy the tasting part, too." I looked at Meadow's workstation, but she was already dashing away. I needed to find out where she'd gone during her filming breaks.

Although Meadow hadn't hidden her hatred for Fawn from me, and surely she'd do that if she had something to conceal. But then neither had Troy. They were vying for joint first place on my suspect list for Fawn's murder.

And then there was Cade. I needed to speak to him. He was such a quiet guy that he'd slipped under my radar. Maybe that was how he'd managed to sneak off set and kill Fawn.

I still had a way to go before I figured out this murder.

Elwin nodded at me as he discreetly slid my burnt cupcakes into the trash can. "I'm sure the next batch will be incredible."

After I'd tidied my workstation, I left the set. I needed independent input into Fawn's murder and the remaining suspects. I'd missed a vital piece of the puzzle by working alone.

I headed to Indigo's house, but the lights were off, and when I knocked on the door, not even her familiars answered. I thought about going to Odessa's farm, but it was on the edge of the village, and my feet were tired from standing and baking. I diverted and headed to Storm's small apartment. It sat over the store she used for her private investigation business.

I hit the buzzer and waited to see if she was in.

"Unless you're free pizza, I'm not interested."

"No pizza, but it's Luna. Are you busy?"

The door buzzed. "Come on up."

I walked up the narrow set of stairs. Storm had already opened her door, propping it with a shoe so I could get in.

After walking in, I shut the door behind me and replaced the shoe in the rack before walking along the corridor and into Storm's open-plan apartment. The walls were bare brick and the floors solid wood.

Fire Fang lumbered over to greet me, drooling and snarling as he bumped me with his huge head.

I petted his coarse dark fur. "Hey, sweetie."

"Fire Fang! No eating the guests. There's food in your bowl if you're hungry." Storm lounged on the couch, a pile of papers scattered on the dark wooden coffee table in front of her. "What's up?"

"I've finished filming on the set for the day." I edged around Fire Fang and toed his food bowl at him, just in case he thought my arm looked tasty.

"And did you make anything truly hideous?" Her eyes glinted with amusement. "Did anyone puke when they tasted your food?"

"Very funny. I'm happy to report, no one got poisoned or choked on my food today." I grabbed a bottle of water from her fridge and sat in the chair opposite her. Storm's apartment was simply decorated. She had comfy furnishings, big rugs on the floors, and pictures of her sister on almost every surface. The heat was always set to high. Storm wasn't a fan of the cold.

"Have you made progress on figuring out what happened to Fawn?" She uncurled her legs from underneath her and sat up straight.

"I was hitting a brick wall until this evening." I opened my drink and took a sip. "I found out something important. The contestants could stop the filming whenever they liked."

"Is that unusual?"

"It is to me. I figured a shoot would be continuous, and then they'd edit out the boring bits. But I got talking to a camera guy, and he said Meadow, one of the bakers, took at least three breaks during filming on the day Fawn was killed."

"You think Meadow killed Fawn during one of her breaks?"

"She had enough time to do it. It's only a few minutes' walk to the play park from the set. Meadow could have ordered a break when she saw

Fawn leave, snuck out and followed her, and killed her."

"What's her motive?"

"They didn't get along, and they argued. Meadow thought Fawn was up herself and should have known her place."

Storm arched an eyebrow. "What was Fawn's place supposed to be?"

"Running around after the contestants. She had a talent for baking but struggled to get a foot in the door."

Storm shook her head. "You bakers are such snobs."

"Hey, I don't make the rules."

"Rules are made to be broken. If Fawn could bake, she should have been allowed to have a go, not stuck on the sidelines because of her family name."

"Elwin was helping her." I tucked my feet under me. "I wonder if Meadow was jealous of Elwin's interest in Fawn. She claimed not to pay their friendship any attention, but she must have noticed they were close."

"It was just a friendship?"

"I reckon so. I've heard nothing other than a spiteful rumor from Troy that they were more than friends. Elwin seems like a genuine guy."

Storm was quiet for a few seconds. "What are you going to do with this information?"

"I need to ask more questions before I take anything to the Magic Council. I have to be certain I'm right about Meadow."

"Do you think Devlin will work with you on this? You two aren't exactly best buds."

"No. And he'd hate it if I solved this murder before him, which makes me even more determined to figure it out."

"That little squirt would flip if you got the jump on him. You should do it." Storm's grin was wicked. She had little time for rule obsessed bureaucrats.

"I'm not deliberately excluding him from what I'm doing, but I've barely seen Devlin since Fawn's murder. According to the contestants, he's been asking questions, but he's not spending any time on the filming set. He's missed a lot."

"Maybe he's avoiding you."

"He hasn't in the past. Devlin's always made a point of getting in my face and making things difficult for me."

Storm smirked. "You know, Odessa could be right. Devlin could be into you. He gets shy when you meet, so he keeps out of your way. Maybe that wolf pendant was from him."

I tucked the pendant inside my sweater as I wrinkled my nose. "He's not my type."

"Is anyone your type at the moment?"

I looked around the room. "Nope. I'm keeping my options open."

"Uh-huh." Storm rested her feet on the coffee table.

"What are you working on?" I nodded at the pile of papers.

"Dead ends and time wasters." Her expression hardened. "I got a tipoff about Eden, but nothing came of it."

I made sympathetic noises as Storm grumbled about false leads and losers wasting her time. She'd never give up looking for her sister, even though it had been five years since she'd gone missing.

"It's the reward money. It makes people say stupid things in the hope of getting their hands on the cash. I'm withdrawing it," Storm said.

"You're not giving up the search?"

"No! But not a single lead has paid off since I increased the reward." Her gaze shifted down. "If anyone has genuine information, you'd think they'd want me to know."

"They would. And one day, you'll find something that'll get you on the right track to finding Eden."

"I'm not giving up until I do." Storm rested her head back against the couch and closed her eyes. "Is there anything I can do to help with your murder mystery?"

"I think I'm almost there. There's one more person to speak to, but the more I find out about Meadow, the more I'm convinced it was her. She had the chance to do it and she had a good motive."

Storm tipped her head forward. "If Meadow channeled her magic into messing up the play park and killing Fawn, would she have had any left to do her baking? What did her cakes look like?"

I frowned. "Like they were created by angels and blessed by a unicorn."

She grinned. "The spells that wrecked the play park were intense. Whoever cast them would have burned through their power. And you always get drained if you do too much baking. Wouldn't that have happened to Meadow? She used her magic on the murder, so her cakes would have been a flop."

"I'm different to other bakers. Most of them get energized when they've done a whole day of baking."

Storm stared at me. "Not you. Why is that?"

"Because I'm a unique snowflake."

"You're a unique something. And you're the first baker I've met who doesn't enjoy making desserts."

"Not true. And how many magically talented bakers have you met?"

"Your uncle. You. Your parents. And I get around. I sample the baked goods when I'm in a new area." Her gaze flicked to the window as lightning streaked across the sky. "We're not expecting more bad weather."

I stood and walked to the window. Sheet lightning blinded me for a few seconds, lighting the gloom in a dazzling flash. "You don't think it's a natural event?"

Storm joined me. "There's nothing natural about this weather. Just like the tornadoes that almost hit Witch Haven, someone is doing this. They're messing with the village by sending weird weather our way."

"A dark magic user? Indigo's mom and her crazy demon lover had their sights set on the place. You don't think they're back, do you?" I peered into the gloomy evening, which was full of dense ominous shadows.

"Their magic was damaging but sneaky. It slowly influenced everything so we didn't know what was going on until it was almost too late." She flinched as thunder cracked. "This feels bolder. Like the magic user doesn't care if they get caught. They want to go out with a magic clap of thunder. When I was battling the tornadoes, the power felt raw, as if whoever cast it wasn't sure what they were doing."

"An inexperienced spell caster couldn't do this to the weather. It takes years of training to get this strong."

"There was a ton of power behind the magic. I wouldn't want to get on the wrong side of whoever's using it."

"You could take them. You can take on anyone."

She nudged me with her hip. "True, but being caught in a tornado and slammed to the ground a few times is no one's idea of fun."

"Hopefully, it'll pass. It needs to. I want no more delays with the baking show. The sooner the filming gets done, the sooner they'll clear out, and life can get back to normal."

Fire Fang whined as the lightning intensified. He tried to crawl under the couch and tipped it over.

Storm walked over and ruffled his fur. She righted the couch then headed to the fridge and pulled open the door. "You can stay for dinner if you like. I've got half a lemon, some cheese that's growing a new kind of mold, and eggs that are almost in date."

"Cheese omelets sound perfect," I said with a grin. "Hold the lemon. Do you want me to make them?"

"Sure. I know you can handle cheese omelets without setting my kitchen on fire. Let's do it."

I checked the eggs were still fresh enough to use before whisking them in a bowl, while Storm cut the mold off the cheese.

I felt positive about solving this puzzle. I'd almost nailed Meadow as the killer. This mystery would soon be solved.

Chapter 14

I was still bleary-eyed as I stumbled down the stairs to grab a strong coffee the next morning. I'd stayed late at Storm's apartment, just hanging out and chatting about nothing in particular. It had been great to have a night off from worrying about Fawn's killer. I'd eventually left when the weather worsened, so I could get home before the rain started.

Earl rolled out from under a counter and lay on his belly, his eyes squeezed shut and his furry nose wrinkled.

"What's up with you?"

"I ran out of my catnip and caffeine blend, and I feel terrible. I have the shakes and a headache. I've caught something gross."

"You're not sick. You're going through caffeine withdrawal. It gets us all." I stared into the delicious dark brown brew I was about to sample. "But it's worth it. And there are health benefits in coffee."

"I'll go back to my regular catnip. You don't get the weird side effects."

"You mean, the drooling, rolling about, excessive sleeping, and then passing out kind of side effects?"

I scooped him up and cuddled him. "I'll order some in. It'll get here by the end of today."

He was already yawning, his eyes closing as he wrapped himself around my shoulders and snuggled down. "Wake me when it gets here. I'm going to sleep off this detox."

"Aren't we supposed to be solving Fawn's murder together? You said you'd help. I haven't seen much evidence of that."

"I don't remember saying that. And you never need my help. I'd only get in the way."

A knock at the front door had me looking up. I was surprised to see Cade standing outside. He lifted a hand, but his expression was glum.

I took a welcome sip of my coffee then headed to the door and unlocked it. "Morning. You're up early."

"I was sent over by Elwin." Cade scraped a hand over his shaved head. "He said if you want to do your baking again, you need to do it before the judging takes place. You should get about an hour. Is that enough time?"

I forced a smile. "Thanks for letting me know. That'll work. Does Elwin want me on the set this morning? I really need to get some baking done here."

"No, it's just us being filmed. You'll be needed about seven o'clock."

"Great. I won't be late."

He sighed and lowered his head. "I'll let Elwin know."

I bit my bottom lip. Cade seemed to have the weight of the world on his shoulders. "Do you want to come in? I've just brewed fresh coffee, and it looks like you need one."

"I wouldn't mind. I didn't sleep well last night." He trudged through the door and slumped into a seat.

I hurried to the kitchen, pulled out two almond croissants, and headed back to the counter. I made Cade a strong mug of coffee before putting everything on a tray and carrying it to the table, where I sat opposite him.

I passed him a pastry. "This might make you happier. It's one of my uncle's recipes. Almond croissants are a specialty of his. I always struggle to stop at one."

"Looks great. Thanks." He picked off a piece of toasted almond and nibbled on it.

"I hope you don't mind me asking, but you seem to be having a tough time. Are you missing Fawn?" I took a bite of my croissant and gave him an encouraging smile.

Cade glanced up at me. "Did she talk to you about me?"

"No, Fawn didn't mention you, but other people said you used to date. It must have been horrible when you learned what happened to her."

He heaved out a sigh. "I can't believe she's gone. I keep expecting her to show up on the set and stomp around like she used to."

"Stomp? Fawn didn't enjoy her job?"

He shrugged. "She didn't hate it, but it wasn't what she wanted to do with her life. She was frustrated and felt stuck. That made her grumpy."

"Elwin mentioned Fawn was good at baking. Did you get a chance to taste anything she made?"

"Sure, she was always trying out new stuff. Fawn didn't like to share too often, because she was always striving for perfection. Which, as you know, is impossible in our line of business." Cade straightened in his seat and poked at the croissant. "There are so many variables and things that can go wrong. I see baking as an alchemical science rather than simple magic. A few grams of the wrong ingredient or a spell not focused, and you get mediocre. Do you know what I mean?"

"I absolutely do. I struggle with that."

Cade chuffed out a disbelieving laugh. "Sure you do. You Brimstones are legendary. I was hoping to meet your dad, but it's good to meet you, too."

"Thanks. That's nice of you to say. My dad is ridiculously busy, though. I barely get to see him."

"That must be tough. When you get a gift like ours, it pulls you in too many directions." Cade bit into the croissant and chewed. "I haven't seen my mom or dad for three years. They're always being asked to cater for exclusive events and whisked off all around the world, all expenses paid. They make a ton of money and enjoy themselves, but they never see each other."

"Mine are in the same position. I guess that's what happens when you get a chance to live your passion every day. I'd love to see my parents more often, but I understand why they're not around. And they don't see much of each other, either. They often take jobs in different countries for months on end."

Cade munched down the rest of his croissant, looking less forlorn. "I worried where Fawn would end up. She was always looking for new opportunities and was determined to make it big."

"Do you think she'd have achieved her ambitions?"

"I'd like to think so, even with her disadvantages. Fawn was amazing. I used to tease her that she'd been secretly adopted because there was no way you could learn to be that incredible." Magic sparkled on the ends of his fingers, and the scent of orange filled the air. "We have the edge over everyone else."

"What did Fawn think about that?"

"She said she was a fluke. But she practiced for hours and still never thought what she did was good enough."

"I bet it didn't help when the other baking contestants were unkind to her when she made the effort to bake. She didn't seem popular."

"It made her doubt herself. Although it also lit a fire under her butt. Fawn was so determined to prove herself." Cade shook his head. "I was always telling her to keep quiet about what she did because people wouldn't understand. But she was so passionate about her food and wanted to learn from everyone. Some of the previous contestants were okay and humored her, but most of them saw her as a joke, and they didn't hide their disdain."

"But you supported Fawn?"

"Of course. And I thought we stood a chance of making it together." His shoulders slumped.

"What went wrong?"

"Cakes, pastries, tarts, and puddings." Cade blew on his coffee. "Fawn was so focused on her career that I got in the way. She said I freaked her out because I was always hanging around and watching what she did. I just wanted to be with her and was interested in her baking. She could do amazing things. I mean, world-class efforts. Her talent was unique."

"Did she end things with you?"

"Yeah, Fawn dumped me." He glugged down his coffee.

"You still liked her?"

"I loved Fawn. I wanted to be with her, but she'd had enough of me. I tried to get her to see sense and stay, but I was wasting my breath." Cade swiped at his bloodshot eyes. "It was painful to see her every day and not be with her. And she used to blank me, which hurt. She didn't even want to be friends."

"Did that make you angry?"

"I was devastated. I was planning to take her out for a surprise meal, one I cooked myself. I hoped we could talk and figure out a compromise. I was planning the meal for after the show ended, but now, that'll never happen. I'll never see her again."

"I am sorry for your loss. It sounds like you really cared for her." I finished my croissant. "Did you see Fawn on set the day she was killed?"

"A few times. I always kept an eye on her to make sure she was doing okay. Fawn must have slipped out when my back was turned. The other contestants were always getting her to run around after them, so she used to sneak off for a few minutes break when she could."

"Did you see any of the other contestants leave the set around the time she died?"

"No, but I was filming all day, just like the others."

"You took breaks like everyone else, though?"

"No. Some of the other contestants are always stopping, but when I'm in the zone, I forget everything else and focus on the food. You must know what that's like. You get an idea and it takes over. The magic flows out, and before you know it, you've created fifty cupcakes and your wrists are sore from all the beating."

"Um, yes. That happens to me all the time."

He nodded. "That's how I do my baking. Once I've got my ingredients and the idea, the camera rolls and I go for it. I power through until the treats are ready."

I leaned back in my seat as I mentally ruled out Cade. If he hadn't taken a break during filming, there was no way he could have killed Fawn.

"Was there anyone in the show who had a real problem with Fawn? Someone must know what happened to her," I said.

Cade didn't speak for a long minute. "Some of them were mean to her. Troy hates everyone other than himself. He's always unhappy about something. Did you know, he burned Fawn?"

"He burned her?"

"She was bringing him a coffee, but she got his order wrong. She used to do it on purpose, just to annoy him. He threw the hot drink over her arm, and it burned her skin."

"That's awful. Did Fawn report him?"

"No, but she was angry, and her arm was sore for about a week."

"Troy should have been kicked off the show for doing that. That's assault."

"He should, but it would have been Troy's word against Fawn. Troy has the Morelli baking empire supporting him and a family reputation that means he's untouchable. If Fawn reported it, he'd have said it was an accident. And if she'd told anyone else what happened, he'd have gotten his revenge. It would have been much worse than a coffee burn."

"But you don't accidentally throw an entire cup of scalding coffee over someone. He's a jerk. Other people must see that."

"Troy would have found a way around it, and Fawn knew that. She didn't even want to tell me what happened, but I dragged it out of her. I made sure her arm was less painful, but I'm not great at healing magic. My spells only work well when it comes to baking. Yours must be the same."

"I'm more of a generalist. I can use my magic for different things."

"Really? Wow! That's rare. If I try any kind of magic that's not food related, it's a fail. It always goes wrong. You're multi-talented."

I ducked my head. "Something like that. What about Meadow? I heard from some of the others that Fawn and Meadow often argued."

"Oh, yeah. All the time. Meadow was jealous of Fawn. She'd seen some of her baking creations and knew they were better than hers. It made her green with envy."

"Meadow said she's getting a co-credit on a recipe she created with Elwin. She must also be a talented baker to achieve that."

He groaned and tipped his head back. "Meadow doesn't stop bragging about that. It's not even that much of an achievement, and the recipe book hasn't been finalized. It's only going in a limited print run book in about a year. Low key. No big deal. The way she talks about it, it's like she's getting her own chain of patisseries and a huge publishing deal."

"It sounds impressive to me."

Cade tipped forward in his seat. "You know, Meadow only got this far because of her mom."

"Who's her mom?"

"Henriette. The show's sponsor. That was a part of the deal. Henriette's family is providing most of the funding for the show, so Meadow got a spot in the final."

"But Henriette's surname is DeVere. Meadow's surname is Eclair. And they don't even look alike. Are you sure they're related?"

"Henriette remarried a few years ago, but Meadow kept the Eclair name. She looks just like her dad. And keeping his name gives her a better reputation in the baking community."

"Why did the marriage fail?"

"From what I've heard, Henriette tired of never having a husband who was around, so she found someone who paid her more attention. Her second husband is something big in the tech industry. And he's loaded. It's his money behind this show."

"So Meadow has even more to prove and wouldn't want any competition getting in her way."

"There's no way Meadow would have gotten that co-credit or been a finalist in this show if it wasn't for her mom's involvement. Meadow's not even that great a baker. I mean, she can make a mean cupcake, but anyone can do that. Well, most of us." Cade tilted his head. "What happened with your cupcakes yesterday? I saw Elwin throw them away."

"Oh! I got distracted. It was nothing."

"Didn't you get the tingles? You must have known when the cupcakes were ready to come out of the oven."

"I was having an off-day. And I reckon there was something wrong with the oven. I'm not sure what happened."

There was a flash of lightning outside the bakery.

Cade looked over his shoulder as he munched on the last of his croissant. "You get freaky weather in Witch Haven. It's my first visit here, but so far we've had tornadoes, high winds, and now it looks like some crazy storm is setting in."

"We think someone is messing with us. It's probably their idea of a joke. We'll deal with it. We saw off the tornadoes, no problem. We've got powerful weather witches living here."

"I'm glad the tornados were stopped. If one had whipped through the place, we'd have never known someone killed Fawn." Cade's eyes clouded with tears. "I hope the Magic Council finds who did it soon. I haven't been sleeping well, and when I do, I have dreams about her."

"I'm sure you'll find someone right for you. It wasn't Fawn, but you'll find happiness again."

He drained his coffee and stood. "I was happy with Fawn. I'd have done anything for her, and I really loved her. I cared nothing for her lack of connections. I'd have looked after both of us. Even if I don't win this competition, I've already had three job offers. I'm also thinking about setting up my own patisserie."

"That all sounds wonderful. I'm sure you'll be a huge success."

"It wasn't enough for Fawn, though. She was aiming for queen of the cupcakes. Nothing was standing in her way. Not even me."

"You'll be someone's perfect guy one day." I led Cade to the door and unlocked it. "Don't get too distracted by your loss. You have a competition to win."

His smile was small and lasted half a second. "Thanks for talking to me about Fawn. Everyone else gets awkward and changes the subject when I bring her up. It's been nice to speak about her. Even though Fawn could be difficult, she had a good heart. She just had a tough life and deserved better. Way better than what she got."

I blinked away tears. My conversation with Cade made me even more determined to find out what happened to Fawn. "You're right. It was terrible what happened to her."

He briefly touched my arm. "Thanks, Luna. And have fun with the judging. Keep an eye on your oven the next time you bake."

"Will do. I'll see you on set." I said goodbye to Cade and closed the door behind him.

I'd need to check with the camera crew to make sure Cade had told the truth, but I could pretty much eliminate him from this investigation. It was clear he'd cared for Fawn and was suffering because of her murder.

That left me looking straight at Meadow. Maybe Fawn had confronted Meadow and told her she shouldn't have been on the show. Meadow was using her family influence to get what she wanted, and that must have stung. Fawn was working hard to make a name for herself, and then someone swooped in and grabbed an opportunity they didn't deserve. If I'd been in Fawn's position, I'd have been unhappy, too.

The more I learned about Meadow, the guiltier she looked. Meadow's unfair inclusion in the show must have been the reason Fawn wanted to meet with Henriette. She planned on exposing their connection and discrediting the show. That wouldn't have pleased fans. There would have been protests and complaints.

And since Henriette couldn't have killed Fawn, it had to be Meadow.

As I got ready for the day, I almost didn't mind that I'd have to bake again this evening. It would give me another chance to get on set and poke around some more. And this time, I was determined to get my cupcakes and the killer right.

Chapter 15

I was feeling proud of myself. I'd spent the day baking in Fandango's, and everything I made turned out well. Sure, the scones were a little uneven, and the caramel cream had a tart aftertaste, but it was all edible. My magic seemed stable for the first time in a long time. I'd turned a corner, and everything was coming good.

It was just a shame the storm was sticking around. Lightning and thunder had been cracking and booming across the sky all day. It meant we'd been quiet in the bakery, with most people deciding to stay away, rather than risk being struck by the lightning that kept pounding the ground.

Uncle Albert put his arm around my shoulders and squeezed. "It's been a good day. I've given all the cabinets a clean out and thought of a few new recipes we can try. And I've been looking through that copy of Elwin's book. It's inspirational."

"I haven't had a real chance to look at it. Are there recipes in there that would work for the bakery?"

"Definitely. Although there is a page that's marked as unfinished. What's that about?"

"That's part of the show contest. Elwin said the finalist who discovers the missing ingredient in that recipe gets a prize. That's what everyone is working on."

"How intriguing. Do you think Elwin knows what this ingredient is? He's holding it back to see if anyone can get it right?"

"I'm not sure. He's been elusive about it. But he's promised whoever finds the ingredient will get profits from the book and a credit on the recipe."

"That's odd. How can you not know an ingredient in one of your own recipes?" Uncle Albert shook his head. "When I get inspiration, I instinctually know the ingredients to make the perfect combination of flavors."

"It could be a test. A way to weed out the winner. I'm sticking with my lemon drizzle cupcakes. I know Elwin wanted me to solve his missing ingredient challenge, but I don't have the time to focus on it. I keep thinking about what happened to Fawn."

"Of course, considering you saw her body, that's understandable." Uncle Albert squeezed me tighter. "Is the Magic Council any closer to figuring out what happened?"

"They must be, but Devlin Goody doesn't tell me anything." I looked around the empty store. "Since it's quiet, I wouldn't mind heading off early. I want to speak to Devlin and see how he's getting on. I've got a few ideas to run past him."

"You be careful around him. He's not your biggest fan. And I still haven't forgiven him for thinking you killed Jinti Calrook."

"I know, but I should keep him informed. I might have a clue about who killed Fawn."

"It's nothing that'll get you in trouble, is it?"

I kissed his cheek. "Of course not. I'm always careful."

"Off you go, then. We haven't had a customer in half an hour. I might close early, especially since the storm is getting worse." He walked me to the door. "If it starts to rain, come back here. I don't want you outside soaking wet when there's fork lightning around."

"I'll keep an eye out." I grabbed my jacket and headed out of the bakery. I walked to Olympus's office, hoping to find Devlin there.

I knocked on the door and headed inside. Monty was sprawled on the floor, and Olympus was behind his desk.

Monty bounced up and ran over to me. He jumped up and rested his huge leopard paws on my shoulders before giving my face a lick.

"Get down," Olympus said. "You'll crush Luna."

I ruffled Monty's fur before easing his paws off my shoulders. "It's nice to see you, too."

"Have you come to play? I'm so bored," Monty said. "Olympus has been staring at those papers for hours. He must have read the information a dozen times. I think he's having a stupid day, since he can't keep the facts in his head."

"I'm reviewing a long, complicated report from the Magic Council." Olympus glared at Monty and pointed to his fluffy bed in the corner. "They have some interesting modernization plans, and I want to make sure I don't miss anything."

"It sounds riveting," I said.

"It's the opposite." He eased back in his seat. "What can I do for you?"

"I was looking for Devlin. I don't want to make a trip to the Magic Council headquarters to speak to him unless I have to."

"He was here about an hour ago. He'll be back tomorrow. What do you need him for?"

"It's about what happened to Fawn. I think I know who killed her."

Olympus's eyebrows shot up and he gestured to a seat. "Tell me everything."

I settled in the seat and clasped my hands together, taking a few seconds to gather the pieces of the puzzle in my head. "It was Meadow Eclair. She's been keeping secrets. She hated Fawn, and she had the chance to kill her."

"Did she confess to you?"

"Nothing like that. But she's Henriette's daughter, and Meadow's only on the show because of her connection to her mom."

"You think Fawn found out about their connection and they fought?"

"I don't know for sure, but they were seen arguing not long before Fawn was killed. It could have been about that. Neither Henriette nor Meadow mentioned they were mother and daughter. They've been keeping secrets."

His eyes narrowed. "It sounds like a lot of good guesswork but not much proof. What else have you got to convince Devlin that Meadow is the killer?"

My mouth twisted to the side. "Meadow took regular filming breaks on the first day of production.

She could have timed it so she followed Fawn to the play park."

"Did anyone see her go after Fawn?"

"No, but I haven't asked everyone. It's possible." My reasoning behind Meadow's guilt was slipping.

"Anything else?"

"Um, not really. Cade is a no, and so is Henriette. Troy's a jerk, though, and he did injure Fawn."

"How?"

"He scalded her arm with coffee. It was deliberate."

"So why aren't you considering him as a suspect?"

I shrugged. "He's horrible to everyone, not just Fawn. And Meadow has more to lose if her secret gets out. She could even be removed from the show, and her career would be over. She wouldn't stand for that. You can get seriously wealthy off cake."

"Is Meadow strong enough to create that kind of magic? The play park was destroyed. Can you do that with your baking magic?"

"I could. Meadow must have found a way to channel her power. It has to be her. Meadow needs to be formally questioned. She's my prime suspect."

"She might be your prime suspect, but..." Olympus rubbed his hands together.

"But it's not enough?"

"You're speculating. I'm not saying you're wrong, but you need evidence."

"If you don't believe me, there's no chance Devlin will." I sank into my seat. All my hard work felt like a waste of time.

"I can pass the information to Devlin, but this needs to be handled carefully. He hates it when people get involved in his cases. He even tells me to keep my nose out, and I'm his superior."

"Would you do that? Devlin never listens to me, so maybe the suggestion could come from you. I don't care, so long as Meadow is properly investigated."

"I'll get in touch with him and see what he thinks. Although he's not been sharing everything about this case. He seems worried I'll take over and solve it for him."

"Devlin sounds like Fawn. He's trying to prove himself." I smiled at Olympus. "I'm surprised you didn't take on this case."

"I would have done, if it wasn't for this." He pointed at the report on his desk. "It's one of the pleasures of being in a senior position in the Magic Council. And I've been having to attend several hours of tedious meetings most days. They're considering me as the lead on this modernization project."

"I never thought I'd hear you say the Magic Council was tedious."

He grinned and glanced at a photograph of Indigo on his desk. "My career is no longer my only focus."

I returned his grin. Olympus had softened since he'd started dating Indigo. "I'm happy for you."

"You're happy I'm stuck with this modernization project?"

I laughed as I stood. "No, I'm happy you've got a life."

"It's not much of a life," Monty grumbled. "He still doesn't play with me enough."

I grabbed a big furry pink ball off the floor and tossed it for Monty.

He growled and flew through the air, catching it in his mouth. He shook it, and then raced over and sat by my feet, swishing his tail.

I threw the ball several more times until it was sticky with leopard spit.

"That's enough. Luna isn't here to play with you." Olympus's gaze cut to the window as the wind howled outside. "You be careful out there. I don't know what's going on with this weather, but everyone should batten down the hatches and wait for it to pass."

"I spoke to Storm last night, and she doesn't think it's natural."

"There's talk of setting up a regular weather watch to see if someone is using their powers against us." Olympus recoiled as thunder rumbled nearby. "You should get home."

"I'll head home soon. I want to do some research in the library before I have to judge the cakes."

"What are you researching?" Olympus walked me to the door with Monty beside him.

"How to make the perfect cupcake."

"I'm surprised you need help with that."

"Oh, you know, I like to be on top form. I have to make sure everything goes right for the contest. I don't want to embarrass myself."

"I'm sure you'll be great. If there are leftovers, I'd love to sample some."

"You're on." We said our goodbyes, and I headed out, turning up my collar against the sharp wind that messed with my hair and made my eyes water.

I dashed down the road to the Witch Haven library. It was a magnificent gothic building with tall spires and small, dark leaded windows.

I ran through the door, gasping as I pulled it shut behind me to stop the wind catching it and smashing the glass. I turned and walked into Nazan Grizig, the scary half-dragon who ran the place with a scaled fist.

He looked down at me, his amber eyes pinning me to the spot and making sweat break out under my arms.

"Hi! I'm here to get books." I went to step around him, but he blocked my path.

"You'd better not be here to cause more trouble." His voice was a deep grumble in his barrel chest, and the scales that ran up the side of his neck flared red.

"I never cause trouble when I'm in here. I'm always respectful of the books. I love books."

"You broke in."

I batted my eyelashes. "You're mistaking me for someone else."

His scales flashed a warning hint of red. "I've made sure you can never get into the basement. I have the ghosts guarding it."

"You control the library ghosts?"

"There's no need to control them. They loathe intruders as much as I do. You were lucky to get out in one piece."

"If I was here, and I'm not saying I was, would it make you less angry if I told you there were extenuating circumstances?"

"No. I'd still ban you for life. I should."

My heart sank to my boots. "But I love the library. I'd be lost if I didn't have this as my sanctuary. Coming here is always so peaceful. Please, don't ban me."

Nazan huffed out a breath and smoke curled from his nostrils, although his scales had stopped changing color, which I took to be a positive sign. "Libraries are sanctuaries. They're not to be abused or taken advantage of. They should also never be broken into. Do we have an understanding?"

"A complete understanding. I'm not saying I did it the first time, but I'll never sneak into your basement again. Or if I do, it'll be because a life or death situation is occurring and I have no other option."

He growled at me. "And don't send any more of your rude friends here."

"Who are we talking about?"

"The one who smells of cinnamon rolls. She must be one of your cake friends."

"Um... I'm lost. What does she look like?"

"She behaved almost as strangely as you sometimes do. She was small, blonde, and stubborn. She stamped through the door, refused to sign in, and left without any books."

"Perhaps this mysterious visitor didn't find what she was looking for."

"My library has everything a bibliophile needs. She came in with a book and left without it."

"Are you sure?"

"I always watch strange visitors. People steal."

I raised a hand. "Not me. And of course, all visitors must sign in at the front desk. I know the rules.

I've brought plenty of people here over the years to show them your beautiful library."

Nazan snorted again and more smoke curled around his head. "Which is why you're getting off with a warning. You're usually respectful of the library services. I appreciate that."

"I always will be. We'll put the basement incident down to a lapse in judgment."

He finally stepped to the side. "Go in but don't stay long. The bad weather has damaged the roof, and the top floor is out of bounds because I'm monitoring for leaks."

"Is it that bad up there?" I fell into step beside him as we headed into the main foyer of the library. The vaulted ceiling soared above us, giving the space an airy feel.

"If there's any risk to the books or library users, I won't keep the place open. You've got half an hour to get what you need." Nazan stopped by the foyer's semi-circle counter. "What are you looking for?"

"Recipe books."

"You know where they are." He turned his back on me.

"Thanks. I won't be long." I dashed to the second floor, passing several people who were heading down the stairs, their arms full of books.

The cookery section was empty as I strode along the book stacks. I browsed several books, taking note of their cupcake recipes, and selected half a dozen before placing them on a table. I'd love to get my cupcakes right this evening. I needed a killer recipe to wow the other judges and contestants. Every time I mentioned my baking magic wasn't perfect, no one believed me, so I couldn't let the family name down.

"We're closing in five minutes," Nazan's voice boomed up the stairwell.

Hurrying along the final row of books, I grabbed two more that looked interesting. I put them on a pile and then picked them up, taking a few seconds to get them balanced in my arms. I'd just taken a step toward the stairs, when the room was plunged into darkness.

There was a huge flash of lightning outside, and thunder rumbled around the building. Nazan wouldn't have turned off the lights and left me in the dark. The storm must have taken out the power.

I inched toward the stairs, being careful not to bump into tables and chairs on my way out.

I was juggling my books, reaching for what I hoped was the door handle, when I heard shuffling behind me. Turning, I peered into the darkness. "Is someone else in here? Do you need help to get out?"

No one replied.

"If you follow the sound of my voice, I'm right by the door. We can go down the stairs together."

There was still no reply.

It must be a library ghost. I was just turning, when a fast moving shadow caught my eye. I sucked in a deep breath. There was no need to panic. Everyone knew the library was haunted, and the ghosts liked to play games, but they were rarely mean.

"There's no need to scare me. I'm already spooked by this storm." When I talked to the ghosts, they usually appeared, but this one was lurking in the darkest shadows of the library.

What sounded like a book thumped to the floor.

I tilted my head. Maybe there was someone in here, after all. Opposite the cookery section were the academic non-fiction books for teenagers. Someone could be huddled in the corner, too afraid to move. Even my heart was thudding faster than it should due to the thunder and the dark.

I crept back to the book stacks. "It's okay. The weather can't get you, but we need to leave. Nazan wants to close the library." I peered along each book stack, but the rows were empty.

Another crack of lightning slammed into the ground close by the building, making me jump. It was time to leave. I'd let Nazan know someone needed help getting out. He'd be sure to chase them from their hiding place.

I turned and tiptoed back toward the door, my arms aching from carrying so many books. I was halfway toward it, when more lightning cracked across the sky.

My eyes widened. Cole stood in front of the door.

I blinked, still dazzled by the lightning, and when the flare faded from my eyes, I couldn't see him.

"Cole? Are you stalking me?" I whirled around, but the place was inky black, and no lightning flashed to help me.

I dropped the books on the nearest table and raced to the door. I flew down the stairs, hoping Nazan would protect me from the angry werewolf. "Nazan! It's Luna. I could do with a hand."

The main foyer was quiet, and no one was around. I needed to get out of here.

I raced to the door and grabbed the handle. It wouldn't open.

"No!" Nazan wouldn't have locked me in. He knew I was still here. Taking a step back, I frowned. Maybe he would, and this was his way of getting back at me for breaking into the basement.

The top floor! He said he was monitoring for leaks. That was where he was. Nazan must have locked the main doors to stop anyone from getting inside.

I raced up four flights of stairs, gasping for breath and not daring to look in on the second floor for fear of seeing Cole. I reached the top floor and grabbed the door handle. It wouldn't budge. Nazan had locked this door as well.

There had to be a way out. Nazan loved this library, and he wouldn't leave me here alone. Maybe he'd gone out for materials to stop the leak from getting too bad. Yes, he'd be back.

I turned and stared down the stairs. Should I wait here or creep to the first floor? If I went back to the foyer, I'd see Nazan as soon as he returned, and I could get him to protect me from Cole.

I headed back down the stairs, slower this time. I got to the second floor and peeked through the glass door. I squeaked and backed away. Cole was stalking toward me.

There was a huge slam of lightning, which lit the room, revealing Cole's angry face. His fists were clenched and his teeth bared.

Glass smashed, and the wind howled through the broken window. It was so strong it slammed open the door, almost knocking me in the face.

Cole barely flinched. He was so intent on getting to me.

There was another growl of thunder and more lightning.

I got my feet to move, but only made it a couple of steps before I screamed.

A book stack was falling toward Cole.

"Look out!"

Chapter 16

Cole saw the falling stack a second too late. He was turning when it landed on him and slammed him to the hard wooden floor with a jarring thud.

I waited for more lightning to show me just how bad the accident was. It didn't oblige. Then I heard a low, pain-filled groan.

Cole was hurt. I inched through the door, my arms held out in front of me. "Are you okay? I mean, of course, you won't be okay. A ton of books just slam dunked you, but at least you're not dead. Unless that was a ghost moaning. Moan again if that was you."

He grunted once in reply.

"Good enough. Grunts I can handle. Give me a minute to find you. I don't want to tread on you in the dark. Where's a good blast of sheet lightning when you need it?"

There was a flash of lightning, and I saw the reason the book stack had toppled. A huge branch of the giant oak tree that used to stand outside the library poked through the window. It must have knocked the book stack off-balance.

Using the lightning to my advantage, I raced to Cole and landed on my knees in front of him.

His head whipped up, and his eyes glowed amber. He tried to push himself up using his arms, but the book stack pinned him down at the waist.

"Don't do that. You'll hurt yourself."

"The books have already done a good enough job of that," he growled.

"I tried to warn you."

He grunted again. "So, what's your next move?"

"Err... my move? What do you mean?"

"I'm injured, and you know I'm coming for you. My wolf is trapped, and he hates being trapped."

"You're... coming for me?"

"I gave you a warning. You saw it."

"Yeah, I got that message, but I hoped you'd calmed down since you smeared that on the wall." I peered under the book stack. "Did you write that message in your own blood?"

"I couldn't find any paint lying around."

"You should have checked the shed." My gaze ran over the book stack. Cole didn't seem badly injured since he was talking, well, growling at me. "If I help you get out, will you promise not to eat me?"

He lay face down on the floor for several seconds, simply deep breathing. "I was never going to eat you."

"You want to make me pay, though. I mean, I didn't treat you well the last time we met."

"No kidding. You chained me up like a wild dog and stole my power."

"Yeah, not my proudest moment. But I was desperate."

Cole didn't reply.

"So, what now?"

"It's your move, witch. You have me where you want me. I guess it's time to get rid of the werewolf."

"I... no. I don't want to do that." I couldn't abandon Cole. Even though he'd been hurt while stalking me, it was wrong to leave him trapped and struggling. "I can get you out, but we have to work together."

He huffed out a breath. "We do?"

I didn't miss the note of surprise in his voice. "If you use your werewolf strength to lever up the book stack, I can put books underneath it and lessen the pressure on your back and legs. Then you can wriggle free."

"I should be in my werewolf form. I'm stronger on four legs. But if I change, I'll make my injuries worse."

"Don't injure your wolf. We can figure this out." I grabbed fallen books and shoved them under the stack until they were almost level with the ledge pinning Cole. "I think I saw you in your werewolf form. You were outside my farmhouse. You followed Bram when he ran off."

"Did you? You sure it was me?"

"No, but I don't know of any other werewolves interested in my hidden farmhouse. The local pack doesn't hang around that part of the woods." I bit my lip. "Did you catch Bram?"

"I didn't confirm it was me in the woods."

"Oh! Sure. Whoever it was, he seemed determined to track Bram, though. And that wolf was kind of handsome."

"Are you trying to make me jealous?"

My eyebrows shot up. "Would you be, if I admired another werewolf?"

A deep growl rumbled through Cole.

Heat flushed across my cheeks. It seemed he would be jealous. Maybe Cole didn't hate me, after all. "You're always welcome in those woods, so long as you're not hunting me."

"That's good to know."

I shoved in more books. "Have you been spending a lot of time hanging out near the farmhouse?"

"I stop by and keep an eye on things."

It should be terrifying that Cole was checking up on me, but it made me feel warm and fuzzy. "I saw your paw prints in the mud. You could have gotten me any time you wanted. I didn't even know you were staking out the place."

"I wasn't. It's on my regular route."

"You're still living in Witch Haven?"

"For now."

"Werewolf business?"

"Witch business."

Oh, boy. I was in trouble. "Are you ready to try lifting the book stack?"

He eyed the book I had in my hand. "You'd better not club me on the head with that when I move."

I looked at the large hardback. "Nope. This one's a classic. I wouldn't want to damage it on your thick skull."

Cole growled out a laugh. "On three." He counted us down.

As he attempted to do a press-up with a ton of books and wood on top of him, I held the book out.

The second there was a big enough gap, I shoved it in.

Cole dropped on the floor, panting. Pain was etched across his face.

"It worked!" I stood back and grinned. "We have a gap. See if you can move."

"My legs are still pinned. One of them is broken."

I sucked in a breath. "You should have said."

"Why? Are you planning on nursing me back to health?"

"I... No. But we have to get you out." I rubbed my hands together. "I could try magic to move the book stack."

"Don't use any magic around me. I never know what you're handling, since it's not yours."

I scowled at him. "I know how to do a basic spell."

"They're my legs, and I'm not risking it. Let's keep going with the books."

We repeated the exercise six more times, with Cole doing a press-up and me ramming books onto an increasingly precarious stack.

He slumped to the floor and wheezed out a tight breath.

"We shouldn't go any higher." I peered under the book stack and gagged. Cole's left leg was bent at a freakish angle.

"I need a minute." His words came out more growly than human.

"We can take as long as you need."

"No, we can't. I heal fast, and if I don't get the bone in my leg set right, it'll never heal properly."

I winced, and my stomach flipped over. "That's bad."

"No kidding. A werewolf with a limp won't last long. We don't tolerate weakness."

"Your pack mates won't turn on you because you're injured."

He looked up at me and arched an eyebrow. "They would. A weak werewolf is no use to anyone."

"You'd be of use to me. When you're not stalking me or thinking about eating me, I'm happy to have you around. And there's always a place for you in my farmhouse."

"I'm no one's lap dog, sweetheart."

My heart did a funny flip-flop at the term of endearment, even though the words were spoken sharply. "I wouldn't expect you to be, but you'd have your uses since the rest of you still works fine."

Cole's grin morphed into a feral snarl. "I reckon I would. Is there a particular part of me you want to take for a test ride?"

My cheeks flushed, and I looked away. "I need to drag you out from under the stack. Can you move your uninjured leg? If you can get purchase on the floor, we can do it together."

"The right leg has some wriggle room. I'll give it a go."

My heart was beating too fast as I edged toward Cole's head. "I'll hook my arms under your armpits and pull. Will that work?"

"Let's do it."

"Promise you won't eat me. I don't want you turning full werewolf because I'm hurting you."

"My wolf is under control. He knows what you're doing."

"He still might want to bite me."

"He definitely wants to bite you." Cole snapped his teeth at me. "But he won't."

I held in a squeak as I grabbed Cole. There was no delicate way of doing this as his head pressed against my bosom and I wrapped my arms tightly around him.

"Comfortable?"

"I've been in worse situations. You smell good."

"I smell of terror and a lifetime of mistakes." I gritted my teeth. Pulling a two hundred and fifty pound adult male werewolf from under a book stack should be an Olympic sport.

I inhaled and caught the scent of grass and smoky fire. It was Cole's unique scent.

He butted his head into my cleavage. "Sorry."

"No worries. Just get settled and don't squirm too much. You ready?"

"All set."

I was in a semi-crouch, so couldn't use my full weight, but I tipped back on my heels and yanked on Cole.

"Go again. I moved an inch."

I sucked in a deep breath, bumping my chest even harder against Cole's face. "Sorry! There's nothing I can do about my fun bags." I leaned back, and this time, Cole used his uninjured leg to lever him forward.

"One more pull," he said. "Can you manage that?"

I looked at the books holding up the book stack. It was moving. "Get out of there. Now!" I threw my weight behind the pull, leaning back and grunting. There had to be veins popping all over me as I

Hulked out in an effort to stop Cole from being crushed.

A second later, he flew out from the book stack and landed on top of me. His lower stomach smooshed against my face, and I was pinned to the floor.

Neither of us moved as there was a loud thump as the book stack slid off the pile of books and hit the floor.

"Is there any chance I can get some air?" I mumbled against his hard stomach.

Cole responded by lifting himself up on his arms so I could roll out. He slumped to the floor. His face was pale, and he was sweating.

"That was a close call," he mumbled.

"How's your leg?"

"It itches."

"There's no need to be a tough guy. I'm terrible with pain. I once sliced my finger on a knife when I was cutting onions, and I was convinced I was going to die. It took me a week to recover, and I still can't look at onions without wincing."

He snorted a laugh.

"I'll see if Nazan has any medical supplies. There must be something around here. Will you be all right if I leave you on your own?"

"I'll be peachy. I might do some light reading while you're gone."

"There's plenty of choice." I hurried down to the main foyer and hunted around. There was a basic medical kit under the desk, but it only had bandages, plasters, and antiseptic wipes. I grabbed it anyway then discovered a staff kitchen that had a bigger medical supply closet. I grabbed everything I thought might be useful then raced up the stairs.

Cole hadn't moved, but he was being watched by two female ghosts. One of them was about to poke his butt cheek with a finger. The second they saw me, they vanished.

I hurried over and dropped the supplies next to him. I pulled open a packet of pain meds, dropped some in his hand, and gave him a bottle of water. "These should take the edge off."

He swallowed them down without protest. "We need to deal with my leg."

"We do? What can I do to help?"

"You need to break it again."

It was suddenly hard to breathe. I stared at his face, and then his leg. "Why would I do something so horrific?"

"It's healing wrong. I can feel it. It's the only thing that'll work."

I shook my head and shuffled back on my knees. "I can't break your leg. It'll hurt you."

"It'll hurt me more if it heals wrong." He circled my wrist with warm fingers to stop me moving. "Luna, you owe me. You have to do this. Find something heavy and slam it against the side of my leg. Aim for below the knee."

"I can't! There has to be another way. Maybe it'll heal okay and you'll only have a slight limp."

"That won't happen. Do this for me."

I stared at his leg again. Cole wouldn't be here if he didn't have a score to settle.

"Stop thinking and start breaking," he growled out.

I shook my head. I couldn't leave him like this. The book stack wouldn't have fallen on Cole if he hadn't been following me. And he was only following me because I'd chained him up and taken his magic against his will.

"Luna!"

I jumped. "Sorry, I'm figuring things out. Is there no other way?"

"No. Go grab that fire extinguisher."

I muttered curses under my breath as I raced over and unhooked the fire extinguisher from the wall. I'd never deliberately hurt anyone. I didn't have it in me.

The floor was cold under my knees as I lined the fire extinguisher up with his leg.

"Do it."

I breathed through my nose. "I'm like a doctor, fixing a broken bone. They do this, don't they? Break bones to make sure they heal properly."

"It happens all the time in the werewolf community."

"Has this ever happened to you before?"

Cole's eyes flashed amber. "Plenty of times."

"You won't turn werewolf when I do it?"

"He knows what's about to happen. He's not happy but accepts it. Now, break my leg."

My heart was thudding so loudly, Cole must have been able to hear it. I lined up the bottom of the fire extinguisher. "About here?"

"That'll work."

I took a swing and stopped an inch from his leg. "Luna! Just do it."

"Sure. I will. That was a practice swing." I licked my dry lips. "Do you need something to bite down on?"

"I'll bite down on your arm if you don't do this."

"Right. Just swing and break. It's easy."

"It's as easy as snapping a twig over your knee."

It so wouldn't be that easy. I rolled my shoulders and lined up the fire extinguisher again. I swung it back, and it flew out of my hand and rolled across the floor.

Cole groaned and closed his eyes. "You did that deliberately."

"My hands are sweaty. This is a first for me. I'm not finding it easy." I raced over and grabbed the fire extinguisher and returned to Cole's side.

"It's not exactly a walk in the park for me." His gaze settled on mine. "You have to do this. Please."

I couldn't chicken out any longer. Cole deserved a fully functioning leg, and if that meant I had to break it, then that's what I'd do.

I didn't look at him as I lined up the fire extinguisher and slammed it as hard as I could against his lower leg.

A werewolf howl echoed around the room as the sickening snap of bone made me turn away and dry heave. I dropped the fire extinguisher and kept my eyes closed as I leaned my hands on my knees.

"Are you good?" Cole's voice was quiet and full of pain.

"Yep. I'm having a great time. Best date ever."

"Date?" He chuckled. "This one's definitely up there in my top ten of weirdest dates."

"I mean, it's not a date. More of a stalk with intent to kill." I glanced back at him.

Cole shook his head. "Hand me those bandages and find something hard and straight for me to use. I need it to set the bone in place."

I was glad to have a distraction, because all I could hear was that bone snapping repeatedly. It took me a few minutes, but I found some meter rulers. There were several in a pile in the children's area, so I grabbed them and returned to Cole.

A flash of lightning revealed how pale his face was, and his eyes were burning amber. He'd also moved his leg, and it was at a normal angle as he held it on either side of his knee.

"Will these do?" I thrust the rulers at him.

"Perfect. You need to remove my boot and cut off my jeans so I can get the wood close to my skin and then wrap the bandage."

I found scissors in the medical kit. I eased off his boot, only getting sworn at twice, and then made a small hole in Cole's jeans just above his knee. I sliced around his thigh as far as I could without moving the leg. I flapped open the jeans to reveal a toned thigh. I didn't look below the knee because it would make me heave again.

I eased two rulers either side of Cole's leg, keeping my focus on his toes. They were nice toes. Some men's feet were horror shows, with gnarly yellow nails and callouses that would scrape the skin off your chin, but Cole's toes were attractive. I wouldn't object to him in a pair of flip flops.

"When you've stopped staring at my foot, you need to elevate my leg so I can slide the bandage underneath."

"I wasn't staring. I was just admiring."

"Have I got it in me to be a foot model?"

I grabbed bandages and grinned at him. "I wouldn't mind looking at your feet while you model a pair of high heels."

The next five minutes were spent sweating, cursing, and taking the greatest care of Cole's leg.

I sat back and swiped my hand across my forehead. His leg was swathed in bandages, and Cole had only passed out once while I'd worked on him. I handed him another bottle of water, which he downed in one go.

I grabbed my own bottle and took a sip. "Now that you're not going to die from being squashed under a book stack, what shall we do next?"

Chapter 17

Cole's smile made him look so delicious that my heart forgot to function for a few seconds. "We're not going anywhere in this storm. And my leg needs time to mend."

"So we're stuck here?"

"With each other. Is that so terrible?"

"It depends how angry you are with me."

"I'm working that through in my head."

"I owe you an apology." I draped the remains of Cole's jeans over his healing leg. "It was wrong of me to chain you up in the farmhouse."

He eased back on to his elbows. "It was."

"I thought you'd see the sense in it."

An eyebrow raised. "I'm struggling to see sense in abducting people and chaining them up."

"It's not like that. There was no abduction. Other than you. Technically, that was me taking without an agreement in place." I sighed. It was difficult to explain my situation and not make it sound odd.

"An agreement? How about you help me up, and we can work through why chains, draining magic, and magic barriers lead to trouble."

I pursed my lips. "Shouldn't you stay still? It'll only hurt your leg if you move."

"Sure. You want to lie down with me and get comfortable if we're spending the night?"

My heart forgot its purpose again. "Err... let's get you up."

He grinned. "I get it. And we've got time."

"For..."

"For this." He gestured from his chest to mine.

Oooh! I was in so much trouble it was making me dizzy and breathless. "I can prop you up if you're uncomfortable."

"I can feel the bone knitting together, and the pain's fading. By tomorrow morning, you won't even know I broke my leg."

"Do you heal that quickly?"

He nodded. "It's one benefit of being a werewolf. All I'll have is another scar."

My gaze flicked over him. "Do you have a lot of scars?"

"Sure. And I'll show you them if you ask real nice."

Oh, boy!

Between the two of us, I got Cole standing on his good leg.

I wrapped an arm around his waist. The guy was all muscle. "Lean on me. I'll get you to a chair."

A strong arm wrapped around my shoulders, and I resisted the urge to snuggle into his embrace. It felt good to be held. I wriggled my shoulders, adjusting to the extra weight. I had to remember Cole had been stalking me, and I'd yet to negotiate that tricky path and get out the other side.

"I really did want you for my harem," I said. "You'd love Gloria and Faye. Ridley's fun, too. He misses having male company around."

"It's never going to happen. I don't share my mate."

I stopped moving and stared at him. "Your mate? Is that how you see me?"

His steady, intense gaze settled on me. "I do. Even after you snared me."

"But I chained you up and drained your magic. You should hate me. I should be on the top of your list of witches you want to eat."

Cole grunted out a laugh. "Maybe I liked the chains. You never know, you could have a kinky werewolf on your hands."

A cross between a laugh and a snort shot out. And my heart still hadn't recovered from him calling me his mate. He couldn't be serious.

Cole chuckled. "Honestly, I wasn't thrilled about the chains. But you're different. And you care about those magic users in the farmhouse. You're always spending time there and taking care of them. I even saw you do movie night with some black and white feature."

"We did! We watched the Wolf Man." I laughed, amazed he'd been paying me so much attention. "Was it factually accurate?"

"I've seen worse. And it's a classic."

I should be freaked out that Cole had been close by all this time, but I wasn't. I liked my strapping werewolf nearby. "They're happy. And my little magic harem have reasons for needing to keep a low profile. They aren't prisoners."

He nodded and gestured to the chair. "I ran background checks on them. I know who they are and what they've done. You're running a risk hiding people who committed such serious crimes."

"They had no choice. Ridley would have been killed by that demon who came for him, and Gloria was in an abusive relationship. Her husband was a monster, and she had to stop him. And Faye... Well, her muggers didn't realize how powerful she was. They surprised her, and she retaliated." I shuffled Cole to the chair. "Faye doesn't use her magic much because she's ashamed of what she did."

Cole eased into the seat and stretched out his healing leg. "It's good to hear both sides of their stories. Do you see yourself as a protector of these magic users? You keep them hidden in exchange for their power?"

I settled in the seat next to him and checked his leg was comfortable. "Pretty much. They'd all be in prison or dead if I hadn't given them sanctuary. They're decent people, and they'd never hurt me."

He shrugged. "It's not a terrible deal you offer. But you'll find yourself in trouble if the Magic Council ever discovers what you're doing."

My eyes narrowed. "Are you going to tell them?"

"I've no plans to do that. But I've also got no plans to join the farmhouse. Like I said, I don't share." Cole reached forward and lifted the wolf pendant that had slipped out of my shirt. "This looks good on you. I knew it would."

My cheeks flushed. "I knew it was from you. He's beautiful."

"He is. And he's also been keeping track of you."

I jerked back in my seat. "What do you mean?"

"I figured I needed to keep tabs on you. I couldn't work you out. One minute, you're this sweet, disarming witch who chases down bad guys, and then I find you with a hidden farmhouse full of criminals you're sucking the magic out of. I couldn't decide whether you were a good girl or needed taking out."

I lifted the wolf pendant and stared at it. "Does your tracking magic make the pendant warm?"

"You noticed that?"

"I did." I went to take it off, uneasy with having a tracker stuck around my neck.

"Leave it on. I'll remove the tracking magic. I don't need to use it anymore." Cole clasped the pendant in his fist and closed his eyes.

A wave of warmth shot down to my toes before fading away.

"It's gone." He leaned so close my vision blurred. "I had to know more about you before I decided what to do."

I sucked in a breath, not sure how I felt about Cole tracking me. I didn't have to put the pendant on, but I'd wanted to. "Have you made a decision? Do you think I'm one of the good girls?"

Cole's intense gaze settled on me, and my heart gave a quick thud. "I'm leaning in that direction. You don't hurt the residents in the farmhouse, and you could have left me under that book stack. I'd have figured a way out eventually, but my leg would have been a mess. Even though I was after you, you still helped. That took guts. It was a risky move."

"I couldn't leave you injured. And you were only in the library because of me."

"Are you saying this is all your fault?" A sly smile spread across his face.

"No! I mean, I had nothing to do with the oak tree smashing through the library window. That was the storm." I glanced at the shattered window and the rain pouring through. "Nazan will be mad at the mess the storm's made. I don't think he's coming back tonight."

"We can get out without his help, but I need to rest my leg before we bust out of here. And we should wait for the storm to blow out." Cole's stomach growled almost as loudly as the thunder. "Something to eat would be good. It takes a lot of calories to heal a broken leg."

"There's a vending machine in the hallway, but we need power to get it to work. And I'm desperate for a coffee." I peered around the room. "Some light would also make this whole place less intimidating."

"You're afraid of a few shadows?"

"More like the werewolf lurking in them."

"I'm friendly, if you know how to stroke me right."

I blushed. "I remember seeing a generator in the basement. And while we're here, we can do some work."

Cole scrubbed a hand across his stubbled jaw. "Why have you been in the library basement?"

"Um, I'm nosey. I'll see to the generator. You get the snacks and drinks." I glanced at his leg. "If you're up to it. Can you hop?"

"So long as I have you by my side, I can do anything."

I looked away and smiled. Cole was only teasing.

It took a few minutes of negotiating, but I got him to the vending machine, and he only cursed twice when he landed awkwardly on his healing leg. I left him some money and headed to the basement. I guided myself along the wall since an inky darkness covered everything, only bumping my knee a few times.

I risked using a light spell, and it sort of worked. I got a tiny ball of light hovering in front of me that chased away some of the shadows. I took a minute to get my bearings before spotting the backup generator in the corner of the basement.

Fortunately for me, the instructions on how to turn it on were printed on a neat label on the front. After going through each step, I sent out hopeful vibes, pressed the power button, and it rumbled to life.

That was easier than I'd expected. And Nazan kept the basement clean and tidy, so I had no giant spiders or their creepy webs to deal with.

I hurried back up the basement steps and re-joined Cole, who'd limped his way from the vending machine and back to his seat. There was a table full of snacks laid out in front of him, and he was munching on a chocolate bar.

He pointed at a glowing wall light. "You did it."

"I did. Good choice of snacks. We could do with some coffee, though."

"I didn't want to risk limping with hot coffee."

"Of course. I'll get it." I dashed back to the vending machine, grabbed two coffees, and returned to my seat.

Neither of us spoke for several long, contented minutes as we sipped coffee and munched on chocolate and chips. Despite the wind howling through the broken window, this felt almost cozy.

"We should be careful with the generator," Cole said, "and only power up essential things."

I nodded. "None of the lights were on downstairs, and we'll keep the lighting in here to a minimum."

"If you get too cold, you can always snuggle with me."

I pursed my lips. "Maybe I don't want to snuggle with you."

His grin turned wicked. "You do. A werewolf knows these things."

"Would that be okay? You wouldn't object to some cuddling?"

"I wouldn't object to anything you're offering me. I'll take it all."

I was speechless, so I opened another chocolate bar and bit into it. Cole was confident, but that was the werewolf way. At least I knew where I stood with him. This wasn't just teasing. This meant something. Maybe even something with the potential for a long-term future.

Cole screwed up the wrapper of the flapjack he'd consumed in three bites. "So what's going on with this murder? I know you're involved. Is that what you want to work on while we're here?"

"Yes. And before you ask, I didn't do it."

He grinned. "I never said you did. But you've been poking around to find out who the killer is. What's your interest in the victim?"

"I'm mainly poking around to make sure the Magic Council doesn't stuff things up. Devlin Goody's in charge, and we have a complicated history."

Cole's eyes brightened to a glowing amber. "Relationship style history?"

"No! As in he wanted to arrest me for murder kind of history."

His shoulders relaxed. "Sure. The poisoned witch. I remember. That's good."

"That I was a prime suspect in a murder? Not from my point of view."

"No, it means I won't get an uptight member of the Magic Council hounding me because I'm dating his ex."

Again, I hit speechless mode for a few seconds. "We're dating?"

"Isn't this a date?"

"It's more a rescue and research mission, with breaks and chocolate."

"I call that a date." Cole tossed back a small bag of cookies. "Who are your suspects?"

"I've got one in mind. Meadow Eclair. She's hiding information, including who her mom really is. She's sponsoring the baking show and fixed it for Meadow to get a place in the final."

"Meadow doesn't deserve her place?"

"I've never tasted her food, but it looks nice. According to one of the other bakers, she's not that talented. Plus, she had a motive and an opportunity. She hated Fawn. And Fawn was about to blow the show apart with information she had. That was why she went to the play park. She'd planned on meeting Henriette and revealing this big story."

"Who's Henriette?"

"Sorry, Meadow's mom and the show sponsor."

Cole was quiet as he took in this information. "Who discovered Fawn's body?"

"Henriette. Then she found me and Storm, and we went to see what was going on."

"So your prime suspect's mom found Fawn? Wouldn't she have covered up the murder if she knew her daughter did it?"

"Maybe she didn't. Meadow could have snuck out of the filming and murdered Fawn without knowing her mom was due to meet her. Meadow could have seen Fawn leave the set and took a chance."

"It's possible, although risky. Anyone else on the suspect list?"

"I've discounted Henriette and Cade. He's another baking contestant, even though he dated the victim and she ditched him. Although I need to double check his alibi. Elwin La Croix, who's a judge, also doesn't seem likely. He looked out for Fawn and helped her after her dad died."

"Anyone else?"

"There's one more contestant. He's a rude jerk, but he has issues with everyone. I'm focused on Meadow."

"Do you think Fawn planned on blackmailing Henriette about the show being rigged?"

"I doubt that was her motive for meeting her. Fawn wanted a foot in the door of the baking community."

"Could Henriette have done that for her?"

"Probably not. But it might have led to Meadow being removed from the show because she didn't get her place fairly. Maybe Fawn figured she'd offer herself as a substitute, thinking they'd be desperate to fill the slot so the show wouldn't be delayed." I sank back in my seat. "Or I'm getting this all twisted up in my head and it has nothing to do with the show. I need proof."

Cole drank his coffee. "What's with all the books you were collecting? More research to solve the murder?"

"Oh, no! Let me go get them." I grabbed the books and sat back down. "I was looking for inspiration. My cupcake recipes have been hit and miss recently."

"Because of your magic issue? The blunting thing?"

"Yep. It should be as simple as clicking my fingers and casting a spell, but it takes so much effort to get anything to come out tasting like it should. The only time my magic clicked into place was when—" I pressed my lips together.

"When what?"

My cheeks flushed. "When I took your magic. I've never felt so alive, and my cakes came out amazing."

He grinned. "Werewolf energy is something else. Your magic harem doesn't give you the same kick?"

"Not anymore. They used to, but it's getting harder to make it work."

"Which is why you want me."

I wanted him in lots of ways, not all of them appropriate. "What I've made for the baking show hasn't been great, and I need to make sure I don't go wrong. I've got a final chance to bake the perfect cupcake. I was supposed to be filming tonight, but that must have been canceled. There's no way they'd film while the storm is so bad." I toyed with my empty chocolate wrapper. "Maybe I won't have to do it."

"If you do, will these books help?"

"Most likely not, but I'm desperate. I'm in a room with the world's next top baker, and everyone is expecting great things from me. They all think Brimstone bakers never have any struggles." I rested a hand on the books.

"Are you the first in your family to struggle with your magic?"

"That I know of. Maybe there are other members of the family who have had problems, but I don't know about it. After all, I've been covering this up for years, so they could have done the same."

"You should talk to your parents and ask them about it. They'd want to help."

"There's no way I'm asking my mom or dad if they struggle with baking spells. They'd think I was crazy." I rested my elbows on the table. "I was always in awe of them when I was a kid. I'd sit in the kitchen for hours and watch them create these amazing desserts. It was effortless. And they enjoyed doing it."

"You don't enjoy baking?"

"I don't hate it, but it always feels like a struggle, and it's exhausting. It's as if I'm not meant to make desserts. Which makes no sense, because that's what my family does. And you've tasted the food from Fandango's. Uncle Albert is another natural baker, although he's a Black, not a Brimstone. My auntie, when she was alive, had so much fun with him in the kitchen. They'd romance each other by creating incredible recipes."

"That sounds like fun."

I chuckled. "It used to get steamy in the kitchen. Food can be sensual when you get it right."

"I'm liking the sound of this even more. We could get steamy in the kitchen together."

"You don't want to eat anything I make. And there wouldn't be steam. There'd be smoke." I closed my eyes and tipped back my head. "I just need something to give me an edge. I can't mess this up."

"You need something special. A recipe no one has used for a while."

"That could help." I looked at him. "What have you got in mind?"

"I smelled some old recipe books tucked away at the back of the book stacks," Cole said.

"You can smell cook books?"

"Sure. They smell of the recipes inside them. I got a whiff of a sweet spice. They pick up the scents while they're lying around. Maybe you've been hunting in the wrong place for inspiration. The books you've selected look modern."

"They're the latest recipes. I picked the books from the best bakers around. But I'm open to trying anything."

"I'll go grab them. They were tucked on a high shelf and looked like no one had taken them out for ages."

"What were you doing looking at recipe books?"

"I wasn't. I was nosing around and killing time while I watched you."

"And figured out when to make your attack?"

He grinned. "You got it."

"Do you need a hand? Or should that be leg?"

"No, I want to test the bone and see how it's healing. Give me a few minutes."

I smoothed my hands over my hair and made an attempt to straighten my disheveled clothing. Cole was being nice to me, and I didn't deserve it, but I liked it. And he wasn't hiding his interest, which was weirdly enjoyable and scary. When a werewolf sets his sights on something, it's rare he deviates from that path.

I wasn't sure what I was getting into with Cole, but I was intrigued to know more.

He returned a few moments later with three dusty, plain covered books. He dropped them in front of me and eased back into the seat.

"How's the leg?"

"Complaining. But it's on the mend."

I flicked through a couple of the books. "These are ancient. Some of the ingredients I've never heard of." I grabbed another one and read through the list of recipes. "These look familiar, but I don't think I've ever taken this book out."

"Maybe you used it when you were a kid. Or your parents could own a copy."

I looked through the pages. "I don't think so, but I've seen thousands of recipe books." I set the book to one side.

Cole leaned forward and took hold of my hand. "I've got an idea to kill time while we're here."

My heart stuttered, and I stared at our joined hands. "What have you got in mind?"

"Follow me. You're going to love it."

Chapter 18

Four hours later, the moon was high in the sky, and my eyes were gritty from lack of sleep and staring at a computer screen.

I hadn't loved Cole's idea of researching online. I'd been happy eating chocolate and getting to know him. But it had been useful.

Cole was a genius when it came to finding information, and he'd unearthed dozens of cookery videos made by Fawn, which we'd been watching.

He let out a low whistle and stretched his arms over his head. "Can you do that?" He pointed to the amazing display of glitter magic that shot from Fawn's hands and covered a five-tiered iced cake.

I wrinkled my nose. "In theory."

"What happens in reality?"

"The last time I used glitter magic, I was scratching it out of my hair three weeks later. The spell worked, but it blew back and covered me. I had blue and purple glitter all over me. I haven't used that spell since."

Cole chuckled. "I bet you looked cute covered in glitter."

"Maybe, but I felt like an idiot." I stared at the screen. "That's real baking talent. And look at Fawn's face. She's in her element. She's literally glowing." The videos showed Fawn making stunning, mind-boggling cakes and desserts. She'd made summer berry ice cakes with ease, revealed delicious mandarin orange and white chocolate floats, and reveled in stacking sponges high and turning them into works of art.

"She makes a decent teacher, too. I've learned a few tricks to use in the kitchen."

"You bake?"

"I might now."

"Fawn is great. And she's patient, talking through each step as she goes. If someone asked me to tell them what I was doing in the kitchen, I'd end up with the bowl on my head and icing in my hair." I hid my envy as Fawn turned to the camera with a huge smile, her eyes alight with pleasure.

We watched a video of her creating a six-layer children's birthday cake with free-standing characters and moving waves. It was so beautiful, it made me tear up. I wanted to be that amazing. I should be that good. This was what I was born to do.

Cole squeezed my knee. "Are you okay?"

I sniffed back tears. "I gave up making complicated desserts a long time ago. Whenever Uncle Albert gives me something challenging, I pretend I'd rather watch him do it. He keeps saying I need to learn because he's planning on handing the business to me."

"You don't look happy about that."

"Fandango's will be shut down within a year when I'm in charge. Uncle Albert makes that place amazing. And he covers for my mistakes. He might not be aware of what he's doing, but I'm not good enough to wash the pots there. There's no way I can run the place. The reputation will be ruined, and then my secret will come out." I gasped in a breath. "I'm a fraud."

Cole turned fully to face me and caught hold of both of my hands. His warm, smoky scent drifted up my nose.

"You're not a fraud. You're just struggling. Everyone's allowed to struggle."

"Do you struggle being a werewolf?"

"I did when I was younger. The first time you change, it's terrifying. You have no control. I'd have paws and a tail, and the rest of me would still be a gangly kid. Or my ears would sprout fur and I'd start howling. Changing is led by emotion when you're young. I'd flip from human to werewolf in the blink of an eye and spend hours figuring out how to morph back."

"I bet you made a cute werewolf pup."

He growled at me. "Werewolves aren't cute."

"Not even the puppies?"

"Even they bite."

"I'd have ruffled your fur if I'd known you when you were a puppy."

"And I might have let you." His gaze settled on my mouth. "I have a theory about your magic."

"Is it that I'm a Friday afternoon?"

"What's that?"

"You know, when something gets made on a Friday afternoon, it's done in a hurry because whoever is making it wants to get home and enjoy their weekend. You never buy anything made on a Friday afternoon because it's bound to go wrong."

"Luna, you're not broken."

"No, but I don't work quite right. I've accepted that."

"You shouldn't. And you shouldn't hide it." Cole cocked his head. "Have you ever thought your baking magic is being blocked by something?"

"It doesn't feel blocked. It feels wrong. I try not to be envious of other magic users who blast out spells naturally, because that's not me." I huffed out a breath. "Take my friend, Odessa, as an example. She's a genius with earth magic. She grows prize-winning pumpkins and can channel the power of the earth into her scarecrows. She makes hundreds of them and never tires, and she only needs a little down time before she's ready to go again. It's almost too supernatural to be natural."

Cole grunted. "I've met some of those scarecrows while I've been hanging out in the village. Those things are lethal. Maybe your friend's magic isn't as great as you think. Does she mean to make them so aggressive?"

"They're meant to be. Though recently, Odessa's had a few problems with them. She figured it was all the dark magic creeping around the village that was having a negative effect on them. But she can still control them. And I see the joy on her face when she's making a new scarecrow."

"And you're missing that joy because you think your magic is broken?"

"What else could it be?"

"A curse? Have you crossed someone powerful who'd want to mess with you this badly?"

"This has been happening most of my life. So unless I annoyed someone when we were in school, I don't think that's likely. And no one was powerful enough to curse me at that young age. Most of us don't come into our full powers until we're older."

"Maybe it's not directly linked to anything you did. Could one of your parents have picked a fight with the wrong person, so they're messing with you for revenge? Have you got any siblings who might experience the same thing?"

"No, I'm an only child. My parents are always busy and didn't have time for more kids." My mouth twisted to the side. "They didn't have time for me. I spent a lot of time at the bakery growing up. I even had a few nannies when I was tiny and used to travel with my parents, but I don't really remember that. I much preferred being at the bakery."

"It sounds like your parents hang out with powerful people. Could something have gone wrong there? They offended someone, so you got cursed?"

"It's not impossible, but it seems unlikely. And wouldn't my parents have told me if a curse was headed my way? It wouldn't be fair to hide that and expect me to muddle through."

"You should ask them."

"It's not an easy topic to drop into the conversation. It would reveal how long I've been hiding this and what I've been doing to cover it up. Just like you, not many people would understand."

"I get why you do it, but I don't agree with it."

I lifted my chin. "It works. Sort of."

Cole raised a hand. "If your magic isn't blocked, and you're not cursed, could it be you?"

"That's what I'm telling you! I'm the problem."

"Your problem is your self-doubt. What if you really believed you could do this magic?" Cole glanced at the screen where Fawn was twirling her magic around a huge blue fluffy edible bear and his cute duck companion. "If you believe in yourself as much as Fawn did, your desserts would be just as magical."

I shook my head, frustration lodging in my throat. I'd once believed I could do baking magic, but it never went right. How many times did a witch have to screw up before she realized she was bad at something?

"You're better than you know." Cole's tone was soft, as if he realized he'd pushed too far. "And you have a good heart, even though your actions are misdirected."

"You still haven't forgiven me for the abduction attempt?"

"Almost. But if you're ever desperate for a hit of werewolf energy, you could just ask. I don't mind sharing with you. Only you, though."

My eyes widened. "You'd really do that? Your energy was incredible. I've never felt so full of life."

He smiled so wide his dimples popped. "Maybe you took to my power so well because you're part werewolf. Now that would be fun."

"I've never gone part furry, and there's no wolf on the family tree." We were still holding hands, and a warmth ran through me as I squeezed his fingers. I had an ally. Someone who offered me help and wasn't judging because of my choices.

"I'm not saying I'll always be available so you can drain me," Cole said. "I often have werewolf business that requires my full strength. But when I have down days, you can make use of me."

"I'd love that. It would be a great help."

"On one condition."

"Which is?"

"We figure out what's going on with you. I'm sure it's a magic block. You get rid of that, and your magic will be as extraordinary as you are."

"I'm extraordinary?"

Cole leaned closer. "No question about it. You're fearless, determined, beautiful, and quirky. What more could a werewolf want?" His lips brushed against mine.

The lights blinked on, and I jerked in my seat, my forehead slamming into Cole's nose.

He groaned, and his hand went to his face.

"Sorry! The lights surprised me."

Cole pinched his nose and moved it from side to side. "Nothing's broken. Do you always headbutt guys who kiss you?"

I rubbed my aching forehead. "I... We could always try..." My gaze moved to the computer screen as Fawn's words drifted toward me.

"You won't want to miss what I'm about to reveal." Fawn's gaze cut to the side before she focused on the camera. "I have information that'll blow apart this snobby, elitist baking establishment."

"Cole, listen to this." I turned up the volume.

Fawn's face was set in an expression of grim determination. "If you've watched my vlogs, you've seen how talented I am. This magic is all mine. I've had these abilities since I was a child, but because I don't come from the right family or have the money to pay for six years of education, I'm not able to work in any of the top tiered baking establishments."

"You have to train for six years?" Cole whispered.

"Only three years if you're in the top tier of baking families."

"Are you?"

"Yep. My family is number two."

"In what?"

"The magical baking dynasty." I glanced at him. "We're a big deal. Everyone wants a bite of our muffins."

His gaze shifted to my chest. "I can see why."

I nudged his attention back to the screen.

"Don't think I haven't tried to get a job and training." Fawn's tone grew harsh. "I've sent hundreds of applications, and they all come back rejected. My lack of name is all they care about. They're not interested in the recipes I send or the videos showing my achievements. They don't want new talent to shine, and they stick to the old ways because they're terrified of change."

"She's building up to something big," Cole muttered.

I nodded, my attention totally on Fawn.

"That's about to change. I have proof the baking community is rotten, deceitful, and full of lies. Everyone in it is so entrenched in their elitist beliefs. Talent and opportunity are wasted because the old ways refuse to bend." She jabbed a finger at a book on the counter. "I'm done with that. It's time to let people with talent have a chance. Soon, I'll reveal exactly what I know, who it involves, and let you make your own decision about this stuck up, damaged tradition. It's time for change, and I'll be leading it."

My heart thudded. "How many people have viewed that video?"

Cole scanned the page. "It's had over half a million views."

"Are there more videos after that date? We need to know what she was going to reveal."

He took a moment to check. "That was the last one."

"So what was the secret?"

"We'll never find out," Cole said. "Fawn never got a chance to tell her fans."

"Her killer must have watched this and stopped her before she revealed the truth."

This was an important piece of the puzzle, but I wasn't yet sure where to fit it.

Chapter 19

I was up early the next morning. Cole had sweetly limp-walked me to the bakery after the storm died down and the thunder stopped trying to shake Witch Haven apart.

I'd had trouble sleeping, partly because I was mulling over what happened to Fawn, but I couldn't stop thinking about Cole. It had been a weirdly perfect evening, despite having to re-break his leg and worrying he might chew on my arm as punishment for chaining him up. I'd had fun. Cole was great to work with, and he had a dry sense of humor that always had me laughing.

Uncle Albert walked into the kitchen. "I thought I heard you up."

"I didn't wake you last night, did I? I didn't get back until the early hours of the morning."

"No, but I waited up for you for a while. I was worried."

The door slammed open, and Earl raced through. He did zoomies around the kitchen six times before skidding to a halt, his fur puffed out and his eyes wide.

I glanced at the door. "Is something invisible chasing you?"

"He's been doing that since yesterday evening," Uncle Albert said. "I thought the storm had upset him."

"It's my new extra strong catnip." Earl did another circuit of the kitchen at record speed. "I might have had too much."

I tried to grab him as he raced past, but he was too fast. "You need to lay off the catnip. Too much is bad for you."

"It's an herb. It's natural. There's nothing bad about it." He was going so fast, smoke was coming off his paws.

"Out of the kitchen, Earl." Uncle Albert opened the door. "You'll crash into something and break it."

Earl raced out the door, and Uncle Albert closed it behind him. "I've never met a more useless familiar. He needs an intervention."

"He's got a few issues, but he tries his best. I'll talk to him about the catnip again."

Uncle Albert looked like he wanted to say more but simply nodded. "You know how to handle him. So what happened to you last night?"

"I got trapped in the library." I pointed to the pile of books I'd brought back and left on the kitchen table. "Nazan locked up early when the storm got bad, but I was still inside. Then the power went out, and a window got smashed."

"You weren't hurt, were you?"

"No, I'm fine. But I was there with someone else, and he was injured. I stayed with him until the storm eased, and then we left." I glanced around the kitchen. "You didn't get any damage to the bakery?"

"No, and I made sure everything was locked tight." He walked over to the stack of books and looked through them. "I heard from that judge, Henriette. They postponed the filming because of the power cut. She said to tell you they've moved everything back to today."

"Oh! That's good. I was worried I'd missed it all." Secretly, I'd hoped the bad weather would mean I'd get out of the whole thing. Even after I'd done my cupcake research, I felt no more confident about making anything on the show.

Uncle Albert picked up one of the books and turned to the contents page. "Henriette said to drop by the set this morning and she'll tell you the new filming arrangements."

"Are you sure you don't need me here? I could always say I'm too busy to keep being a judge. I don't want to neglect my duties."

He lifted his gaze from the book. "You're not enjoying yourself?"

"It's not that. It's just different. And the world of TV isn't as glamorous as I thought it would be. There's lots of standing around and not doing much. And after everything that happened to Fawn, it's not much fun."

Uncle Albert shook his head. "It's a tragedy, but you shouldn't let that put you off. And I can't wait to see the finished show. I hope they mention Fandango's plenty of times."

"I'll make sure they do."

There was a crash in the upstairs living room.

Uncle Albert raised an eyebrow. "You really need to do something about Earl. He's bored."

"I will. As soon as the show has left the village and everything's back to normal, I'll concentrate on my baking and Earl. I'm all for a quiet life."

"So long as it's not too quiet. You don't want your life to get dull."

"Dull sounds ideal right about now."

He picked up one of the other books and turned it over several times. "I don't believe it. This can't be real."

"What have you got?" I brewed coffee as he continued to flick through the book.

"I'd forgotten about Perry Marshall. She was an obscure high witch who lived alone and shunned society. Everyone thought she was unhinged, but they kept her included in the baking community because of her extraordinary recipes."

"Is that one of her books?" I brought over two mugs of coffee and placed one on the table for Uncle Albert.

"Yes! She disappeared over a hundred years ago. No one ever found out what happened to her. There were lots of rumors, but one day, her home was cleared out, and she destroyed all her recipes."

"Destroyed them? Are you sure it's the same baker? That book was in the library."

"There's only ever been one Perry Marshall. I'm surprised you haven't heard of her. She's legendary."

"And before my time."

"Mine, too, but once you've experienced a Perry Marshall recipe, you don't forget it. This was in our library?"

"Tucked away in the back. I'm not certain I should have taken it because it wasn't on the cookery shelf, but Nazan trusts me with books. Is it really that good?"

His eyes gleamed. "There are probably only a couple of copies of this recipe book left in existence. Her recipes were usually passed down orally. Perry despised fame and never authorized any of the books that came out with her recipes in them. She said baking was an art and shouldn't be exploited for fame and profit."

"Is that why there are so few of her books in circulation?"

He leafed carefully through the pages. "She never intended for her recipes to be public. I've heard stories about her younger years, when she was less jaded. Perry would hold enormous feasts and invite hundreds of people. She'd create incredible dishes and serve them to her salivating guests. People begged for the recipes and offered gifts, money, and a golden future if only she'd share her secrets. She wasn't interested in that. For her, it was about creating the perfect dessert. She's on my list of dinner guests."

"Dinner guests?"

"The six people I'd most like to share a meal with. Perry Marshall would be there, making the dessert." Uncle Albert grinned like a school boy on his first day of summer break. "This is extraordinary. We shouldn't keep this. It must be protected. People would do a lot to get their hands on these recipes."

"I didn't realize it was such a big deal. Cole found it hidden away on some dusty library shelf."

"Cole?"

"Oh, he's the guy I got trapped in the library with."

"Your werewolf friend?"

"That's right."

"Will you be seeing him again after spending the night together?"

"Uncle Albert! It wasn't like that. We were trapped, and he was injured. It was all innocent."

"Of course. So..."

"It's possible." I flapped a hand. "Tell me more about this book." I wasn't ready to explain my relationship with Cole, especially since I wasn't sure what was going on between us.

Uncle Albert's appraising look suggested he wouldn't forget about Cole, but his excitement about the book soon overtook him. "I tried a variation on her recipe for Tuscan Strawberry Tart. It was delicious."

"What shall we do with it? Should we give it to someone or take it back to the library? Maybe Cole found it in a restricted section. He wouldn't have known the recipes were valuable."

"Let me do some research. I know a collector who'd be interested in this. He wouldn't sell it, but he'd make sure it was looked after and the recipes given the proper care and attention." Uncle Albert tore his gaze from the page. "I recall there was talk of an exhibit for Perry's work. I'm not sure what came of it. If it ever happened, this book must be included."

"I'm sure you'll find it the perfect home."

He glanced at me. "Why were you looking for recipe books in the library? We've got dozens here."

"I was brushing up on my technique. I wanted to get things right when I bake on the show."

"It's important we keep perfecting our art." Uncle Albert hadn't touched his coffee, which was rare. He usually sucked down a huge mug before he was ready to bake. Instead, he settled in a seat and continued to look through Perry's book.

I leaned close so I could look at the recipes. Some of the ingredients sounded archaic.

"I'd love to try some of these, but somehow, it doesn't seem right," he said. "Although customers love traditional recipes, and they'd adore these. Of course, they wouldn't have Perry's unique magical taste, but I could market them as Perry Marshall inspired desserts."

"That sounds fun."

"We could create a whole new range." Uncle Albert shook his head. "I'm getting ahead of myself. This doesn't belong to me. It would be wrong to exploit your find."

"There's no harm in trying out one recipe." I grinned at him. "I can see you're desperate to get out your mixing bowl."

"Maybe just one. We should do it together. Between us, we can create something spectacular. It's been a while since we combined baking magic."

I bit my bottom lip. "I'll leave the spectacular to you."

The warmth in his eyes faded and was replaced with concern. "You used to love baking with me. It's been such a long time since we've done anything together."

"It's not been that long. We made a batch of donuts just the other week."

"I meant something challenging. A recipe that'll test our abilities. That was why you were getting these recipe books, wasn't it? You want to make sure you're at the peak of your baking ability."

I toyed with my mug. "Sure. And I don't want to let the family down."

"Luna, that would be impossible. I'm always so proud of everything you make."

"Yeah, I know." I didn't deserve his support or praise.

"We could do one of the easier recipes and work on it for an hour this morning."

I finished my coffee and stood. "You have fun. I need to go next door and see what the plans are for today." I didn't miss the flicker of sadness in his eyes nor the way my heart lurched, but I couldn't let Uncle Albert down by messing up this recipe.

"Of course. You don't want to miss out on that. Enjoy yourself." His nose was soon buried in the book, a smile returning to his face.

I left Uncle Albert to his delighted musings as I grabbed a pastry and headed to the front door. I should be as excited as he was about this recipe book, and I should have known about Perry Marshall and drooled all over the rare find, but it stirred nothing in me. I didn't care. I was a poor example of a Brimstone baker.

But I couldn't worry about recipe books. It was time to pin down the evidence on Meadow and solve Fawn's murder.

I stopped when I got outside, surprised by all the debris lying around. The storm had done a number on the village. Several windows were being boarded, and half a tree lay across the road. Tiles from roofs were scattered around in shattered pieces, and several trash cans rolled slowly from side to side.

After a quick check of the bakery roof, relieved to find it all looking intact, I headed to the set, which was buzzing with activity.

I slowed and ducked behind a set piece. Devlin was in there, and he was talking to Elwin.

Someone tapped on my shoulder, and I squeaked and spun around.

Odessa stood behind me with a grin on her face. "Who are we hiding from?"

I grabbed her and pulled her out of view. "Devlin. I could do without him being here."

"Is he pestering you again? I'm convinced he wants you as his girlfriend."

"I guarantee he doesn't." I watched him for a few more seconds. "I think I know who killed Fawn. I was planning on quizzing the camera crew and Elwin this morning, so I can prove it was Meadow Eclair who snuck out and got her."

"How exciting. You sound like a real detective. You'll be joining Storm's detective agency if you keep this up."

"It would beat baking for a living."

Odessa pursed her lips. "You're still having problems?"

"Only every day." Devlin and Elwin were still talking. "How's the farm? You didn't get any damage from the storm, did you?"

She huffed out a breath. "It's a mess. The storage barn lost half its roof, three of my scarecrows escaped, the pumpkin patch was decimated, I lost fifty percent of my baby crop, and all the fencing on the east side has gone."

I did a low whistle. "If you need a hand getting it fixed up, I can come over and help later."

She grinned at me. "Thanks. I've got my boys working on patching up the barn and securing the fencing. The bad weather freaked them out. And I spoke to Indigo and Storm last night before the power went out. They're convinced this wasn't natural weather."

"Who is screwing with Witch Haven? And why do they keep sending bad weather our way?"

"No one knows. It's being looked into, though. Did the bakery survive okay?"

"Yes, but I wasn't there. I got trapped in the library with Cole, who was almost killed when a tree crashed through the window."

Odessa gasped. "You were trapped with Cole! How thrilling. Tell me everything."

"There's nothing to tell. We got trapped. Cole got injured. Then we lost power—"

"You were in the dark with a sexy werewolf? Did you make out?"

"No! He was injured. A book stack fell on him, and he broke his leg."

"Oh, that's less romantic. Did you at least get to know him better? Is he as sexy as he is gorgeous?"

"Isn't that the same thing?"

"No! And I meant his personality, not his delicious werewolf abs."

"You've seen Cole's abs?"

Odessa sighed and fanned her face. "Only in my dirty dreams. Go on, spill. I plan on living my love life through your encounters with this furry hunk of gorgeous love."

"Is that healthy?"

"I don't care if it's healthy. It's happening."

"He's a decent guy. I like him."

She squeaked out a noise of delight. "I sense furry love in the air. You and a werewolf, I didn't think you went for the alpha possessive guy. It's not a bad thing, but you've always gone for guys who were more docile and easy to control. Like Englebert."

"Believe me, when Englebert had a few drinks, he wasn't docile. And his hands were almost impossible to control."

Her nose wrinkled. "I don't want to hear those nasty details." She nodded at Devlin. "Shall I distract him so you can tie up your loose ends and catch your killer?"

"That would be great. I don't need long. Five minutes."

Odessa adjusted her cleavage and pushed out her chest. "I've got two things to distract Devlin Goody with." She waltzed over to where Devlin and Elwin stood and tossed her hair over one shoulder.

Both men stopped talking and watched her approach. Their eyes were drawn like magnets to her chest. Odessa always knew how to work a room.

After talking to them for a couple of minutes, she caught hold of Devlin's arm and moved him away from Elwin.

I waited until they were far enough away before hurrying over to join Elwin.

He smiled when he saw me. "I'm glad you could make it today. I was beginning to think this show was hexed, and we'd never finish. Witch Haven has been a challenging place to film."

"It's not always like this. Although I have my own worries, which I hope you can clear up."

"Of course. Anything to keep a judge happy. What's your concern?"

"Meadow Eclair. What's your opinion of her?"

His eyebrows rose a fraction. "She makes excellent desserts."

"Not her baking, I'm sure that's great. Do you trust her?"

Elwin's brow wrinkled. "Will my answer influence your judging?"

"No. When I judge, I'll do it on the food alone."

He sighed. "You've found out about her connection to Henriette, haven't you?"

"You know about that?"

"It's not exactly a secret, but you can see how Meadow's involvement in the show might be misinterpreted as favoritism."

"I do. Some people might go as far as to say she doesn't deserve her place here. Was that a part of the deal? Henriette sponsors the show, and in exchange, her daughter got a place in the final?"

Elwin glanced around and stepped closer. "Not officially, but Henriette has connections in our industry, and her second marriage added significant wealth to her personal fortune. She's not someone you say no to easily. And I saw no harm in being flexible. Meadow's a capable baker. She has a solid family history and has taken the required classes to gain her qualifications. If anyone looked into her application and the process she went through to get her place in the final, they'd seen nothing untoward."

They might not, but that didn't make it right. "Henriette persuaded you that Meadow should be here over someone more talented?"

"Yes, that would appear to be the case." He pinched the bridge of his nose. "You're not going to say anything to anyone, are you? It would ruin the show, and we've worked so hard to get this far."

"I won't. And that's not the reason I'm asking. But I'd like your honest opinion of Meadow."

"Oh, well, that's good. And I appreciate your discretion." Elwin smoothed a hand over his hair and relaxed a fraction. "Certain bakers, particularly the younger ones, let all of this go to their heads and get over-inflated in the ego department."

"You're saying Meadow's high maintenance?"

"She can be. But it's a phase. I expect when you were a bright young thing, fresh in your baking abilities, you got full of yourself. I did. I thought I could rule the world. But I mellowed as I matured. Meadow will be the same. She is excellent at what she does. And if I didn't think she could make something of herself, I'd never have let her on the show."

I wasn't sure I believed that. And it made sense now why she was taking tips off me in the hope of improving her baking. She was a fraud, the same as I was. "I look forward to trying her final entry."

"I'm glad we have an understanding." Elwin gripped my elbow. "We do, don't we? This goes no further?"

"We do. I'll judge her fairly."

"Of course. I never doubted you." He broke out a false looking smile. "Have you had a good look through my recipe book yet? Is there anything in there to tempt your taste buds?"

"My uncle has been looking through it. He's excited to try the recipes."

"That's excellent. I'm pleased to have yet another satisfied customer. Now, if you'll excuse me, I need to talk to the lighting crew. We'll be starting soon." Elwin hurried off.

I headed over to Dave, who sat behind his camera.

"Hey, Luna. Back for another go on the camera?"

"Not today. I'm just here to do my baking and then get out of here. I'll be glad when this is over."

"Yeah, me too. A few days off is just what I need. And I need to go on a few long runs to burn off some of the cake I've been stuffing down."

"It's a tough life."

He chuckled. "My waistline agrees with you."

"I wanted to check a couple of things about the filming on the first day, if you've got time."

"Sure. I'm doing nothing but sitting around and waiting for the baking to begin. What do you need?"

"Do you remember when everyone took their filming breaks?"

"Not offhand, but I can check. Most of the film has already been edited, and we make a note of the cuts to make. What do you want to know?"

"I want to make sure the finalists stuck to the rules. The judges want to ensure they weren't using anything unauthorized in their baking." I was making this up on the spot, but needed a valid reason to look at the information.

"Oh, sure." He hopped off his seat. "Right this way. We keep the reels in the production van."

I hurried out behind Dave and into a large white van parked outside the set. It was crammed full of equipment, with two stools set in front of large screens.

"Take a seat. It won't take me a minute to look." Dave rifled through a folder. "Here it is. This sheet is Cade's, this is Troy, and there's Meadow."

I checked Cade's sheet first. As he said, he'd filmed the whole time and hadn't taken a break, which discounted him as Fawn's killer. Troy took one short break, almost at the end of his filming. It would have been impossible for him to leave the set, kill Fawn, and get back in time. Meadow took three breaks of twenty minutes each.

"Did you film Meadow on the earlier rounds of the baking show?"

"Sure. She's been with us since the beginning."

"Is it unusual for her to take so many breaks during filming?"

"Give me a few minutes to check the records." Dave pulled out a file and flicked through it. "Yep. It's standard Princess Meadow behavior. She's always flouncing off to do something with her hair or make-up."

"Does she always leave the set?"

"Not always. Sometimes, she stays and complains about something. Does that break the rules?" He grinned wickedly. "Are you going to chuck her off the show?"

"No, I can't disqualify Meadow for that." Twenty minutes would have given her enough time to race to the play park and kill Fawn, but it would have been cutting it fine. But she was the only suspect who could have done it.

"I'd love it if you found out she was doing something dodgy. That would bring her down a peg or two."

"You don't like Meadow?"

"She orders me around like she's the Queen of Sheba. Meadow's just a jumped up little baker with a posh baking name, same as the rest of them." His cheeks flushed. "No offence to bakers. You're nice. Nosey, but nice. Are all Brimstones this friendly?"

"Not always. And I'm not offended. You're right, though. It doesn't seem fair some people get a foot in the door because they got lucky with who their parents are."

"You're one of the good ones, though. You're down to earth. I like working with you." Dave shook his head. "Meadow thinks she should be treated like someone special. We all have our own set of skills. If Princess Meadow sat behind a camera and was told to hold a static shot, followed by a pull back and then a tracking tilt, she wouldn't have a clue."

I patted his shoulder. "Thanks, Dave. You've been a great help."

"I'm always happy to help those who feed me delicious treats."

I stepped out of the van and came face-to-face with Devlin.

Chapter 20

"Luna. I have questions for you." Devlin loomed so close, I could smell the cranberry muffin and coffee he'd had for breakfast.

I tried to sidestep him, but he matched my movements. "You can ask me later. We're about to start filming, and I need to get ready."

"No, I can't." His sharp gaze cut to Dave, who'd slunk out of the van and was hurrying away. "What were you doing in there?"

"We were just preparing for recording the final day of the baking show. If you stick around until the end, there'll be plenty of dessert to try." I made another dodging move.

Devlin blocked me. He caught hold of my elbow and led me away from the van so we were out of earshot of anyone. "Every time I ask questions about Fawn's murder, people say you've already asked them. Why do you think that is?"

"How strange. I can't imagine. Are you sure you've got your facts right?"

"Yes."

I bit my bottom lip and looked as innocent as possible. It didn't work. Devlin continued to glower at me until I sighed, admitting defeat. "I might have asked a few tiny questions. I was curious about what happened to Fawn."

"Your job isn't to be curious about a murdered assistant. That's why I'm here. You're interfering with my investigation."

"I promise I'm not. I just want to make sure the killer is found."

"What do you think I've been doing?"

I eased my elbow out of his tight grip. "I don't know. It's the first time I've seen you here in days. Which is a surprise, since the murder suspects are all on set."

His nostrils flared. "You've gone too far. By poking around and asking questions, you could have tipped off the killer. They could have run off or hidden vital evidence."

"No one has left the set and not returned. And all the suspects are still here, including the prime suspect."

His eyes narrowed. "What do you know about our prime suspect?"

I sucked in a breath. "I know who killed Fawn. At least, I'm ninety percent sure. But I need more proof."

Devlin heaved out a sigh and shook his head. "Stop! You're only making this worse for yourself."

"Or I'm making it better for you." Devlin had to see sense. I was on his side, even if I felt competitive about finding the killer before he did. "Who do you think killed Fawn?"

"I'm not sharing confidential details of a murder investigation with a civilian."

"Do you think it was Troy? After all, he burned Fawn. He hated her enough to injure her. He could have taken things further."

"How do you know about that?"

"I asked around."

"You interfered and snooped where it isn't wanted."

"Or how about Cade? Fawn broke up with him, and he didn't take it too well. He loved her. Love can turn dark when someone gets rejected. Was it a lovers' tiff gone wrong?"

Devlin crossed his arms over his chest and continued to glare at me.

"No, I also don't think it was Cade. And it couldn't have been Henriette or Elwin."

His lips pursed. "Why couldn't it have been either of them?"

"Henriette found Fawn's body. If she did it, she'd have hidden the murder until after the storm passed. And I saw Elwin on set when I took a break. Which leaves us with Meadow."

"No! No more. I'm dealing with this investigation. If you keep getting in my way, I'll sentence you to more community service."

"For helping solve a murder? That's hardly fair."

"You're obstructing a member of the Magic Council. I'm unable to do my job competently because of you."

"Are you sure it's because of me you can't do your job properly?"

"I've had enough of this." Devlin grabbed my arm and dragged me toward the bakery.

I stumbled against him. "What are you doing?"

"I've had my suspicions about you for a long time. Your magic worries me."

"You're only saying that because I've almost solved this murder and you haven't."

"I'm saying it because I've been keeping tabs on your activities at the bakery. Whenever you bring out something you've made, I buy a sample."

"You sneaky... You've been testing my food again? Don't you need a warrant for that?"

"Technically, yes, but this is an experiment of my own choosing. And I still have those complaints on file and evidence to show you've been using strange magic. Magic that doesn't belong to you. I must know where it comes from and whether it's safe to have in food items."

"That's been explained away. There's nothing harmful in my magic." It hadn't been explained, not properly. I knew this would eventually come back to haunt me.

"It has never been explained to my satisfaction. And a week ago, just before this murder happened, I had another five complaints about the food from Fandango's."

"Impossible. I barely make anything in the bakery. Uncle Albert's been in the kitchen most of the time, and everyone loves his food."

"These complaints relate to a carrot cake. Did you bake that?"

I winced. Uncle Albert had been busy one day and begged me to make a huge carrot cake since it was one of our most popular lines. I'd tried to get out of doing it but had had no option other than to roll up my sleeves and get stuck in. I figured I'd gotten away with it.

"Your silence speaks volumes."

"I'm thinking! Maybe I did make that cake. Or maybe these serial complainers bought it somewhere else and they have a grudge against Fandango's. I've also heard a rival bakery is thinking of opening in the village. I bet that's it. They're putting in false complaints to ruin our reputation."

"It's not that. You're making it up." He pointed to the bakery door. "Get inside."

"Why?"

"Because I need you to prove you're not deceiving customers."

"I'd never do that. I always have honest intentions when I make my food."

Uncle Albert pulled open the door. "Is everything okay, Luna?"

"Yes. Devlin's just being his usual difficult self," I said.

"Your niece is refusing to cooperate with my investigation."

"What are you investigating?" Uncle Albert said. "You don't think she had anything to do with this murder, do you?"

"No, but Devlin's made up complaints so he can cause trouble."

"About the bakery?" Uncle Albert gestured us inside then swiftly shut the door. "I have all my certifications. They're on display behind the counter. And we have the highest hygiene rating."

"It's not you I'm worried about. It's Luna. She's still using unstable magic and serving it to customers. If this isn't stopped, you'll have a death on your hands."

"I'd never kill anyone with my food. You're making something out of nothing." I was overheating as panic overwhelmed me. Devlin wasn't letting this go. He was determined to ruin me.

"There's a simple way to resolve this," Devlin said. "Show me a baking spell. I need to witness your ability to make sure you're not putting anything odd in your food."

"That's the perfect solution," Uncle Albert said. "And once you see how incredible Luna's baking is, you'll know she does nothing strange with her food. I rely on her. She makes delicious cakes."

"Then she can make one for me right now," Devlin said.

"I don't have the time." I backed to the door. "We're about to get to work on the baking show, and I can't miss the last day of filming."

"This is your reputation at stake. Make time," Devlin said. "All I want is a simple cake. Surely that's within your ability."

Uncle Albert nodded encouragingly. "You can do this. Let Devlin look at what you do, and then the Magic Council will be off your back once and for all."

I squeezed my hands together. I hadn't had a top up of magic for a while and had no idea how stable I was. What if I made something, and it poisoned Devlin? Or it tasted disgusting? It would be all the proof Devlin needed to shut Fandango's, and that would destroy Uncle Albert.

"Let's schedule this for another time. Perhaps one day next month." I edged away.

"We do it now, or I'll take these complaints to the next level," Devlin said. "I have enough evidence against you to bring a request to close order on the bakery."

Uncle Albert's eyes widened. "We can't afford to close. We'd lose too much business, and we're about to get a huge boost from Luna being on the baking show."

"If Luna won't display her magic ability, she leaves me with no option. This is a simple solution, yet she's reluctant to take it. That's suspicious."

Uncle Albert turned imploring eyes to me. "Just a quick cake. What's the worst that could happen?"

I couldn't let down Uncle Albert. "Of course. But it'll need to be something easy. I really should be on set."

"You choose the recipe. I'll watch each step and see how you channel your magic. If I'm satisfied nothing untoward is going on, I'll leave you alone," Devlin said.

"No more bothering me?" I said.

"I have to investigate these complaints. But once I've watched you bake, I'll inform the complainants that there's no basis for concern." Devlin adjusted his hat. "I know I sound harsh, but my top priority is people's safety. I'm a fan of Fandango's, and I don't want to close it, but I will if I find you behaving inappropriately with your magic."

I grabbed my apron and tied it around my waist, hiding my shaking hands from Devlin. If this went wrong, my secret would be revealed to Uncle

Albert, and I'd be so ashamed. I'd have to leave. I couldn't stay at Fandango's once he knew I couldn't really bake with magic.

A coil of anger wrapped around me as I glared at Devlin. I'd concealed my secret for so long, and he was ruining everything. All my careful plans were being torn apart.

"What will you make?" Uncle Albert said. "I'll get the ingredients out for you."

"No, Luna must do this on her own." Devlin sounded disgustingly smug. "I need to see every step she takes. Albert, this doesn't concern you. I suggest you leave."

"I'm not leaving my niece alone. And this is my kitchen, so I'm staying."

"Then stay out of the way," Devlin said. "You're not to help."

Uncle Albert grumbled under his breath as he settled in a seat as far away from Devlin as possible.

I set out my tools. A favorite mixing bowl, a wooden spoon, my weighing scales, and measuring cups. I went to the pantry where we stored a huge array of baking ingredients and carried out everything I needed.

"Is it important you weigh everything? Shouldn't your magic detect the right amount of each ingredient?" Devlin's gaze ran over everything I'd set on the counter.

"You can, but I like to be doubly sure. After all, I don't want to poison the customers."

"Luna is always thorough when she bakes," Uncle Albert said. "She knows what she's doing."

"I'll be the judge of that," Devlin said.

I took my time measuring everything, mixing it together and making sure the batter was the perfect consistency. Once I was certain I had a winner, I greased the cake tin and slid the batter into it. So far, so good.

"It'll take twenty-five minutes to bake." I turned to Devlin once the cake was in the oven. "You could always wait outside if you need fresh air. You'll be bored waiting here."

"I intend to watch that cake." Devlin pointed at the oven. "And I've yet to see you use any magic on it. Why is that?"

"It's not so unusual. We use our magic at different stages of the baking process," Uncle Albert said. "It's up to the individual baker when they put it in. I infuse mine during the process. Luna puts it in at the end."

"Perhaps that's the problem," Devlin said.

"I don't have a problem," I muttered. "We all do things differently. That's what makes our food unique."

Devlin got to his feet and folded his arms over his chest. "You can wait with me if you like, but I'm going nowhere. I plan to get to the bottom of my suspicions about your magic."

Uncle Albert's expression was full of worry as he gestured me out of the kitchen.

I jabbed a finger at Devlin. "Touch nothing."

"I'm only here for your cake."

I hurried after Uncle Albert and closed the door so Devlin couldn't hear us. "I'm sorry this is happening. Devlin hates me, but it's not fair he's dragged the bakery into his vendetta."

"You're doing well. Don't let him intimidate you."

"It's hard not to. The guy is holding the future of the bakery in his hands and enjoying trying to destroy it."

Uncle Albert pressed his lips together. "I hate to say this, but he is doing his job."

"You can't be on the side of the Magic Council. I've done nothing wrong."

"I'm not. And if Devlin keeps bothering you, you can make an official complaint. But your cake will prove your baking is perfect."

I ducked my head. "I'll do my best."

"That's all I ever ask of you." He hugged me hard, and I leaned against him. "I'll go set up the counter, and you keep an eye on Devlin. Or would you like me to deal with him?"

"No, this is my mess. I'll make sure Devlin doesn't get up to trouble in our kitchen." I grabbed a strong coffee from behind the counter. I was tempted not to get one for Devlin, but it caused me physical pain not to be hospitable. I made him a weak coffee with lots of milk, since that was his regular order.

I headed back to the kitchen and thumped the mug down in front of him.

He stared into it. "What's in this?"

"It's coffee."

He sniffed it then took a tentative sip. "This is good. Just how I like it."

"You've been to Fandango's plenty of times. I always remember customers' orders." I drank my own coffee.

We spent the next fifteen minutes in a tense silence as we stared at the oven as my cake slowly rose.

The oven timer pinged, and I put on oven mitts and took out the cake. The top looked golden. It was the perfect sponge.

I set it on the table in front of Devlin. "Satisfied?"

"Not yet. You need to insert your magic. That's the reason I'm here. Anyone can make an average looking cake."

"I'd like to see you try."

Uncle Albert bustled in. "I heard that. And Luna's cakes are never average."

I'd hoped Uncle Albert would have gotten busy behind the counter, but of course, he'd have sensed the cake was ready and wouldn't want to miss me proving Devlin wrong.

I removed my oven mitts. "We should let it cool first."

"That'll take too long. Use your magic on it now," Devlin said.

Uncle Albert nodded at me.

My palms were sweaty. I clenched and unclenched my fingers several times, staring at the cake and willing my magic to behave.

"I'm waiting," Devlin said. "I'm asking to see one basic spell."

"Don't hurry Luna," Uncle Albert said. "Baking is an art. It can't be rushed."

"It's a simple sponge cake."

I held my hands over the cake, closed my eyes, and let the magic flow into it. It didn't want to come and felt stuck on my fingertips, making them itch and burn.

My shoulders hurt as I rolled them, trying to get the tension loose. I tried again, this time keeping my eyes open. The magic shot out and bounced into the cake in a jagged wave, threatening to carve the sponge in half. But it worked. The spell was in the cake, and it was holding.

I let out a quiet sigh and lowered my hands. "Are you happy now, Devlin?"

"You seemed to struggle. Did you find that spell difficult?" His gaze was latched on the cake.

"I don't do well under pressure. I got nervous."

He lifted his chin, a sour expression crossing his face. "I'd better do a taste test."

"It'll be too hot to eat."

"Cut me a small piece and leave it on a plate to cool. Why are you making this so difficult?"

I grabbed a plate and a sharp knife, gripping it tight as I marched back to the table and thumped down the plate.

Devlin's eyes widened a fraction, but he wisely said nothing as I lifted the knife over the cake. I stuck it into the middle of the sponge and paused. The cake had just wobbled.

"Is there a problem?" he said.

"Nope. No problem, just give me a—" The cake exploded.

I yelped and staggered back as hot cake batter splattered everywhere. Uncle Albert ducked, but even he got sprayed with flying cake. Devlin hadn't moved, and his face was covered in gooey cake mix.

A blob of cake dripped off the end of my hair. "Would you believe me if I told you it was supposed to do that?"

He swiped a hand down his cake splattered face. "Was that your idea of a joke? Do you think what the Magic Council does isn't important?"

"No! I don't think this is funny. But I was nervous. I lost focus when I channeled my magic into the cake."

Uncle Albert's face was set in a mask of horror as he looked around the kitchen. "It's the weird weather magic. It must be."

Devlin whipped his head around. "Explain yourself."

Uncle Albert caught my eye for a second before focusing on Devlin. "I've also found things challenging, recently. I'm sure it's the odd weather magic in the village. It's affecting our powers."

"I've not heard about this. You're making excuses for Luna." Devlin pulled off his hat and scraped off cake. "You're behaving like you want this place shut. Every time I come here, you block me."

"We don't. We can explain this." Uncle Albert gestured to me. "Luna has been under pressure. The murder, the baking show, and add in the strange weather magic. Anyone could make a mistake."

Devlin shook his head. "There's something wrong with you, Luna. And I intend to find out what it is."

"I'll try again. I'll make you another cake. And I'll get it right this time." My voice wobbled. How had I gotten this so wrong? It was a simple sponge cake.

"It's too late. This is an assault on a member of the Magic Council, and I won't stand for it." Devlin thumped his gooey hat back on his head and then turned and stomped out of the kitchen. The front door slammed a few seconds later.

I gulped in a breath before grabbing a cloth and wiping cake off the table and into the tin.

Uncle Albert caught hold of my hand. "Leave that. Come sit with me. I want to talk to you."

"I should clean this before it sets. Cold cake batter is like cement." I was too ashamed to look him in the eye.

"Luna... I know."

I placed the cloth down and glanced at him. "What do you know?"

He steered me to a seat, then sat next to me, keeping a tight grip on my hand. "I know you struggle with your baking magic."

"I don't. This was a mistake. You could be onto something with the weather magic. It's messing with my power, just like you said."

There was a kind expression in his eyes as he shook his head. "I only said that to get rid of Devlin. And I've been around you all your life. I was there when you made your first batch of rock cakes. Those things were so hard, I almost chipped a tooth."

"I was a kid. We all start from zero and learn how to do things."

"That's just it, you shouldn't. Baking magic is as simple as breathing in and out. It's automatic."

I gulped and looked at my cake splattered clothing. "Not everyone gets their full powers in one hit."

"No one in your family came to their powers late." He was quiet for a few seconds. "Tell me what's going on. I want to help."

"It's stress. Fawn's murder, the baking challenge, and the Magic Council after me. I don't handle stress well. Maybe I need a vacation."

"You haven't always been stressed, though. And you've struggled to control your baking magic for a long time."

Shame tinted my ears pink, and tears filled my eyes. I'd always thought I'd done a great job of hiding my failings from this wonderful man.

"I've never said anything because we've always managed." Uncle Albert sighed. "But Devlin has it in for you, and now he's witnessed this, he'll pursue you even harder. I'm not sure I can hold him off."

"You don't need to. Once Devlin's calmed down and cleaned himself up, I'm sure he'll realize this was an accident."

"It might take more than that. He knows something is wrong."

"I'd suggest baking him a I'm sorry-for-exploding-a-cake-in-your-face-cake, but I doubt he'd accept it." I risked a look at Uncle Albert and almost cried. "I'm so sorry."

"No apology is needed." He squeezed my hand. "You'll always have a place here. You do know that, right?"

"Until you get bored with me hogging the single bathroom?" I tried to blink away the tears, but more took their place. I didn't deserve such acceptance.

"Luna, I want to be clear on this. You're my niece, and I love having you here. We're family, no matter if your magic doesn't work quite right. It's you I love, not your spells."

I struggled to swallow past the lump in my throat. If Uncle Albert knew how terrible my magic was, he wouldn't say that. And I could never reveal my failings to my parents. They'd be humiliated to have a daughter who couldn't even bake a basic cake. I was a Brimstone baker. How could I be such a tragic mess?

"Luna, talk to me. Please don't shut me out."

"I need inspiration," I blurted out. "That's what I struggle with. Something different from the usual recipes. I still haven't found my niche. Once I've found it, everything will be fine." I grabbed the cake splattered recipe books I'd borrowed from the library and set them in front of me. "These are the solution."

Uncle Albert's forehead furrowed. "Do you really think it's that? You need an area of expertise to excel in?"

"I'm certain of it. Maybe desserts aren't my forte. I could look into doing something savory."

"The Brimstones are one of the best baking dynasties in the world. Don't you have a passion for desserts?"

"I don't mind eating them." I kept my attention on the books.

He patted my shoulder. "I'm here for you whenever you're ready. There's no pressure. I just want you to be happy."

"I am. I'm happy here with you. I'm happy in the bakery." I forced a smile. "How about we forget this exploding cake episode?" I grabbed the Perry Marshall recipe book, which only had a small amount of batter on it, and flipped it open.

Uncle Albert was quiet for a moment. He stood slowly. "I'll make us breakfast. Is there anything special you'd like?"

"Chocolate chip pancakes?" I always wanted them when I was under the weather. And, right now, I felt like retreating to my bed and never getting out again.

"Then you shall have them. I'll be back in a few minutes."

My eyes closed, and I tipped back in my seat the second he left the kitchen. I'd been an idiot to think I could hide my problem from Uncle Albert. Of course, he'd noticed my baking mess-ups over the years but had been too kind to say anything.

I hurried around and cleaned up the kitchen and then returned to my seat. The smell of sugar and melting chocolate filled the air, and my stomach grumbled. Uncle Albert's pancakes made everything better.

The Perry Marshall book was still open, so I flipped through it. I turned the page and discovered the bottom right corner was ripped off. It was a recipe for lemon meringue cupcakes. I ran my finger down the list of ingredients and discovered one had been struck through with thick black pen.

Perhaps someone tried the recipe and didn't like that ingredient.

This recipe looked familiar. I grabbed the copy of Elwin's new recipe book and opened it then set the books side-by-side. I flicked through, my finger stopping on the lemon meringue cupcake recipe. The same recipe in both books. That wasn't so unusual. Bakers always borrowed from each other.

I read through the ingredients and instructions. They were identical, apart from the one missing ingredient. It was the ingredient Elwin was holding the challenge for on the baking show.

My stomach jolted, and I sucked in a deep breath. I checked the page numbers and nodded. I'd just discovered who'd killed Fawn and why.

Chapter 21

I gulped down my chocolate pancakes so quickly I gave myself indigestion. Once I'd finished eating, I grabbed the recipe books and jumped up.

"Luna!" Uncle Albert said. "What's the hurry? There are more pancakes."

I kissed his cheek. "Thanks for breakfast. I need to get to the set." I dashed out and hurried next door.

Devlin was there when I arrived. Olympus was also with him. The discussion looked heated as Devlin waved his arms around and pointed at cake batter on his clothes.

It looked like Olympus was trying hard not to smile.

Even though Devlin was one of my least favorite people, I was glad he was here. He needed to hear what I was about to say. I'd been wrong all this time. Meadow hadn't killed Fawn, but I knew who had. It all came down to cakes and greed.

I clutched the recipe books against my chest as Elwin walked over.

His gaze ran over me. "Luna, is everything okay?"

"No, not really."

"You look flustered. Are you unwell?"

"I'm fine."

"Have you had a mishap in the kitchen? That looks like cake batter in your hair."

I lifted my hand and discovered several gooey lumps stuck to me. "It is."

"You have time to clean up before we get started." Elwin looked at the recipe books. "Or is there something else you need?"

"Is it time for the judging?" I wanted everyone gathered together so they could hear what I was about to reveal.

"Not yet, but we were about to do a recording of the cakes the finalists made and get the judges' initial reactions. Did you get a chance to make your entry?"

"No. I won't be entering anything."

"That's a shame. Still, you can judge everyone else. And I'm sure you'll do a fine job. We're starting in just a minute. I'll round everyone up." Elwin's expression was puzzled as he looked me over, then he walked away.

My nerves jangled as I waited to reveal my discovery. Cade, Troy, and Meadow stood by their workstations, covered trays of cupcakes in front of them. Henriette was speaking to Devlin and Olympus, and the crew were setting up to film.

It was crucial I get this right. Fawn deserved justice.

Elwin clapped his hands. "Now we're all here, we'll get shots of the finalists with their cupcakes and a first reveal of the judges' reactions. It's always fun to see their faces when they view the entries for the first time." He beckoned me and Henriette to join him.

I stepped forward and placed the recipe books down. "Before we do that, I have something to say."

Elwin gestured to me. "We let all the judges have an opportunity to talk about their experience and how much they've enjoyed being a part of the show. Now's not the right time, though. Cake reveals first."

"It's not that. I need to talk about Fawn." I shifted my weight from foot to foot as all eyes focused on me. "I've been weighing up motives for who'd want to kill her, sampling everyone's alibis, and... prodding opportunities."

Devlin marched over with Olympus beside him. "What are you doing, Luna? You've been told to stay out of this investigation."

"I chose to ignore you. And I know who murdered Fawn and why."

Devlin opened his mouth, but Olympus stepped forward. "Do you have new evidence?"

I nodded, grateful for his intervention. "The killer is on this set." I looked around the group. "One of you murdered Fawn."

"This is outrageous," Devlin said.

"If Luna has information to share, she has a right to tell us," Olympus said. "Go ahead. What have you discovered?"

"Thanks, Olympus." I took a few seconds to collect my thoughts. Dave slid onto his camera seat and discreetly started recording. "I didn't know Fawn well, but she was kind to me."

Troy snorted and shook his head.

"I understand she wasn't always good to everyone else, but she had a right to be frustrated. Fawn had a natural talent for baking. I've seen her baking, and she created things that were out of this world incredible."

"Fawn probably stole the recipes from someone else," Troy said.

"She didn't. And her social media following was growing. She has hours of videos online for anyone to view. It was all her own work." I checked everyone's reactions, but no one flinched. "In her final video, Fawn promised a big reveal. One that would blow apart the baking community. I believe the knowledge she had was the reason she was murdered."

"You should have shared this with me," Devlin muttered.

"I've only just put the pieces together," I said to him. "I've spoken to everyone here who had a connection with Fawn, and nearly all of you had a reason to want her dead." I looked around the group again. Troy no longer had a smug expression on his face, Meadow seemed angry, and Cade looked defeated.

"It wasn't any of us," Meadow said. "We were all being filmed when she died."

"That's what I thought at first. But I got chatting to Dave. Hi, Dave." I waved at him. "And he told me you could all take breaks whenever you liked. And Meadow, you took several breaks. Long breaks that gave you enough time to leave the set, kill Fawn, and return without raising suspicion."

"No! It wasn't her." Henriette hurried over and placed an arm around Meadow's shoulders.

"You're right. It wasn't. But I was suspicious of Meadow for a long time, especially when I learned of your relationship. Meadow got here because you're sponsoring the show, Henriette. I thought for a long time that Fawn had discovered this and was planning to reveal it to the viewers. They wouldn't have been happy to learn this."

"That's not true," Henriette stuttered. "Meadow has talent."

Meadow scowled at me. "Fawn hated that I was here and she wasn't. She made it clear how much she resented me. She either ignored me or was rude to my face. I'm glad she's gone."

"That's not kind," Henriette whispered to her daughter.

I turned my focus to Henriette. "I also ruled you out. You found Fawn's body. The killer staged the murder scene to look like a tornado had hit, and Fawn got in its way. But thanks to the skills of our residents, that problem was diverted. If it had been you, you wouldn't have told me about Fawn."

Henriette nodded. "Of course it wasn't me. And although Fawn could be sharp, I never wanted that to happen to her."

I turned to Cade. "You loved Fawn, but she wasn't interested in you. She dumped you to focus on her career."

He nodded. "Sure. Everyone knows that."

"It's so humiliating," Troy said. "Ditched by a wannabe baker who'd have never amounted to anything."

"Keep your mouth shut," Cade muttered. "She was a much better baker than you'll ever be."

"Is that how you got her into bed? You pretended she knew what she was doing in the kitchen?"

Cade scowled at him and shook his head. "Fawn was incredible."

"I ruled Cade out as a suspect because he was on the set the whole time." My gaze shot to Troy. "Unlike you. You took a break during filming on the day of the murder."

His eyes widened. "You think I did it?"

"You've openly admitted you disliked Fawn, and you burned her arm."

"I don't know what you're talking about." He stuffed his hands in his pockets.

"You threw a mug of scalding coffee over her arm because she got your order wrong."

"Don't deny it. I know what you did," Cade said. "You were jealous of her."

"There was nothing to be jealous of." Troy kept his gaze down. "And that was an accident. Fawn got in the way, and the coffee got knocked over."

"You lost your temper and deliberately hurt Fawn. Maybe it happened again when you found her in the play park," I said.

"I didn't do it." Troy's panicked gaze shot around the group. "I only took one short break. I couldn't have done it."

I sighed. I sort of wished it had been Troy. "You didn't. Which leaves us with only one person." I looked at Elwin.

"Me?" He gave a high-pitched chuckle. "I'd never hurt Fawn. She was an incredible talent."

I tapped the two books I'd brought with me. "You saw her talent and knew about her lack of opportunity. Fawn had no family reputation or qualifications, and she desperately wanted to make it in the baking community. Did you discover her videos online or simply see her baking one day and realize her untapped potential?"

"I recognized Fawn's ability and encouraged her. I even worked with her on some recipes."

"Fawn was vulnerable after her dad died, and you took advantage. You pretended to look out for her, but the whole time, you were exploiting her."

"This is ridiculous." Elwin looked at Devlin. "Are you going to put an end to this? You can't let this young woman dictate what goes on here."

"Luna, why do you think Elwin killed Fawn?" Olympus said.

"I only just realized his motive," I said. "The recipes in his new book are unusual. I've never seen anything like them. That was until I discovered an old Perry Marshall recipe book hidden in our library."

Elwin laughed. "Now I know you're making this up. There are no Perry Marshall recipe books in circulation. They were all destroyed."

"Not all of them," I said.

"What has this got to do with Fawn's murder?" Devlin's sharp tone suggested I was almost out of time, and even Olympus was looking at me with concern.

"I'd have never linked the two together, but Fawn left behind a clue. In her pocket, she had a piece of paper with a number and a recipe ingredient."

Devlin spluttered several odd noises, his face turning bright red. Olympus caught hold of his arm and shook his head.

"The number on the paper was the same number torn out of the recipe book in the library." I flipped open Perry Marshall's book and found the page. "There's also an ingredient scrubbed out in this recipe. It just happens to be the same recipe Elwin set everyone the challenge of completing."

"You're wrong. Bakers come up with new recipes all the time. Sometimes, they're similar." Elwin shook his head. "We're wasting time."

I turned to the page in his book containing the cupcake challenge recipe. "The ingredients are identical, apart from that one missing ingredient you want everyone to find."

"This is meaningless! And every baker knows you can't copyright recipes." Elwin's gaze was fixed on the old recipe book, and he licked his lips. "Perhaps I took a pinch of inspiration from the classics. Let me see that book."

I picked up the recipe book and held it against my chest. "This is proof. And I haven't checked with the library yet, but I'm sure Nazan will confirm Fawn's visit. He mentioned someone coming in with a book and leaving without it. Fawn concealed this in the library to make sure you couldn't find it."

"This is one elaborate fantasy too far," Elwin said. "Fawn was a friend."

I looked at Devlin. "Elwin planned on passing off these recipes as his. There's no mention or credit to Perry Marshall in his new book."

A thin smile crossed Elwin's face. "This is a misunderstanding. And as I said, there are no Perry Marshall cookbooks in existence." His gaze darted to the book I held.

"There are. And you've seen one. That's where you copied all your recipes from. You're a fraud."

"Bakers are always sharing ideas, and ingredients are available for everyone to use. There are literally hundreds of thousands of copies of recipes all over the world in different cookbooks. I've done nothing wrong." Elwin hadn't stopped staring at the book.

Devlin stepped forward. "Elwin is right. You can't copyright recipes."

My mouth dropped open. Devlin was sticking up for the killer?

He glanced at me. "But you can be in breach of copyright if you use the same photos, descriptions, and language. Elwin, did you copy these recipes from this old cookbook Luna found?"

"Of course not." Elwin gulped, and his hand shook as he swiped it through his silver hair.

"If these are your recipes, you must know what the missing ingredient is in the cupcake recipe," I said. "Tell us what it is."

"No! And ruin the surprise?"

"We're done with surprises. If this is your recipe, you'll know what's missing." I arched an eyebrow. "Or maybe Fawn figured out what you were doing and scrubbed out the ingredient so your deceit would be uncovered."

"You have no authority here." Elwin looked at Devlin and Olympus, desperation in his eyes. "Why are you letting this witch do your job?"

"It's a good question," Devlin muttered. "But we can clear this up. Show me the recipe Luna is referring to, and we can compare them."

Elwin's cheeks flushed. "We have a show to complete. Millions of people are expecting us to broadcast."

Henriette touched his arm. "We don't want rumors getting out that you copied a Perry Marshall recipe book. I have too much invested for there to be a scandal."

"There won't be a scandal," he growled through his teeth.

"We can move on as soon as you reveal the missing ingredient," Olympus said.

"It's this recipe." I flipped open Elwin's book and pointed at the lemon meringue cupcakes.

Devlin peered at it. "There is an ingredient missing." He looked up at Elwin. "What is it?"

"If I tell you, this whole show will have to be scrapped."

"We're not filming." I glanced at Dave, who was most definitely filming. He gave me a discreet thumbs-up. "This is between us. The audience won't know a thing about this. They'll still get a surprise."

Elwin's face turned several shades of red before he swung toward the baking finalists. "Reveal the ingredients you used. I'll tell you if you're right."

"Err... I used allspice berries," Troy said after a glance at Devlin.

Elwin's gaze flicked to me, but I was giving nothing away. He was scrambling for an answer. "What about you, Meadow?"

"I used ground hibiscus blossom. Is that right? Did I win?"

Elwin ignored her. "And you, Cade?"

Cade glanced at me, worry in his eyes. "I used a combination of ground agave and a pinch of jamberry clove."

"They could all work." Elwin seemed to be talking more to himself than us.

"But they're all wrong," I said.

He whirled around. "Don't ruin the surprise!"

"Would you like to know what the missing ingredient is? Fawn died with the secret in her pocket."

Elwin scowled at me, his body trembling. "Why would she hide this from me? I was supporting her."

"What you actually did was take advantage of her. You knew her difficult situation and pretended to be her mentor. Did Fawn show you the Perry Marshall book, or did she discover you had a copy and took it?"

Elwin lunged for the recipe book.

I leaped back just as Devlin and Olympus swooped in and restrained him.

He fought to get free, but they had him in a fierce grip. "I must know what that ingredient is. Tell me!"

"So you can make a fortune out of your lies?" I said.

Elwin gasped in a breath. "Why would Fawn be so cruel?"

"To stop you from deceiving people."

He sagged in Olympus and Devlin's hold. "Please, I need to know the answer. It's been haunting me."

Elwin was obsessed, and that obsession had tipped him over the edge. I almost felt sorry for him. "It was Galangal Star."

He groaned. "I'd never have guessed."

"Are you confessing you killed Fawn to protect this secret?" Devlin said.

Elwin's head jerked up. "No! I'm not confessing."

"We'll take it from here, Luna," Devlin said. "Hand over the recipe book."

I glanced at Olympus, and he gave me a swift nod. I handed over the book, and they led Elwin away.

There was silence, then everyone started talking.

I backed away, the stress hitting me as I leaned against the workstation. I'd done it. Not only had I figured out who killed Fawn, but I didn't have to make cupcakes for this wretched show.

After this experience, I'd be finding a new favorite baking show to watch.

Chapter 22

I ambled down the stairs into the bakery. I smiled at the bright, calm morning that greeted me.

I'd just pulled the blinds when Indigo, Odessa, and Storm walked up. Indigo had Nugget, her cat familiar, draped over one shoulder, and Fire Fang strode alongside Storm, his eyes glowing red.

Earl bashed into my calf as he zoomed by. "Can't stop!"

"You're still using that caffeine blend of catnip?"

"I found a spare packet, and I can't throw it away," he gasped out as he bounded around the floor. "It would be a waste. That stuff is expensive. I sold my collection of fluffy mice to get it."

"You shouldn't sell your things. I've got a regular delivery set up for you. Isn't that enough?"

"It doesn't last as long as it used to. I reckon it's being cut with something cheap." He leaped up the wall and scrambled along the top of the cabinets.

"Don't be manic when everyone's here. They'll think something's wrong with you." I unlocked the door and welcomed everyone inside. We exchanged hugs and fist bumps, and I risked a tickle of Fire Fang's chin, which he accepted with only one fierce growl.

I petted Nugget, who struggled off Indigo's shoulder and mooched away with Fire Fang beside him.

"Any news from the Magic Council?" I asked Indigo as I brought over coffees and pastries for everyone at the table.

"Elwin's confessed. He held out for a while and kept arguing that he had every right to use the recipes. But that Perry Marshall book has messed with his head. He was desperate to get his hands on it. I reckon it's got some serious magic attached to it. He kept asking to see it like it was his firstborn child."

"Perry was supposed to be a genius with her baking." I set out the food and drink, and everyone dove in. "Maybe her magic came with a hint of food addiction."

"That's why I never eat cheese." Storm inspected her cherry scone.

"You do!" Odessa said. "You had mac and cheese at my place last month."

"That wasn't real cheese. At least, it didn't taste like it."

"It was goats' cheese. I was experimenting."

"Why don't you eat cheese?" Indigo said.

"It's as addictive as hard drugs. One bite of cheddar and before you know it, you're snorting cheese strings through your eyeballs. It sounds like Perry's cakes were just as bad. Or good. I don't know. They sound dangerous."

"Uncle Albert said people were obsessed with her. Perry ended up hiding because of all the attention." I shrugged and ate a bite of almond croissant.

"The Magic Council had an expert look at the Perry Marshall recipe book, and Elwin's new book is identical. He updated the pictures but didn't change any of the recipes or cooking methods."

"He wouldn't dare," I said. "According to Uncle Albert, everyone tried to replicate what she made. He'd have had to keep the ingredients and measurements exactly the same to have any hope of being half as good as her."

"Devlin also checked with Nazan, and he confirmed seeing Fawn in the library not long before she was murdered." Indigo selected a pastry.

I nodded. "I knew that was her. I thought nothing of it when he told me about her visit, but it makes sense."

"Fawn asked where the cookery section was and was in and out in five minutes," Indigo said.

"She knew the library would be a safe place. It's easy to hide a single book among thousands."

"And Devlin checked with the rest of the crew. Several of them reported seeing Elwin go in and out of the set on the day of the murder."

"And I didn't notice what he was up to. I also believed him when he said he was looking out for Fawn." I shook my head. "All Elwin wanted was her silence so he could get rich and even more famous."

"Do you think Fawn planned to tell Henriette about the stolen recipes?" Odessa said. "Was she looking for an ally?"

"I'm not sure she was. I didn't know Fawn well, but she was determined to succeed in this industry. I reckon she planned on confronting Henriette with the truth. She might have forced her to get rid of Elwin or maybe even insisted she be on the show. Fawn was ambitious. She took a big risk to get her shot at the big time, but it didn't pay off."

"Elwin is bitter about being caught," Indigo said. "He was so close to getting a ton of money and fame, and it's been taken away."

"Thanks to Fawn. And it's no less than he deserves. Did he say where the recipe book came from?" I asked.

"Fawn showed it to him but got suspicious when he started working on a new cookbook and the recipes were identical."

"So he had to kill her, or his career would have been over."

Odessa shook her head. "It's such a tragedy. Do you think this will change anything in the baking community? Word will get out about what Elwin did."

"I doubt it. There's such snobbery in the baking business. Even someone getting killed trying to change things won't do anything. You're born into this world, or you'll always be on the outside, no matter how talented you are," I said.

Earl, Nugget, and Fire Fang crashed through the door that led to the kitchen. Nugget had half a kipper hanging out of his mouth, Fire Fang had his nose smeared with buttercream, and Earl was covered in flour.

I hid my face in my hands for a second. "I'm really sorry. I think Earl has introduced the other furballs to the joys of caffeine enhanced catnip."

Our familiars raced around the bakery so fast their movements were a blur.

"Who'd have thought catnip would affect a hybrid hellhound." Storm grinned and shook her head.

"Uncle Albert said I needed to stage an intervention with Earl. All he cares about is his catnip."

A table got knocked across the bakery as our familiars continued their catnip induced mania.

"Talking of an intervention." Indigo glanced at Odessa and Storm. "Did I hear right that you exploded a cake all over Devlin?"

"Devlin told you that?" I busied myself with smearing strawberry preserves all over my croissant.

"He was complaining to Olympus when he didn't think I could hear. Devlin's convinced there's something wrong with your magic."

"He's just got it in for me."

"Maybe. But I doubt you've seen the last of him," Indigo said. "He's convinced you have a problem."

"Is your magic still being weird?" Odessa said. "We can always help."

I chewed on the huge piece of croissant I'd stuffed in my mouth. "Help how?"

"Well, I'm not sure, exactly. We need to figure out why your magic isn't working right and get it sorted. I have a craving for a glittery unicorn cake, and I want you to make it."

I huffed out a breath. "Cole thinks I'm hexed. Maybe he's right."

"Since when does that werewolf get an opinion on your magic?" Storm said.

"They're dating," Odessa said. "They've spent the night together."

Indigo dropped her scone. "Really?"

"Not like that! We got trapped in the library, and Cole was injured, so we couldn't leave. We had to stay until the storm died down. There was nothing romantic about him having a broken leg."

"Did you help him with his bandages?" Odessa cackled a wicked laugh.

"I had to."

"And..."

"And nothing."

"You peeked at his leg. You must have seen his muscles."

I looked away. "Cole has an acceptable body."

Storm snorted a laugh. "Sure he does. I've never met a tubby werewolf."

"He seems delicious, dangerous, and yummy," Odessa said.

Storm's laughter faded. "Be careful around him."

"No! Throw caution to the wind. It'll be good for Luna to have fun," Odessa said. "But why does Cole think you're hexed?"

"Because like you said, my magic can occasionally be weird. My cakes blow up when they're not supposed to, they taste strange, and I never know what I'm going to pull out of the oven."

"You enjoy baking, though?" Indigo said. "This is what you want to do for the rest of your life, isn't it?"

I looked over as the door opened and Uncle Albert came through. He greeted us all before getting to work on filling the counter with breakfast treats. "It has to be. My family is here. What else am I supposed to do?"

"That wasn't the answer I was hoping for," Indigo said. "Do you love using your baking magic? When you wake up, do you get a smile on your face because you know you're spending the day delighting customers and making treats?"

"Or do you cross your fingers and hope you won't poison anyone or blow up a cake?" Storm said.

I licked preserves off my fingers. "Probably the last option. I wouldn't mind doing this if I knew everything would turn out fine, but my spells shouldn't be explosive. I've never seen that happen to other natural bakers."

"Maybe you're not a natural baker," Storm said. "Your talents lie elsewhere."

"I have to be. I work here with Uncle Albert, and I can't go off and try something else. He relies on me. And I have the family reputation to consider."

"Your uncle only cares about making you happy," Odessa said.

"And you don't seem happy," Indigo said. "Your magic isn't happy being forced into desserts."

I ate more croissant. It wasn't happy magic I often cast, and I also wasn't full of joy. I stayed because I had to. Uncle Albert wasn't getting any younger, and he was talking more often about passing the business to me. It was the last thing I wanted.

Storm's gaze shifted to the door. "We've got company."

I turned and smiled as I saw Cole outside. He raised a hand. "I'll be back in a second." I hurried over and opened the door.

"Hey." His easy smile had my heart flipping. "I heard you solved Fawn's murder."

"Yep. We have caught the bad guy."

"Congratulations. If you're free, I'd love to hear about it." Cole glanced over my shoulder. "I thought we could spend the day together, if you're not too busy."

"I'd love that, but I need to work. I've left my uncle on his own for too long."

Uncle Albert, who'd obviously been listening in, walked over. "I can spare you for the day." He held out his hand. "You must be Cole."

Cole shook his hand. "That's right, sir. I was hoping to take your niece on a date. With your permission."

Uncle Albert nodded. "If Luna wants to date you, I have no problem with that. Of course, I expect you to be respectful and not take advantage."

"Uncle!"

"Absolutely, sir. Luna only deserves the best."

My cheeks flushed. "Can we stop with the eighteenth-century chivalry?" I turned to Uncle Albert. "I wouldn't mind a day off but only if you're okay with that."

"You go. I can manage here. And since the date of the baking show release has been put back two weeks, we won't get any crazy rushes. I intend to spend the day trying out a new recipe for a Battenberg cake and chatting with the customers about everything you've been up to. They'll want to hear how my amazing niece caught a killer."

"Thanks. It looks like I'm free," I said to Cole.

"I thought we could head to Troll Mountain. We could grab some food and take a long walk. The views are great up there." He glanced at the sky. "And the weather is holding, so we don't need to worry about any storms trapping us."

"You never know around here. Make sure you pack wet weather gear," Uncle Albert said.

"I'm not dressed for hiking, but give me ten minutes to change." I glanced at the table where Indigo, Odessa, and Storm were watching our every move. "Come in and meet my friends. I expect they have a few questions for you."

Cole grinned. "No doubt. And I'm happy to answer them."

I introduced him to my friends then dashed upstairs to get ready. I changed into suitable clothes for hiking but made sure my hair looked nice and my make-up was discreet but enhanced my eyes.

When I dashed back down the stairs, Cole was sitting on a chair, and my friends surrounded him. There was some intense grilling going on, but he was relaxed and taking it in his stride.

"Just remember what I said." Storm glowered at Cole as I stopped by the table.

He tapped the side of his head as he stood. "I could never forget that. Enjoy your day, ladies."

I said goodbye to everyone then headed out the door with Cole. "I have to ask, what did Storm tell you not to forget?"

"She said she'd rip my arms off and beat me around the head with them if I disrespected you. I like her. I liked them all. It's good you have friends watching your back. It's important you have a pack to protect you."

I looked through the window and waved at them. "They're the best friends a woman could want." Things finally felt like they were back to normal. Elwin had been arrested for Fawn's murder, the filming was over, and life at the bakery could carry on as it had always done.

My gaze cut to Cole. Well, apart from the gorgeous werewolf I was walking alongside. This wasn't so normal, but I was more than happy to have this new addition in my life.

❧───❧

My feet ached, my legs were tired, and I couldn't stop smiling. My date with Cole had been wonderful. We'd walked, talked, and eaten a huge feast and then walked some more. The weather had been glorious. The sun even came out, and I'd had the best date of my life.

Cole was funny, charming, and protective. He looked out for me the whole time and even lifted me over fallen trees that had come down in the storm. I was hoping we'd get to repeat this date soon.

He pulled his car up outside of the bakery, walked around, and opened my door. He held out his hand, and I took it. I would never object to this kind of chivalry.

Cole kept hold of my hand and stared into my eyes. "I had a great day."

"Me too. I've never walked those trails. It got pretty wild out there."

"They're not on any official maps, but I've run them a few times in wolf form. I figured they'd be just as much fun on two legs. And the company made it even better."

I grinned up at him. "I agree. We could try another route next time."

"We will. You can suggest somewhere around here. I've only run in a few places, so a lot of this area is new to me."

"I'll dig out some maps, and we can take a look." My heart thudded as Cole leaned down, his gaze on my lips. He froze and inhaled deeply.

"Is something wrong? I might be a little ripe after all that walking. I worked up a sweat." I sniffed my shirt. I didn't detect anything, but I didn't have a werewolf's keen sense of smell.

He leaned back, his eyes darting around. "It's not you. I smell smoke. You didn't leave a cake burning in the oven, did you?"

I thumped him on the chest. "Not funny. I have no plans to burn anything. At least, not today."

He inhaled again. His eyes glowed amber, and a second later, he threw himself at me. We hit the ground as a massive roar rang through the air.

Even though my eyes were closed, a brilliant light flared behind my eyelids.

Cole remained above me, pressing me against his chest for at least thirty seconds.

I peeked under his arm, and my mouth dropped open. The front of the bakery was gone, and flames licked out of the shattered windows. "Let me up! Uncle Albert and Earl are inside."

Cole looked over his shoulder then rolled off me. "Be careful. There could be another explosion."

I took a step toward the bakery, but Cole held me back. "I have to get them out!"

"It's not safe."

My eyes flooded with tears as fire roared out of my home. "We have to do something. We could try around the back and find a safe way in."

"The flames are already shooting out of the roof. The whole place is on fire. You can't go inside."

I shoved against him, but he wouldn't let me go. "I can't leave them in there. They'll die." It could already be too late. Uncle Albert had probably been dozing in his easy chair, and Earl would have been snoozing somewhere cozy. Neither of them stood a chance of getting out.

"I can hear the fire truck. They'll quickly put this out." Cole hauled me back from the intense heat as the Fandango's sign disappeared behind a thick cloud of black smoke.

I could barely see as tears streamed out of my eyes, and I choked on the smoke. I was numb with horror and shock. I'd just lost everything I loved.

About Author

K.E. O'Connor (Karen) is a mystery author living in the beautiful British countryside. She loves all things mystery, animals, and cake.

If you want to be part of the Witch Haven crew, practice spells, solve a few murders, spend time with amazing witches and their talking familiars, and get a **free** book, join her weekly newsletter.

Sign up today.

Newsletter:
https://BookHip.com/QKGDWJW
Website:
www.keoconnor.com/writing
Facebook:
www.facebook.com/keoconnorauthor

Also By

Spells and Spooks
Hexes and Haunts
Curses and Corpses
Muffins and Moonlight
Cupcakes and Cauldrons
Pancakes and Potions
Hauntings and High Jinx
Hauntings and Havoc
Hauntings and Hoaxes
The Case of the Screaming Skull
The Case of the Poisoned Pumpkin
The Case of the Cursed Candy
Fire Fang
Silvaria

If you enjoyed

Cupcakes and Cauldrons

turn the page to read an extract from the next Witch Haven mystery.

PANCAKES AND POTIONS

ISBN: 978-1-915378-33-0

Chapter 1

I paced the corridor in the hospital for what felt like the thousandth time. Only Cole standing in front of me and blocking my path stopped me from wearing holes in my boots.

He gently cupped my face and wiped the tears off my cheeks with his thumbs. "Your uncle will be okay. They got him out in time."

"You don't know that. And what's taking them so long? He could have serious burns or damage to his lungs because of smoke inhalation. I need to see him. I should be in there with him." My breath came out ragged, my head hurting from so much crying.

"The doctors know what they're doing. And you need looking at, too." Cole lifted the ends of my hair, which were frazzled from the intense heat of the fire at Fandango's.

"I didn't get hurt. You were there to protect me." I slumped against him and wrapped my arms around his waist.

He hissed out a breath, and it was only when my hands slid down his back that I realized part of his shirt was shredded.

Cole gently eased away my hands and settled them on his butt. "Go easy with the tight hugs until my back heals."

"You should have told me you were injured." I hurried around behind him. Bright pink skin showed beneath the tattered shirt.

"You know me. A werewolf can heal from almost anything. I'm more worried about you."

"Are you sure? We can get a nurse to see you." I skimmed my fingers lightly over his hot flesh, so grateful for the power of werewolf magic.

"Positive. They don't need to waste their healing energy on my burns. I'll be fine in the morning."

I leaned against his solid chest. I breathed in the scent of smoke, burned cloth, and spicy Cole.

"What do you think happened at the bakery?" His voice was soft under the bright lights of the hospital waiting room.

"I have no idea. We get the equipment regularly serviced, but maybe something malfunctioned. We have a lot of things that could catch fire." I shook my head. "But Uncle Albert is always so careful about shutting things down. He never leaves anything on. And I know I didn't."

"This has nothing to do with you. We were out for most of the day."

I sighed. "I really want to talk to Uncle Albert. Maybe he saw something."

"Luna!"

At the sound of Indigo Ash's voice, I turned. Right behind her were my two other closest friends, Storm Winter and Odessa Grimsbane. Cole stepped back as all three of them engulfed me in hugs, and in seconds, we were talking over each other. Odessa and Indigo were crying, and even Storm's eyes looked hazy, and she rarely shed a tear.

"How's your uncle doing?" Indigo pulled back from the hug.

"I haven't seen him yet. That can't be a good sign."

Cole's hand rested on my shoulder. "It's a sign the doctors are working hard. They'll let you in soon."

"What happened at the bakery?" Storm's dark hair was scraped off her face in a messy ponytail. "I heard the explosion from my apartment."

I stepped back and rubbed a hand across my face. "I don't know. It all happened so fast, my brain hasn't caught up. I was outside with Cole when the fire appeared out of nowhere."

"Oh! You're lucky to still be standing if you were that close to the flames." Odessa gripped me tight, her round cheeks pink and her eyes full of concern.

"I had someone watching my back." I smiled at Cole before focusing on Storm. "Are you sure about the explosion?"

"It sounded like it. The air was sucked out of my place, and then there was a boom. It took me a few minutes to figure out what was going on. Fire Fang alerted me to the problem. He kept pacing around the apartment and whining. I took him out to take a look, and we discovered Fandango's on fire."

"You must have just missed us. The fire crew found Uncle Albert quickly, and we came in the ambulance." I rubbed my aching forehead. "We have nothing explosive in the bakery. I figured maybe an electrical fire, but I don't know..."

"Do you think magic caused the explosion?" Indigo said.

My friends exchanged a worried glance.

"I... maybe. I hadn't thought."

"Who would do that to you?" Storm said.

Indigo ducked her head. "I was thinking my mom and her freaky boyfriend could be back."

"I can't think about the cause." I caught hold of Indigo's hand. "But it's not your mom. She's gone. All I care about right now is Uncle Albert and making sure he's fine. I'll figure out the rest later."

"We'll stay here until you know how he's doing," Odessa said.

I sucked in a shaky breath, my heart giving a desperately unhappy thud. "Actually, I need help with something else. Earl. They couldn't find him in the bakery. The firefighters were putting out the blaze, but I had to leave with Uncle Albert. I... I think Earl's dead."

Cole's hand tightened on my shoulder.

"We can go look for him," Odessa said. "Would you like us to do that?"

I swallowed. "I have to know what happened to him, but it won't be safe at the bakery. The firefighters wouldn't let me anywhere near the building, even though I begged them to let me find him. They were having trouble controlling the blaze."

"Not anymore. The fire's out," Storm said. "Haven't you checked outside? It's raining buckets."

I glanced at the window and only then noticed the torrential rain pounding the glass. I'd never been so happy to see a rainstorm in my life.

"We can find Earl." Odessa squeezed my hand. "You know him, he always tucks himself away. I expect he was protected on top of a cupboard or inside a mixing bowl out of the way of any trouble."

"I hope so." I could barely get the words out. Earl wasn't the greatest familiar in the world, but I couldn't imagine him not being in my life. He was my adorable, lazy furball, and I had to find him.

"We'll get him. You'll be fine and so will your uncle," Indigo said. "Then we'll figure out what happened at the bakery."

The main doors slammed open. Zek, one of the teenage gremlins I was teaching at the reform school, staggered through the doors clutching something black and smoking. Trotting beside him was Fire Fang, who growled at anyone who got too close.

Zek dropped to his knees and wheezed out a breath. "I need help here. I have an injured familiar."

My eyes widened as I took in what he was holding. "Is that Earl?"

Zek looked up at me. "Yeah. I saved him for you."

I raced over, almost colliding with a nurse as she stopped and peered at Earl.

"Oh! I thought that was a baby. It's just an animal," she said.

"He's more than that. He's my familiar." My hands shook as I touched Earl. "And he's been in a fire. He needs medical treatment."

"Then he needs to go to the vet. We don't treat animals here."

I rounded on her. "You'll treat him. And Zek."

Zek lifted a hand. "I'm good. Just got messed up from the smoke."

The nurse pursed her lips, a shimmer of indecision in her eyes. "Maybe some pain relief, but the vet is the specialist for familiars." She strode away.

I gently rested a hand on Earl's side, relieved to feel him breathing. I gripped Zek's shoulder. "How did you find him?"

"We heard about the fire at the reform school and went to look. We were worried about you. You're our least worst teacher, so we didn't want you getting crispy around the edges." He gave me a sharp-toothed grin. "When the firefighters pulled back, one of the others said he heard a noise inside. The guys distracted the firefighters, and I crept in. I found this little dude and remembered you saying you had a black cat familiar."

I wrapped my arms around Zek, being careful not to squash Earl, and hugged him tight. "Thank you. I thought I'd lost him."

"No worries. You saved me from choking to death on a cupcake. It's only right I repay the debt. I always do."

More tears slid down my cheeks. "You're incredible. I don't know how I'll ever thank you."

"No need. I owed you, and now we're even. Although if you give me a couple of extra marks on my next assessment, I wouldn't mind."

I smiled at him as I carefully stroked Earl. I couldn't see any burns, but his eyes were closed, and he didn't respond, no matter how many times I said his name.

Fire Fang nudged me out of the way with his enormous head and wiped his huge pink tongue across Earl. He did it several times, occasionally pausing to spit out black bits of charred fur he'd scraped off.

"Is that a good idea?" I inched away as Fire Fang growled at me.

Storm nudged me. "He knows what he's doing. There's more to that hellhound mutt than meets the eye. He knows things. It's freaky. And he's still levitating when he sleeps."

Earl made a hacking cough, and his eyes flew open. Fire Fang backed away and lowered himself to the floor, giving a gentle whine.

"Earl, can you hear me?" I knelt in front of him.

He coughed up a huge ball of gross looking black goo and slow blinked at me. "Am I dead?"

"You came close. Zek rescued you from Fandango's. Do you remember anything about how the fire started?"

Earl looked at Zek. "Huh! You saved me?"

Zek puffed out his chest. "Yeah. I found you wedged in a dented tin. You were under a table at the back of the bakery."

"How did I get there?" Earl uncurled himself and inspected each paw. "I was taking a nap in my favorite brownie tin under the counter when there was a bang. That's all I remember. I wasn't under a table when I dozed off."

"Do you know where the bang came from?" I said.

Earl flopped out of Zek's arms and dropped to the floor. He shook himself and sniffed his fur. His nose wrinkled. "Maybe the kitchen. I don't know. It happened fast. I was sleeping, there was a noise, and that was it."

"Whatever it was, it must have been violent enough to propel you across the bakery," Indigo said.

Earl nodded. His head shot up. "What about Albert? He was upstairs after he'd shut the bakery for the night."

"We're still waiting to find out," I said.

Zek stood and brushed down his soot covered clothing. "I'll leave you to it."

I hugged him again. "You're my hero. You were so brave."

He pulled back and grinned. "Make sure that goes down on my assessment. Maybe I'll get out of the reform school early for such heroic behavior."

"I'll make sure it does. I'll see you in class soon."

He nodded at me and strode away, his chest puffed up and a swagger in his step.

The nurse returned. "I'll look at your familiar now."

"Nope. No need for any medical probing. I'm okay," Earl said. "I feel good. Although I smell weird. I could do with a bath, and I don't say that often."

"Luna Brimstone?" A middle-aged doctor in a white coat appeared in the waiting room.

"That's me." I raced over.

His smile was reassuring as he nodded at me. "I've been with your uncle. He's going to be fine."

A huge weight lifted off my shoulders when I heard those words. "Thank you. Can I see him?"

"Yes. He's awake and talking, but he's going to need rest. And he got burned. Healing spells have already been applied, but we want to monitor him for smoke damage and shock."

"Of course. So long as I can see him."

"Just for a few minutes. And only you." His gaze cut to everyone lurking behind me.

I looked back at my amazing group of friends, and they waved me away.

"Go. We'll be here when you come out," Indigo said.

I hurried along with the doctor and into a quiet room along the corridor.

Uncle Albert was sitting up in bed. I sucked in a breath. He looked so small and pale tucked under pristine white sheets. Both his hands were wrapped in thick bandages and a pale pink glow shimmered around them.

I hurried to his bed, determined not to burst into tears and worry him.

"Five minutes," the doctor said from the doorway. "Then he needs to rest for the night. So do you. It must've been a shock seeing what happened to your business."

I nodded, but my attention was on Uncle Albert. I went to grab his hand but pulled back, not wanting to hurt him. "I'm not sure where's safe to touch."

His smile was wobbly. "It's best not to grab my hands. I got burned moving things. I was upstairs when the fire started, and I made it down the stairs, but hot metal blocked the way."

Tears filled my eyes. "How are you feeling?"

"Numb and giggly. I have amazing healing magic pulsing through me. I'm sure I won't feel this good tomorrow when it's worn off. How about you? And Earl?"

"Earl's okay. Someone found him. He's in the waiting room. I was outside the bakery with Cole when the fire started." I pressed a hand against his arm. "I couldn't get to you. The flames were so intense. They came out of nowhere."

He nodded. "One minute, I was snoozing in my easy chair listening to the radio, and the next, there was a bang and smoke poured into the room. The flames moved so quickly."

"I'm so glad you got out in one piece." I looked at the bandages and bit my lip. "Your poor hands."

He sighed. "I won't be able to do any baking for a while. How bad is the damage to Fandango's? Do we still have a business?"

"I didn't wait around to see. I came straight to the hospital with you." My bottom lip jutted out. "But the flames were already out the roof as we left. I'm not sure we can save it."

His gaze lowered, and his shoulders sank. "Oh, well, I was thinking the place needed a makeover. Now, I've got no excuse. Although this will be more than new tables and chairs and a coat of paint. Perhaps we can come up with the new design together. This could be a fresh start."

Uncle Albert always looked on the bright side of things, no matter how grim it got. "It'll get the best makeover."

He nodded. "And we're insured, so we don't have to worry about the money. But if it's as bad as you think, it'll take a long time to rebuild. We'll be out of business for months."

"Don't worry about that. We'll figure something out. You concentrate on healing. We need to make sure your hands are able to knead that magic dough. Otherwise, customers will complain."

His gaze ran over me. He opened his mouth as if he was going to say something then simply nodded. "You're right. There's no rush. Are you sure you weren't hurt?"

"Cole protected me. His back got burned, but he's already healing."

"Then thank him for me. He's a good man. I trust him with you."

"I trust him with me, too. Cole's always looking out for me."

"When I'm up to it, I'll make him a thank you meal. And it's time I got to know him better if things are serious between you." He tilted his head. "Are they serious?"

"Cole would love that." I smoothed his sheets. "And things are moving in the right direction, although we're still getting to know each other. We had a great date today."

The doctor returned. "Your uncle needs to rest. You can come back and see him in the morning."

I kissed Uncle Albert's cheek. "Make sure you get plenty of sleep. I'll be back first thing."

"You rest, too. And don't worry about me. I'm in the best place. The doctors here are amazing."

After giving him a careful hug, I left his room and gently closed the door behind me. It was only then I realized I had nowhere to sleep. My home was gone. Where was I supposed to go?

Pancakes and Potions is available in e-book and paperback

ISBN: 978-1-915378-33-0